MW00932093

THE FORGOTTEN HOME

VS Gardner

Despite its hardships life
is all about family, togetherness
and love! Enjoy my story!

VS Gardner

i

Copyright @ 2023 VS Gardner

All rights reserved.

This book is a work of fiction.
Names, characters, places, and incidents either are products
of the author's imagination or are used fictitiously.

Scripture quotations are from The Holy Bible,
New International Version® Copyright© 1973, 1978, 1984
by International Bible Society. Used by permission of Zondervan.
All rights reserved.

Cover Painting by Steve Gardner
Cover by Amber Park

ISBN 9798376434673

Printed in the United States of America

This book is DEDICATED
~ to *each one* of my grandchildren ~

Here are some things I want you to know....
- I began asking God to give you everything you will need to get through the hard times of life and to bless you with joy before you even existed.
- I will pray for you until my last day on this earth.
- My desire is for you to know God, love God and live out His plan for your life ~ in this you will find joy! Joy is deeper than happiness.
- The relationship we share has added great joy to my life.
- *I am proud of you!*

The best advice I can offer you is this:
Love God, love others and always be kind!

I am so thankful...
...to be your grandma.
...for the precious miracle that is *you*.
...for every hug we have shared. *I marvel at you!*
...for each time you include me in your life and give me your love.
...to be a part of your life for as long as I live.
...to live in your memories.

Remember this~
nothing's going to happen today
that you and God together cannot handle.
You are never alone! God is always with you!
He promises never to leave us alone
and He keeps his promises!

Grandma Nessa will always love you!
God loves you even more.

~ ACKNOWLEDGEMENTS ~

~ **Readers** – The most fulfilling part of my author journey is having folks share their reactions to my stories. Knowing my story has perplexed, touched, brought joy, spoken to a heart or impacted a life gives my writing meaning. *Thank you for choosing to read my novels.* If my story has moved you to laugh, cry or gain a new perspective I would love to hear about it! My deepest thanks to any reader who chooses to give feedback, refer my books, rate or post a review, follow/friend me on my Facebook Author page (VS Gardner) or follow the author on Amazon. A special thanks to those who've waited patiently during the writing process – *you are my treasured fan base!* Your support means the world to me! I've had such fun hearing from and/or meeting so many of you! *Thank you for enjoying my stories!!*

~ **Merchants** ~ To each merchant making shelf space for my books: *Thank you!* Your support means so much to me!

~ **Family** ~ You are my life's best blessings! I could fill a book with what you mean to me; *I am so thankful we're family. I love each of you beyond words!*

To the following, for the investment of your time, input and guidance –
THANK YOU!
~ **BETA Reader:** T Moise,
~ **BETA/Proofreader:** Steve Gardner
~ **Proofreaders:** Mitch and Morgan Webber, Monica White
~ **Something Else:** Deb Troiano –In addition to your usual input thank you for your experience and information on how monarchs grow.

~ Above all I'm thankful to God, my loving Father, for the fulfillment of my lifelong dream of becoming a published author, the blessings He continuously pours into my life and for giving me the gift of faith and a way with words.

~ *My appreciation knows no bounds* ~

ALSO BY VS GARDNER

A Killing on Hardee Street
A Brick to Remember

Author's Note

I've written butterflies into the stories
of my first three novels.

I've always loved my name.
~ Vanessa ~
of Ancient Greek origin meaning butterfly.
In addition to its beauty
the butterfly's symbolism of new life
makes it even more precious.

~ Butterfly ~

The butterfly is a great symbol of Christ
it begins its life walking the ground amongst us.
It then 'dies' and is wrapped in a shroud
until it rises again, glorified!

The butterfly serves as a reminder
of people who have left us,
been made whole and are now
free of the worries of this world.

-copied/author unknown-

THE FORGOTTEN HOME

VS Gardner

CHAPTER 1

The nurse walked briskly back into the nursery and looked again at each bassinet. Once she was certain the baby in question still wasn't there a sense of panic began to rise inside her. She hurried to the main nurses' station and went straight to the head nurse.

"I noticed an empty bassinet in the nursery so I went to the mother's room and she didn't have the baby. Without saying anything I followed the proper procedure and checked with all the other nurses. I've just come from the nursery again and the baby still isn't there. I'm not able to find her."

The head nurse immediately sprang to action – cautioning each member of her department to appear calm but move quickly. She initiated a full-scale department search. By sending every maternity ward nurse to a specific area they would soon confirm whether or not the baby girl was indeed missing.

If the baby wasn't located, an emergency code must be called as soon as possible. One nurse covered each patient room in the maternity ward. Another double checked the nursery while yet another went into the examination room to be certain a pediatrician had not come at this late hour to examine the baby. That wasn't likely but they were covering every possibility. Within a few moments all of the nurses had returned to the nurses' station. The missing baby girl had not been found.

The head nurse lifted the phone from its cradle and calmly dialed the numbers 2222 - the line which is always open for this sole purpose. She quickly relayed the situation to the operator. Almost instantly after hanging up the following announcement was heard over the hospital public paging system: "Code Pink – infant female, white gown, pink blanket, maternity ward nursery. Code Pink - infant female, white gown, pink blanket, maternity ward nursery. Code Pink - infant female, white gown, pink blanket, maternity ward nursery."

Before the announcement had even been completed the head nurse had sent one of her nurses to the baby's room to be with her mother. She was now in the process of gathering this important information: when the baby girl had last been with the mother, when she had last been handled by the nursing staff, when she had last been seen by anyone and what visitors had come and gone from the maternity ward.

The Code Pink announcement had set each member of the hospital staff outside of the maternity ward on high alert as well. Many had instantly taken action. Through repeated practice drills they all knew to take this situation seriously. There was never the assumption it was a practice run. All staff knew their role in this circumstance and everyone was strictly following protocol.

Each head nurse had started a search within her designated ward, with all outside exits being checked as well as the inside of stairwells and other isolated areas. Once those had proven clear an appointed person stood guard at the double door access point to the ward to ensure no one left.

Security staff had immediately been dispersed to each and every outside entrance and exit of the hospital and remained at those access points. Anyone carrying a large bag or wearing clothing which could conceal an infant came under suspicion and would not be permitted to leave the premises.

Other members of security were looking around on the outside of the facility. According to protocol all contracted services staff would be prohibited from leaving the grounds until the baby had been found. In the event the infant wasn't located the police would be notified and an official police investigation would begin.

Two minutes later the code pink announcement was again heard throughout the entire facility. This would continue every fifteen minutes for one hour even after the police arrived at the hospital and took charge of the situation.

If the missing child was located the operator would announce, "Code Pink - All Clear" three times. Upon hearing that announcement all hospital staff would simply resume their normal activities.

Sadly, that would not be happening tonight.

CHAPTER 2

After excitedly stepping down into the canoe nine-year-old Jaxson balanced himself as he walked to the center seat and settled onto it. As soon as he sat down, he pulled the zipper of his jacket all the way to the top, lifted his hood over his head and tied it's string at the neck.

The night air was cool, not cold. The wind blew just strong enough to make for a cold breeze. He knew that being on the water it was bound to get even colder as the night wore on.

Matthew was already seated at the front of the canoe facing forward when Jaxson heard Steven's boots splash into the water behind him. He felt the canoe push off from shore as Steven quickly climbed in and took the back seat. Almost immediately Steven and Matthew were working the oars in sync with one another. Working together they propelled the canoe evenly and smoothly out to the middle of the lake.

Never having been out in the canoe this late at night before Jaxson leaned his head back to look up. He couldn't believe how many stars there were and how vastly they spread across the night sky. It was the prettiest thing he had ever seen, until he looked out over the lake and saw those very same stars reflected in the water. It seemed as though they were surrounded by stars at every turn. Jaxson had never been allowed to stay up this late before, let alone to venture out onto the lake, but tonight was special and its mission was important.

The air was thick with excitement but there was also an undercurrent of tension. Jaxson understood the excitement. He did not understand the tension. There was a lot about what was happening tonight that he would not understand. He had only been told what he needed to know. It left him with a lot of unanswered questions. He didn't like that, but he understood it had to be that way.

If he were a man, like Matthew and Steven, he would know exactly why everything had to be done in the dead of night, under cover of darkness. He would know the reasons for what was happening. But that was for the grown-ups to know and for him not to worry about. He had accepted this because he trusted the adults in his life. He loved them and he trusted them. Steven and Matthew and Ms. Amber had given him a home in which he was loved and protected. They were his family now and he trusted them completely.

It was as simple as that.

Jaxson had learned, in his short nine years of life, that things didn't always go the way people might think they would, or even the way they may want them to.

He was just a boy but he had faced things many children his age never had and never would. It made him courageous and strong. Matthew told him this while they worked around their home together, cutting trees for firewood, doing yard work and repairing the railing on the porch. Jaxson was smart, hard-working, funny and fun. Matthew pointed that out as well.

Steven leaned up toward Jaxson and interrupted his thoughts by asking quietly, "you remember what to do, right?"

"Yes," Jaxson answered without hesitation. "I'll stay in the canoe with my head down. I will not watch where you and Matthew go or look at anyone. I will not listen to what is said. Instead, I will count just as Ma has taught me. I will wait right here in the canoe and be ready for you to hand me the bundle. Once I have it, I will hold it tightly to my chest. I will not let it go as we go back across the lake. Although we all know it will not be necessary, I will protect it with my life. We are on a great adventure just like the ones we've read about in our books. I only have one job tonight. It's a very important job and I will not fail. Tonight, I am the keeper of the treasure."

"That's right," Matthew spoke from his seat in the front of the canoe where he had been listening intently. Though he had not turned to face Jaxson his voice, deep and soft, carried back to him clearly.

"Okay. This is it!" Steven said with a hint of excitement as the shoreline came into view.

"You've got this, Jaxson," Matthew said. "No worries."

Rowing smoothly and quickly the two men gently guided the canoe until it ran alongside the wooden boating dock.

Jaxson watched as Matthew reached up and grabbed the bar with his left hand. Reaching across with his right hand he wrapped the rope from the front of the canoe around and quickly made a loose knot in the rope to secure the canoe in place. Steven was doing the same at the back of the canoe.

Both men stepped from the canoe onto the dock and walked silently and quickly into the darkness toward the parking area. Jaxson immediately lowered his head, looked at his tennis shoes and began to count.

"Counting is a wonderful way to occupy one's mind when waiting for time to pass," Ms. Amber had said when she talked with him about his part in tonight's adventure. "As you know there are sixty seconds in one minute and there are sixty minutes in one hour. Of course, you won't be sitting in the canoe for an hour!" she had said with a laugh. "But counting will pass the time for you and when the guys return you will know how long you waited. The best way to count seconds is by saying 'one thousand and one, one thousand and two' so just do that. When you reach one thousand and sixty you will know it's been one minute. Then you say 'two thousand and one, two thousand and two' until you reach two thousand and sixty and you know it's been two minutes. Just keep doing that until the men come back."

The two of them had practiced counting seconds together many times after that day and before tonight.

Jaxson counted to three thousand and thirty before hearing Matthew and Steven coming back to the canoe. They had only been gone for a little over three minutes.

Loudly enough for Jaxson to hear him Matthew whispered, "Okay buddy, it's time to do your job. Look up here now and get ready to receive the treasure."

Jaxson raised his head and saw Matthew kneeling on the wooden dock while Steven stood beside him. Steven leaned down and very gently handed the bundle to Matthew. Matthew then leaned down and handed it to Jaxson who glanced at it quickly before immediately hugging it to his chest.

Steven dropped a good-sized bag behind Jaxson and the two men stepped into the canoe, sat down and began unwrapping the rope from the bar nearest them. By the time another minute had passed the canoe was smoothly and quickly crossing the lake toward their home.

About half-way across the lake Jaxson felt a stirring in his arms. He gently lowered the soft bundle into his lap and looked down at it. By the dim light of the moon, he could see that in the center of the tightly wound blanket was the sweetest little face. Two tiny, bright eyes were looking directly into his eyes. When a soft little cooing sound came from the baby Jaxson leaned his face close to hers.

"It's okay," he said. "Don't you worry. I've got you. You're safe with me. You will always be safe with me."

Jaxson gently lifted the bundle up to his shoulder just as Ms. Amber had taught him to do. As he patted the baby's back ever so softly, he silently vowed that nothing bad would ever happen to this little girl. Not as long as he could help it, anyway.

CHAPTER 3

Approaching the shore Matthew and Steven aimed the canoe perfectly into the little grove in the land where they kept it docked. As they increased the speed of their rowing the canoe ran aground and Matthew jumped out and pulled it further onto shore. Steven stepped out into the water and the two men dragged the canoe with Jaxson and the baby girl still inside until it was secured in place.

Jaxson had never felt more important than he did that night. Steven and Matthew stood aside and watched as he carefully stepped from the canoe with the baby safe in his arms. Steven grabbed the bag he'd earlier tossed into the canoe and the three of them walked together through the woods toward the house. Neither man attempted to take the baby or even asked Jaxson how he was doing. The boy had been prepared for this task and no one questioned his ability to perform it.

Approaching the back of their home Jaxson could see Ms. Amber standing in the window just inside the back door. He knew she was anxiously awaiting the baby's arrival. Jaxson patted the back of the little girl gently. He leaned his mouth to her ear and quietly said, "Welcome to your new home little one. I am your big brother, Jaxson, and I will keep you safe."

Matthew sprinted ahead and opened the back door. Steven stood to the side as Jaxson walked through and went straight to the waiting woman.

After giving him a quick hug Ms. Amber looked down into his face and asked, "Did everything go as planned?"

"It went perfectly. The night and the lake were calm, the moon was bright enough to see all around us. The bundle was delivered on time and

I've held her safely and protected her every moment. Would you like to take her now?"

The smile on Ms. Amber's face radiated from somewhere deep inside her. She stepped forward and lowered her arms, stretching them out toward him with her palms upward. "If you are ready to give her to me, then yes, I would very much like to hold her now," she said.

Jaxson stepped closer and lowered the bundle from his shoulder. When she lay between them on his outstretched arms, he looked at the sleeping baby. He then looked up into Ms. Amber's face.

"She's sleeping," he said simply.

"I see that," Ms. Amber said. "You know what that means, don't you? It means she trusts you. You did exactly as you needed to do. You made her feel secure and safe. If she had been afraid, she would have cried. I am so very proud of you, Jaxson. No one could have done this job better than you have done it. The Lord was with you just as we have asked him to be."

Looking up at Steven and Matthew she said, "I am so proud of all of you. What you've done tonight is very important. We must always be there for one another in this life and we must always protect those who need to be protected. For reasons we do not get to know, this little one's life is in danger and she needs our protection. She now has a temporary new home here with us. God has been with all of you tonight. He will continue to be with all of us as we take on the responsibility and joy of caring for this little one.

There's no way for us to know how long she will be here with us; so, we will just love her until she leaves for another home. When she does, it won't be easy, but God will comfort us and bless us for giving her a home here with us in her time of need."

They had all talked this through before. Still, it was good to be reminded this was a temporary mission of love.

Steven held up the bag he'd been given and told Ms. Amber it was supplies to help with the baby; diapers and formula and such. She asked him to sit the bag on the kitchen table for her to empty later. As he did that her eyes went to the bundle in Jaxson's arms. Seeing the longing on her face Jaxson stepped forward and handed the baby to his mother.

Looking at the three young men she said, "you've all done such a wonderful job tonight. I am so proud of all three of you. Now get your boots and coats off and go into the kitchen and get a cup of the hot cocoa I made while you were gone. Then come and join us in the living room and we'll talk for a while.

The men did as she had asked, each choosing a seat close to the others. Now settled, everyone sat looking down at the precious bundle on her temporary new mother's lap.

"Welcome to our family, sweet girl," Ms. Amber said.

"Welcome to our family," her three rescuers echoed in unison.

The little one's eyes went from one face to the other as if she understood exactly what was happening.

Looking up at the young men, Ms. Amber said, "Now tell me, what is this tiny girl's name?"

Steven and Matthew looked at each other uneasily for a few seconds. Matthew's head gave a slight nod toward Steven as if to say 'go ahead'.

"Well, here's the thing," Steven began. As you know we really had no idea what we were getting into tonight. Matthew got the call that a baby was in danger and we were asked to take her in. The three of us talked it over and agreed to bring her here and the plan was set for tonight.

We still don't know much more.

When we arrived, we were told her parents are in serious danger. They believe those who are after them will either kidnap or kill their baby so they've chosen to give her up to keep her safe. After they gave us the bag of baby items and handed her over, we asked for her name." He hesitated and looked at Matthew who spoke up immediately, "she doesn't have one."

"Oh, my," Ms. Amber said

Matthew picked up with, "I know. We were surprised too. I mean, surely, she does have one? They're just not telling us. I don't know what else to think. But as we crossed back over the lake with her safely in the canoe even that started to make sense to me. If they gave her a name it's probably better for us not to know it. I mean, think about it. If we use her real name, those who want to hurt her have a better chance of finding her. On the other hand, giving her up in secret and without a name makes it a lot harder for anyone to find her, now or ever."

Understanding crossed Ms. Amber's face. "That's true," she said.

A profound sense of sadness came over her as she sat looking at the baby girl. Sadness that such evil should threaten the safety of an innocent little girl; sadness that the baby's parents were faced with such a horrendous and difficult decision, sadness that this little angelic creature not only has no parents and no home but she now has no name either.

They were left with a dilemma Ms. Amber had not expected. How were they supposed to name this baby?

What were they going to call her?

CHAPTER 4

Ma, Matthew and Steven were all looking at him intently. The look on each face mirrored the others. Jaxson wasn't exactly sure what their expressions meant. If he had to venture a guess, he would say curiosity: interest, maybe even wonder.

"I've never heard that name before," Steven said.

"I was just thinking the same thing, but I like it," Matthew added.

They were gathered together to choose a name for the new baby girl they'd taken in to live with them at The Delaney Home for Children.

Jaxson made the first suggestion and the others were now reacting to it.

"I've never heard that before either," Ma said. "How did you come up with it, Jaxson?"

"It's in one of my favorite Christmas movies," he answered, wondering if she liked it. "We don't have to use it. I just really like it."

"I really like it, too," Ma said. "I also like that it's uncommon. It's unique just like our girl here."

All three of them were smiling.

Ms. Amber looked from Matthew to Steven and each of them nodded their heads in response to her unspoken question.

"Well," she said with a huge smile, "it appears this may go a bit quicker than I expected. By no stretch of the imagination did I think we'd come up with a name this easily but it looks like we're all in agreement. Okay then - her first name will be Jovie. Good job, Jaxson!"

Jaxson beamed.

"Now, what shall we do about her middle name?"

"Well, ma, what's your middle name?" Matthew asked thoughtfully.

11

"Oh, that's a great idea," Steven said excitedly. "Yeah, Ms. Amber, what is it?

"Mine?" she answered hesitantly. "My middle name is Lynn.

"Jovie Lynn," Jaxson said. "I like it!"

"I do, too," the others said in unison.

"What do you think, ma?" Matthew asked.

Looking a little surprised, Ms. Amber said, "Well, I wasn't expecting anything like this, but I do like the two names together. If you're all in agreement I'm happy with it. I'm very happy with it, actually."

"I think we're all in agreement," Matthew said, looking from Steven to Jaxson. Seeing their affirmative nods he said, "Yep, looks like it. Jovie Lynn it is!"

"Jovie Lynn it is then," Ms. Amber said as a tear slipped down her cheek. "I've never had a child named after me before. I feel quite honored."

CHAPTER 5

It was just another day like all the others. Prison life offers no variety. Nothing changes from one day to the next, even the sounds become monotonous with the passage of time; from the clanging of the cell doors automatically opening at their appointed times, the footfalls of prisoners moving in single file line formations from one location to another, the clinking of utensils, the clattering of dishes and thudding of trays deposited on tables all overshadowed by the steady hum of chattering voices.

For a good many prisoners the highlight of the day is time in the yard. It's their one and only chance to enjoy being in the open-air walking about or participating in whatever small game of sport may be going on.

The monotony of day-to-day life in prison often adds to the hopelessness of life behind bars. Thatcher had grown tired of it pretty quickly but there was nothing he could do about that. Following his arrest, he spent almost a year in the county jail waiting for his case to go to trial. It had now been just over a year since he was found guilty and sentenced to life in prison. His surroundings constantly wore on his mind and to his way of thinking, he most certainly did not belong there.

He blamed his plight on one man, and one man only: a detective who'd been obsessed with solving a case.

To say Thatcher was bitter would have been a gross understatement. He was beyond bitter and constantly fed his bitterness a steady diet of promises to make that one man pay. It would happen, he guaranteed himself on a daily basis, constantly stewing on the how, when, and where.

Today he was busy analyzing just exactly how he had arrived at this point in his life. For once, his focus was on himself instead of the detective he so passionately hated. Only on a rare occasion did this happen. But when

13

it did, he forgot everything and just followed the path his mind had set itself to. Today it had set itself to thinking over his own behavior patterns, the very actions that had led him to where he now was.

On these rare occasions he went back to the very beginning, his childhood. Who had Thatcher Foreman been way back then and how had he become who he now was?

Remembering his early childhood, he was forced to admit it hadn't taken him long to realize he was different from other children. He wouldn't have known that, but for the reactions of those around him. When he followed his natural impulses, he often found others looking at him strangely. Their uncomfortable silence made it clear he bewildered them. This point was driven home when he accidentally hurt a classmate. When the child cried out, Thatcher's first impulse was to laugh, which he did quite heartily. By the expressions of the other children, he realized they found his amusement not only confusing but unacceptable.

As he grew older, he learned to hide his delight in the discomfort of others. He, also, mastered the ability to cause hurt in ways that appeared accidental but really weren't. On those occasions, suspicion lingered in their eyes. Not wanting to believe the worst of him, the suspicion quickly changed to confusion. Thatcher found pleasure even in that. Convincing them the incident had been an accident was quite the trick when it became necessary. But through his unwavering insistence he always prevailed. After all, no one wants to believe another child means to do them harm.

Young Thatcher was amused not only by the pain of others but by their fear. Through closely studying his own feelings he had to admit, to himself if to no one else, that he genuinely liked seeing the fear in their eyes.

It wasn't easy for him to understand natural human responses so he took on the endeavor of learning them by watching the reactions of those around him. Seeing their sympathy: desire to comfort or help, or simple indifference told him most people react with natural empathy. Upon gaining this knowledge he began his practice in appearing sympathetic since obviously that was what others expected of him.

Reacting true to his own nature drew responses indicating he'd said or done something inappropriate. In those instances, he quickly thought things through and asked questions to gain understanding of what he had done that was amiss. In this way his knowledge grew and he honed the skill of deflection. As a result, Thatcher became a master of manipulation. He collected information that would help him appear to be normal, though he was definitely very different.

Being an exceptionally clever child, he saw the importance of hiding his initial desire to act inappropriately and to adopt the correct responses. Once he mastered putting that into practice, he fit in remarkably well with his peers. By staying alert, he was quick to be sure he didn't commit any social faux pas.

The older he got the more he wanted to follow the path of his misdeeds just to see where they would lead him. If he hadn't reigned that in, he would have been what's called a bully in today's educational system. The only reason he didn't allow himself to really let loose was that he wanted to be well received or at the very least to go unnoticed.

He was smart so he did well in his studies. He was athletic and strong which put him in a good spot with both the boys and the girls through his high school years.

 Girls seemed drawn to him and he learned to use that to his own advantage. Since his reputation mattered to him, he found other outlets for his desire to inflict pain. The mystery of small pets gone missing in his neighborhood remains unsolved. His urges ebbed and flowed to the point where he could somewhat control them. He might go quite a while without inflicting pain but when he began to feel the need, he always found a way.

After graduating high school and while living on his own experimenting with his impulses got easier. He studied the area around him and found a few remote locations to utilize. He clearly remembered the first time he hid in a dark alley with a ski mask in his pocket. He felt powerful hiding there in the dark as people walked by completely unaware of his presence.

That, he now realized, was the real beginning of the end.

CHAPTER 6

By that time, Thatcher was fitting in quite well socially. In fact, he had an air of confidence women found attractive. Why shouldn't he be confident? He was good-looking, smart, well-educated, and strong. He'd learned early in life to display his sense of humor and participate in innocent fun. People are drawn to that. He was actually quite likable.

When standing in the shadows of a darkened alley was no longer enough to satisfy him, he began to take action. Once started, things continued to escalate making it imperative that he not stick around to risk being caught. Thinking everything through he decided to pursue a job that would allow him to move from place to place so as not to be connected with the results of his actions.

That's when he got his CDL Class A and Class B commercial driver's licenses. He attended the truck driving classes required to drive tractor-trailers, semi-trucks, dump trucks, and passenger buses. Upon completion of the training, he chose to become a semi-truck driver and quickly took a job making deliveries across the country.

As a young adult man, it didn't take him long to realize he enjoyed being with well-dressed, professional and confident women. The type that frequented hotel restaurants and bars when they were attending a business conference. It became his practice to locate the hotels that hosted such events on his trucking delivery routes. He would then dress in casual business attire and have dinner followed by a few drinks in the bar of that hotel. Pretending to be traveling on business himself soon became a fun part of scouting out his prey. He had no interest in hurting children, men either, especially since they posed the possibility of overpowering him. His victims were innocent and unsuspecting business women, some he left alive though badly shaken, others he did not.

He successfully stayed under the radar for a good many years until things got a little too close for comfort. After one particular incident he was hauled in for questioning, along with several other truckers. He wasn't certain what had alerted the police that the offender might be a truck driver but he was well practiced by then and felt sure he had left no evidence of his involvement. He was right and after cooperating politely during questioning he was free to go. Still, he didn't like the experience of being treated as a suspect.

While sitting at the police station Thatcher caught on to which particular young police detective first suspected a truck driver's involvement. Although nothing was discovered, the officer remained convinced they were on the right track. His diligence unnerved Thatcher. Though limited, their interactions revealed him to be relentless, like a dog on a bone.

What Thatcher had no way of knowing at that time was that Detective Alan was a highly motivated individual. After graduating high school, he'd begun and completed the required classes to obtain an Associate Degree in Law Enforcement. He then immediately enrolled in evening classes, essentially combining his education with on-the-job experience in an attempt to quickly further his career. At the young age of only twenty-five the then Officer Alan aced the written exam and completed the required interviews with his superiors. As a result, he was promoted to Detective Alan, reaching that achievement more quickly than most.

Just a short few months later while looking over the details of multiple brutal attacks, a few of which had resulted in the deaths of the victims, Detective Alan noted the perpetrator could be transient. As a result, several truckers who were staying near the scene of the most recent attack, Thatcher included, were brought in for questioning.

Following their first interaction Thatcher decided to keep an eye on Detective Alan's career. He wasn't pleased when the detective received several public accolades and a commendation during the following year. He grew irate while watching a press interview in which the detective revealed he was gaining significant ground on a case he'd been diligently working on for some time. The details of his remark revealed to Thatcher that the detective was beginning to close the gap between them. He had no choice but to seriously rethink his movements. In fact, Detective Alan's relentless pursuit soon forced him to be even more precise in his efforts to avoid detection, ultimately even prompting him to make a career change.

After doing a bit of research he decided to apply for a bus driver position with USA Bus Travel & Tour Company which provided guided tours across the United States. He liked the idea of being a tour bus driver. From what he gathered each tour was assigned a traveling tour guide. All he would really be doing would be driving the group from location to location, dropping them off and picking them up at each featured point on the tour and returning them to their hotel for the night.

With the skills he'd practiced all his life he was certain he could blend in well with the travelers. He was sure to be seen as the funny and likable bus driver. The free time afforded to him while the tourists were sightseeing, having dinner and going to featured shows would come in quite handy for his particular pursuits.

He got the job and that's exactly the way things went. Just as he'd hoped would happen, Detective Alan lost track of him and he was able to relax.

It wasn't until about six months later that he decided to check in on the detective's actions. He was not happy to discover that Detective Alan had continued making strides in his career and in his quest to solve the crimes Thatcher was directly responsible for. Believing the perpetrator to be transient he had begun working with police departments nationwide and had requested FBI involvement. As much as this frustrated Thatcher he did find there to be an element of entertainment in the challenge presented by Detective Alan. It was almost as if being able to elude the detective added to his overall satisfaction. He began to see staying one step ahead of the detective as a bit of a game.

Although he didn't realize it at the time, it was this very attitude that was to be his undoing.

Getting caught up in the game made him lose focus. Losing focus led to mistakes. Mistakes that gave the detective the evidence he ultimately used against Thatcher when the case went to trial. With his own determination and the force of the FBI behind him Detective Alan was finally able to put an end to over a decade of Thatcher terrorizing women.

CHAPTER 7

His wife Marissa was crying again.

It had now been over three weeks since their baby daughter's disappearance from the maternity ward of the hospital in Austin Texas where she was born.

Marissa's due date had come and gone when exactly one week later her water broke and she went into labor. Their firstborn child, a little girl, weighed in at eight pounds and ten ounces and was twenty-one inches long. She was a good-sized baby, which made perfect sense since she had taken her sweet time before putting in an appearance.

He and Marissa joked together that she was probably going to run late for the rest of her life. Their daughter was perfectly healthy and absolutely adorable and each of them fell completely in love with her at first sight.

Her birth had come in the wee hours of the night. He stayed at the hospital as long as possible enjoying every moment with 'his girls'. A term he had quickly taken to affectionately calling them.

The baby was immediately taken away to be bathed and weighed. He used that time to tell Marissa what a great job she did and how proud he was. The nurse brought their baby in and assisted Marissa in learning to breast feed her new daughter. When they were finally alone the new parents huddled together marveling over this incredible little blessing.

Once their daughter was returned to the nursery and his wife had fallen asleep, he left. He was filled with wonder and joy as he drove home, showered and fell into bed exhausted.

Awakening the next morning he was excited to go see his girls. 'His girls' he definitely liked saying that.

He and Marissa spent a good deal of time with their new daughter that day and the next.

In the early evening of the second day Marissa told him he could go home. She would enjoy the evening with the baby and get some sleep since they were coming home the following day. He left around seven, stopping off to get a bouquet of flowers and Marissa's favorite Russel Stover candy. Those would be waiting when he brought his girls home the next day.

Little did he know of the devastating change that would come upon their lives just a few short hours later.

If someone had told him, even one month ago, that his baby daughter would go missing from the hospital nursery and he would be unable to do anything to find her, he never would have believed them. After all, he'd spent his entire adult life working for law enforcement. He was now the lead detective of his department for Pete's sake. How was this even possible?

But here he was again. Like so many times over the past three weeks since Marissa had come home from the hospital without their baby, she was nowhere to be seen. But by now he knew where to look.

She always went to the nursery. As had happened repeatedly, he found her slumped in the middle of the nursery floor with their baby daughter's sleeper clutched to her chest. Like all of the other tiny items of clothing in this room it had never even been worn.

A soft moaning escaped his wife's lips as she rocked slowly back and forth. He entered the room and approached her. Lifting her head, she stared at him vacantly through cascading tears. He knelt on the floor and gathered Marissa lovingly into his arms. He had absolutely no idea how to even begin to comfort her.

Never in his entire life had he been so totally incapable of dealing with a situation. He felt completely useless.

He was a good man. He was a strong man. Prior to this moment he had thought himself to be a powerful man, definitely more powerful than these circumstances were revealing him to be.

The police had no idea what had happened to their daughter on the night she disappeared. They had absolutely nothing to go on. No one had seen anything suspicious, at least if they had, they weren't talking.

From that moment until this one he and everyone willing to help him had been combing through his past cases. They were trying to determine if this could be the act of someone out for vengeance against him. It had been their first theory, of course, but how were they to know?

His was a noteworthy career, especially with his recent promotion to detective. He had worked numerous cases and put multiple offenders in jail. In truth, there were any number of people who may want to hurt him, many of whom, probably wanted to see him dead. Without question there was more than one person who hated him with a deep-seated hatred. Everyone in his line of work, especially detectives who testify in court to successfully close multiple cases, knows what pure unadulterated hatred can lead someone to do.

Exhausted and exasperated he now sat on the nursery floor holding his broken wife. It was all he could do these days. Without having some kind of lead, he had no idea what to do despite the many resources available to him.

Lowering his head slightly he lightly kissed Marissa on the top of her head. He felt as if he'd failed her. How did it come down to this? With his successful law-enforcement career and current position as lead detective - how was it possible he had not a single clue of how to find his own missing daughter?

CHAPTER 8

"I love it! I absolutely love it!" Thatcher repeated over and over as he paced back and forth in the small prison cell.

Feeling extremely annoyed, Jamin glanced up at him. The man was impossible to live with and yet Jamin had already survived eighteen miserable months as his cellmate.

Thatcher bent over and laughed himself into hysteria. Finally catching his breath, he skipped around the tight cell in an awkward dance repeating in a sing-song voice, "I said I'd make him pay and now I've found a way." Suddenly he slapped his thigh and laughed heartily before shouting loudly, "Not only that but I've pulled it off to perfection!"

At least this is something different, Jamin thought. Up until now he'd been stuck listening to the endless droning on and on of Thatcher's intense hatred for the detective responsible for putting him away. Jamin had heard that tirade so often that he could, in fact, quote it verbatim.

"He was a thorn in my side for years, literally years! So relentless was he in his pursuit of me, you would think I'd killed his only sister, but he knew not even one, of my prey. And yes, in the end you could say he won. He would certainly say he's won. Oh, how that sticks in my craw!! But he did win, not the war I assure you, but he's definitely the victor in this one battle, after all, here I am rotting away in this stinkin' cell while he's happily going on with his life. I'm stuck here with you, my equally doomed cellmate. And you just love listening as I go on about this day after day. I know you do."

Jamin, his very reluctant cellmate, had been unable to dispute that statement. The bitter man went on incessantly day after day, week after week, month after month. He was constantly berating the absent detective who's apparent relentless pursuit, excellent investigation and damning evidence had finally put Thatcher away for his heinous crimes. Jamin had lost count of the times he'd suffered through the same ceaseless rant as each man lay stretched out on his own pitiful version of a bed; the worn, thin, uncomfortable mattresses on metal frames in the prison cell they were forced to share.

"There's a price to pay for our vices," Jamin had often wanted to point out but never did. He had learned pretty quickly it was better to stay silent during those rantings. Besides, there was no denying the truth. He was doomed to Thatcher's unwanted companionship.

"You're not the only one stuck in this life," he would've added if he had spoken. "I'm sentenced to this god-forsaken place too, but the worst part of my punishment is drawing you as a cellmate."

Generally, he just sighed heavily and turned toward the wall trying for the thousandths time to shut Thatcher out.

"I see I'm boring you again," the insanity had gone on. "Guess you'll just have to suck it up! Someone's gotta hear about it. Looks like you're the lucky stiff who gets to listen while I chew this over and I've got a lot of chewing to do, let me tell ya. He's gonna pay. That's right! I'm gonna make him pay! I don't know how yet but if I've gotta suffer daily he's gonna suffer, too. I'm gonna think about it, talk about it, think about it and talk about it until I come up with a plan and carry it out. That little man who thinks he's a big man right now is gonna find out different. Just give me time. Oh, wait. I've got nothing but time in here. We've got all the time in the world don't we, roomie? Well, that's all right. I'll be putting my time to good use. I'm gonna think about it, talk about it, think about it 'til I figure this out. You mark my words, there's gonna be a reckoning day. That detective will rue the day he set his sights on me. He thinks my games up but he doesn't know who he's dealing with. No one's ever known who they're dealing with in me. If I never get out of this rat-hole I'll find a way to make him pay for putting me here. I promise you that. And when I make a promise - I keep it. You just watch and see. This ain't over. What's that they say? It ain't over 'til the fat lady sings', well, I'm here to tell ya, there's some singing comin' up and it ain't gonna be pretty!"

After over a year of listening to Thatcher's angry rant this new development might actually be interesting Jamin thought. His crazed roomie was now mumbling happily that Detective Alan was suffering now.

Sure, he was walking free in his life on the outside but that didn't matter anymore. All that mattered now was that just like Thatcher he was suffering every minute of every day. Finally, Thatcher had seen to it the man would suffer every day for the rest of his life.

What does that mean? Jamin found himself wondering.

CHAPTER 9

"That kid is amazing!" Matthew said to Ms. Amber shaking his head in wonder. "I've never seen a kid so devoted. There's nothing he won't do for that baby. He's just about mastered diaper changing. He definitely does a better job than I do."

"I know," Ms. Amber said. "He's been such a help with her feedings, too. If I'd realized he was going to dedicate his entire life to her based on that one night's assignment I might have given the gravity I put into all of it a bit more thought. I mean, I did emphasize the seriousness of the task at hand but that boy didn't make a commitment for one night he made it for a lifetime! I don't see what I can do about it now though. I've explained it over and over and every time he says he understands. He assures me he'll be able to handle it when she gets adopted and is taken to her new home. He just keeps saying there's no backing down from his promise now.

'You weren't there,' he says to me, 'you didn't see the way she looked at me when we were in the canoe. I meant it when I promised to keep her safe. All I'm doing now is keeping my promise to you and to her and to God. You want me to do that, right? I know you do so stop fussing about it. I'm not doing anything I don't want to do so just let me. And yes, I know someday God will give her a family who will love her and want her and they will take her home with them. When that happens God will go with her. From then on, I will pray for her and trust God to keep her safe for the rest of her life. I'll be okay, Ma. You'll see. But until then she's mine to watch over and I'm never going to let her down.' That's what he keeps telling me."

"Well, there you have it," Matthew said. "The kid knows what he's doing. At least as much as a kid his age can know what they're doing. As he

25

pointed out at his last birthday, he is in the double digits now. He's a pretty smart ten-year-old if you ask me."

Though Ms. Amber knew his words were meant to reassure her, they didn't. She couldn't help being concerned about her son. The baby had already been with them for six months and Jaxson had grown to love her deeply. He thought he was prepared but Ms. Amber knew nothing could really prepare him for the day he'd lose his baby sister. And the longer they were together the harder that loss was going to be.

She certainly hadn't mastered it but the hard times of life had taught her not to worry, even when it wasn't easy, and sometimes it was really hard.

Right now, for instance. But even when it was difficult, she made sure to practice praying instead of worrying. So here she was again asking God to help her, Jaxson and the rest of the family when the actual day arrived that their precious girl would go to a new home.

Right now, at this very moment she would pray for the adoptive parents.

"I don't know who they are yet," she prayed. "I don't know where they are or why they're going to want to adopt a little girl ~ but you know, God. You know every intimate detail of their lives. You know why they're going to need her and that she already needs them. Please, God, as the loving father you are, please prepare them, even now, to take that precious little girl into their lives and home and to do exactly what Jaxson is already doing. Help them care for and protect her in every way she will ever need. Please bless them for being willing to love an abandoned baby and make her their own."

Coming full circle her prayer then became one for Jaxson. She thanked God for the excellent way he was caring for the baby and for the precious young boy he now was and the good man she knew he would grow up to be. She thanked God, again, that the damage done to Jaxson's innocent mind and spirit in the first six years of his life was slowly but surely being healed here in her home just as the damage that had been done to Matthew had been healed.

She thanked God for blessing this house to be everything she had wanted, dreamed of and worked to make it. It was an oasis, a haven, a place of healing and a home filled with love.

"He's done it again," Steven said, shaking his head in amazement as he walked through the large opening that separated the kitchen from the living room. "No question about it - Jaxson's got the touch. She's asleep. Out like a light. He's putting her to bed now. I don't know about you but I'm beat. I got most of the fencing repaired on the back side of the property today but it was a job. I don't mind sayin'. I'm going to bed. You'll see me in the morning when we'll do it all again." If the words were the only thing heard it would seem a complaint but the statement was said with pure joy. He loved his life.

Steven had come on board around the time Ms. Amber first purchased the house. He was in on it all from the beginning and had helped her make the place into a home where children could safely play. Steven was the only paid employee and room and board was part of his compensation. Being just ten years younger than Ms. Amber he was the only resident of the household who had never been one of her children, but that certainly didn't mean he wasn't one of the family.

Steven was an exceptional man. He was good, honest, and had a great sense of humor and fun. He had a very loving spirit, was kind to everyone he met and had a natural way with children. He made them feel special and loved. He was also a jack-of-all-trades and master-of-many. He instilled good work ethic, honesty and integrity into the children as they worked alongside him. Just as a father would, he had taught every boy who had come and gone through the years about the upkeep of the house and its land. Matthew seemed to have natural skills in those areas so when he showed a greater interest than the other children Steven invited him along more frequently. As the years unfolded the two of them became quite close and Matthew learned a great deal from Steven, not only an excellent work ethic but about life as well. The tradition was now continuing as Matthew mentored the younger children and taught those who showed greater interest in the work, which Jaxson definitely did.

Amber often thanked God for bringing Steven into her life and blessing her home with him.

"Good-night Steven," she called after him. "Thanks for all your hard work today. Rest well."

As Steven left the room Matthew put the last clean dish into the cupboard and hung the drying towel over the oven door. He then turned to where Ms. Amber sat comfortably in her easy chair.

"I've about had it myself so if there's nothing else you need, I'm heading to bed," he said.

"Oh no, I'm fine. You go get some rest. Thanks for all your help today. You know I couldn't keep this place going without you, right?"

"I know you say that. I also know you'd find a way to make it happen. No worries, we're all in this together and with God we'll keep on getting the job done. Rest well, ma," he leaned down and gave her a quick hug.

As she watched her son walk away old memories flooded in. Matthew had come to her when he was just a little younger than Jaxson. At six years old he looked as if he were barely four. He was malnourished, pale and withdrawn. His mother was a drug addict and his mostly-absentee father was very violent when he was around. By the time the police finally took Matthew from the home he had been through it. He arrived at Ms. Amber's timid, traumatized and afraid to trust. She'd had her work cut out getting him to let her in at all. Trust didn't come easy but with consistent love and patience it did finally come. Matthew stayed on once he became an adult, partnering with Steven in keeping the place going and mentoring the children. Has it really been fifteen years since Matthew first came to me? she asked herself in disbelief. Where has the time gone?

CHAPTER 10

As he watched his beautiful wife drying her damp hands on her apron, he couldn't help but notice the sadness that always seemed to overshadow her these days.

He knew she desperately wanted to be happy again. She was trying. Unfortunately, it appeared that despite her best efforts she was fighting a losing battle. Nothing had been the same since the disappearance of their baby. How could it be? They had a little girl somewhere out there in the world - or did they? No, don't do that, he said to himself, just as he did every time the thought that their daughter may be dead crept into his mind. He had to go on believing and hoping she was alive and that someday he was going to find her. He simply had to! It was the only way he could stay above the grief he and his wife were battling daily.

Aprons were a special part of Marissa's childhood which was why she had a bright and colorful collection of them. She wore one every time she worked in the kitchen.

When they were just getting acquainted, Marissa had happily shared her memories of the first time her grandmother put an apron on her. Marissa's grandma Nora was an excellent cook who loved preparing delicious food for her loved ones. She was in the habit of having a weekly family dinner to which all of Marissa's relatives were invited. It was a standing invitation and whoever was able to come came. Whoever wasn't able to come looked forward to the next one.

When Marissa was a very small child her grandma Nora noticed she enjoyed helping in the kitchen. Wanting to spend special time with each member of her family, grandma Nora was always on the lookout for something they could do together. Teaching Marissa to cook was just the thing. And so it was that her grandma Nora made Marissa her very first apron. It was very similar to Nora's, tying at the waist and having huge pockets.

Marissa shared her memories of the day her grandma Nora first tied the pretty apron around her waist. It was just before asking Marissa to help her mix the biscuit dough. Her grandmother soon taught Marissa to embroider and they embroidered their names onto their aprons together.

Marissa now had the tiny apron hanging on a peg in her own kitchen. She often said the happy memories it brought to mind made her smile. The aprons Marissa now wore were full front-coverage aprons meant to protect the upper body from spills. The lower half of all her aprons still had large pockets just like grandma Nora's.

Still to this day Marissa took the time to embroider her name onto each new apron. Yes, aprons were definitely his wife's thing.

Does she still enjoy this, his mind asked him as he watched Marissa take the casserole dish from the oven and set it on the hot plate in the center of the table for their evening meal. He was pouring sweet tea into their glasses and making light conversation with her as he did every evening at this time. All the while his heart ached for her and for himself as they continued to live with the grief of their daughter's strange disappearance.

Despite the passage of time, they weren't getting over it. Do you ever really get over something like this? He asked himself for the thousandths time. You get through it. You keep going on. You survive. He knew that to be true. Still, he found himself wondering if that was the best they could hope for. He hoped not. He wanted to do more than just survive and keep moving forward.

It hadn't been easy and there were still moments in which he wasn't sure they would make it, but they were still here. They were still together.

We're definitely survivors, his mind told him as he thought about how blessed they truly were. Many couples didn't make it through similar circumstances and he could see why. It was overwhelming. There was only one other word to describe it really. Having your newborn baby go missing from the hospital never to be found and returned to you was nothing short of devastating.

He could understand why Marissa was so debilitated. While they were both excited about their coming baby Marissa's entire life revolved around it. She gave up her job to be a stay-at-home mother. She spent months anticipating and planning for their daughter's every need and lovingly decorating the nursery.

When their baby disappeared a huge part of his wife's reason for being disappeared with her. Unfortunately, Marissa's grief kept her from feeling able to return to work. As he looked back over the past year one thing was clear. His sweet wife had come as close as a human being can come to having a complete mental breakdown without actually having one. Thankfully, she was doing better now, but there was no question her grief was still pulling at her, perhaps it always would.

Even as he worked through his own grief God gave him the strength to continue being patient and loving toward his wife. Most of the time he was the strong one. But he'd be lying if he didn't admit there were times when he was close to reaching his own breaking point. Despite her own pain Marissa saw that and reached out to him in his times of need. He was beyond thankful their shared grief was serving to strengthen their marriage instead of tearing it apart.

To say the baby's first birthday, just a few short weeks ago, had been difficult, would be a gross understatement. As the day drew close each of them felt unsure of what to do. In the end they spent a quiet evening at home, just the two of them. Though it wasn't easy they revisited her birth and their great happiness during the first two days of her life. Of course, those memories led to the night she went missing. Holding each other they talked it all through. Crying together they wondered all over again what had become of their sweet daughter. Finally, they prayed together, asking God to continue to give them strength and comfort and to watch over their daughter until they were reunited. Through their faith they firmly believed that would happen, they just didn't know whether it would be during this life or the one to come.

CHAPTER 11

"There you go!"

"You've got it!"

"Hold on tight!"

Hearing the children's sudden shouts, Ms. Amber's hand stopped in mid-air as she looked up from hanging a towel on the clothesline to see what was going on.

Gathered in the clearing just beyond her, the children were just starting to run.

"Don't let go!!" Jaxson shouted to his little sister as he held her in his arms. "I've got you! Just hold onto the string."

"Don't let go, Jovie!" another child shouted excitedly as Jaxson's pace picked up.

Jaxson was tall, and stronger than most eleven-year-old boys, most likely a result of working side-by-side with Steven. Steven had taken the boy under his wing and was teaching him everything he knew about property upkeep.

Jovie held the kite string clutched tightly in her little fist as her big brother began gliding along with her in his arms. The other children ran alongside with their heads turned and eyes keenly watching the kite in hopes it would catch the wind and lift.

Suddenly it did just that!

Everyone squealed in delight, Ms. Amber included.

Jovie cheered loudly as the orange butterfly kite leapt into the air. It twirled on the wind several times as Jaxson's legs carried them swiftly across the field. Once he was certain it would stay up, he slowed and turned bending to lower Jovie to the ground. Gently holding her little arm in his hand, he pulled it toward the ground and back up again in one fluid motion. The kite dipped and immediately leapt with the movements.

It was a rare windy day that Jaxson wasn't in this clearing flying a kite. Practice had made him exceptionally good at it, especially for one so young.

Ms. Amber stood watching with a smile on her face and in her heart. It did her good seeing the children playing so well together. She loved nothing more than for them to be outside running off their excess energy in some fun way.

This wasn't the first time she'd marveled at Jaxson's way with other children. Actually, it was the reason she'd chosen him for such an important mission, almost two years ago. It certainly seemed now that from the moment he'd taken the little bundle into his arms, Jovie had become the most important thing in his world. The care and devotion he invested in her truly was beyond the ability, attention, and scope of a boy his age. And yet, he had done it and continued doing so even now. The patience Jaxson had with children in general, but especially with Jovie, was simply undeniable.

How many times had Ms. Amber been amazed at their relationship? So many, and in so many ways. It warmed her heart and terrified her at the same time. The love between them was a wonder to witness and for those two children to experience. Still, she couldn't help being concerned. Jovie was going to leave one day and when she did it would break both of their hearts.

Of course, other children had come and gone since Jaxson joined the family and he'd done well with it. He seemed to love all children but his bond and devotion to Jovie were above anything Ms. Amber had seen before. It left her to wonder how they would ever come back from being separated.

How can I protect them from the hurt that's coming? She asked herself for the thousandths time. What can I do to prepare them? How can I make them understand something they cannot begin to comprehend until it actually happens?

As she always did when these became her prevailing thoughts she turned to God.

Please give me the wisdom I'll need. This is all on you, God, it's certainly beyond me. I'm going to need you to help me help Jaxson when the time comes, she whispered to her heavenly Father. Jovie will go to her new home where it will be up to her new family to help her adjust. Jaxson will remain here where it falls on me. How am I going to help him get through such a great loss at such a young age? Please God, please help me be ready.

She continued to clip clothing onto the line as she processed her thoughts and prayed for her children. A short time later while carrying the empty laundry basket back to the house Ms. Amber looked toward the clearing. The little ones were taking their turn holding the string as the older ones worked the string further up the line to make sure the kite stayed airborne. It made her proud to see children working as a team. Teamwork was one of the priorities taught in this family.

Fun was another family priority, a very important one. Amber loved seeing the children having fun together. Children were meant to have fun. Listening to a child's laughter was one of the greatest joys of her life.

The majority of children coming to live with her came from a life void of laughter. They'd had to learn self-protection; seeing and enduring things no child should ever be exposed to. For most, self-protection took the form of isolation. It's only natural for human beings to shut themselves off from others after being deeply hurt, abused or abandoned. Isolation is the ultimate avoidance of pain. Not allowing others to get close is the same as not allowing others to inflict hurt.

There were a few, like Jovie, who were so young when they arrived, they brought no memories at all. But for the others, memories were strong and often traumatic.

Ms. Amber had always loved children, even when she herself was one. Being born with a natural capacity to connect with others she never lacked in having friends. In fact, she still stayed in touch with several ladies from her elementary school days, mainly her friend Kate, who made as much of an effort as Amber did to keep the friendship going.

Amber's mother often referred to her outgoing nature as God-given. She nurtured it by encouraging her daughter to include all children and to always be kind. Perhaps this was the reason everyone seemed to love Amber. It was certainly why everyone she knew felt loved.

Amber seemed to inherently know where there is much hurt there must be much patience and unconditional love. The more a child has been hurt the longer it may take to gain their trust and draw them to willingly open their heart. To her way of thinking there was no time limit when it came to giving a child space in which to heal and learn to trust. It was one of the main reasons she was such a good mother.

As a result of Amber's gentleness, acceptance and love, every child with a barrier in place when they first arrived eventually lowered it. With her consistent gentleness each one learned to let her love them, given more time they learned to love her in return.

It took a while sometimes but eventually they came to understand what it meant to be a child. With the constant nurturing, protection and love offered in their new home each child began to let go of their fears. Once that happened, they were able to relax and allow themselves to have fun and that was the beginning of happiness.

The first time Amber heard each of her children laugh a real belly laugh was burned into her memory. Those moments were what life was all about.

Amber loved being a mother, and she was good at it, excellent, in fact. This was why, despite what had brought them there, the children in Ms. Amber's family not only survived, they thrived.

Amber saw others with her heart, not her eyes. This allowed her to love without reservation, a risky proposition at times, for sure. Regardless of her own hurts Amber never lost that ability. For this reason, she was the perfect woman to mother hurt and abandoned children.

Amber loved cuddling little babies, she loved taking care of them, teaching them, playing with them, making them feel safe, and hearing them laugh. And as they grew older, she loved talking with them, hearing their thoughts, working with them and teaching them, knowing their dreams and helping them learn how to make and achieve their goals.

Having had such a home in her own childhood may have been the very reason she was so driven to establish the Delaney Home for Children. It was not only a place where children could be loved and happy, it was a place for her to be loved as well.

CHAPTER 12

One morning at breakfast while reminding the children it was the first day of spring Ms. Amber asked what they loved most about the season. Asher loved seeing the ground turn green after all the brown grass of the southern winter. Lisha loved hearing birds singing in the mornings again. Several other answers were given before Ms. Amber heard what she'd been waiting for.

"It's butterfly time!" Carter shouted.

"Yes, it is," Ms. Amber agreed with a huge smile, "and that means we'll be heading to the milkweed garden to begin the process of growing this year's monarchs. We'll get started right after breakfast. But we need to gather everything else we'll need first."

Just as they were beginning to clear the table there was a knock on the back door. As usual Kate didn't bother waiting for an answer. Being practically a member of the family, she opened the door and called out to let them know she was there. Ms. Amber and several of the children called 'come on in' at the same time and immediately started laughing. Kate walked into the kitchen asking what was so funny which only started them laughing again.

As soon as the dishes were finished, each child was assigned a task and sent on their way with instructions to meet on the back porch in ten minutes.

With all the natural sunlight flooding through its many windows the back porch was the perfect place for growing monarchs, especially since they only grow in temperatures higher than seventy degrees. Natural lighting is very important for monarchs because studies have shown they don't develop the navigational skills they need when they're exposed to artificial lighting.

36

Amber had very purposefully planted milkweed when she moved into the house for this very reason. She wanted growing monarch butterflies to be an annual educational project in the Delaney household. And it was. Amber and Kate had as much fun with this project as the children did. They probably had even more fun seeing the children's fascination in each step of the process.

Children learn best when they're having fun. What could be more fun than watching a caterpillar become a chrysalis and eventually seeing a butterfly emerge and fly away?

As each child arrived, some ten minutes later Ms. Amber ran through the checklist of needed items with them.

Tomato cage, check.

Netting, check.

Vase, check.

Shallow cardboard box, check.

Newspaper, check.

"Very good," Ms. Amber told them all after everything had been gathered and accounted for. "It looks like everything is here."

Now who can tell us what we need to do first?" Ms. Kate asked.

"Cover the tomato cage with netting," several children shouted at once.

"That's right!" Ms. Amber said. "And then we need to?"

"Put newspaper on the bottom of the box," Asher exclaimed.

"Very good! What's next?"

"Put the vase on the newspaper," Robby replied.

"That's right, and then?"

"We set the cage over the vase inside the box. Then that cage is ready, right Jovie?" Jaxson asked his little sister who was standing beside him taking everything in.

"Uh huh," she answered, nodding her head up and down with a bit of uncertainty.

Jovie was the youngest child living in the Delaney Home at that time but her age didn't matter. As was true with everything they did, all of the children participated, everyone learned and had fun together.

Of course, there were kits that could be purchased for all of this, but the family had such a good time making the butterfly cages each year that Ms. Amber never bought them.

37

Over the next hour or so Amber and Kate would work with the children to help them put together the chosen number of butterfly cages. Once they were ready for use, they would all be on the look-out for monarch eggs and caterpillars.

Eggs are the hardest to find. They're so small they're often hidden under the leaf of the milkweed plant. Ms. Amber explained that once an egg is laid it only takes between three to five days to become a caterpillar. Fewer than ten percent survive due to weather, predators, parasites and disease so finding eggs is challenging. Sometimes they are found on a milkweed stem with a caterpillar already on it. What a bonus it is when that happens

A few days later, in the late afternoon, Amber and Kate sat drinking sweet tea and chatting in the gazebo. Suddenly hearing lots of excitement coming from the side yard they hurried to see what was going on.

They found the children gathered around Asher in the milkweed garden. He was telling them about spotting the first caterpillar of the season. The real fun began as he pointed it out. The milkweed with the caterpillar on it was cut, carried inside and put into a vase filled with water inside the cage.

Monarch caterpillars have a huge appetite. They can eat up to two hundred times their own weight in milkweed so extra milkweed needs to be brought in regularly. Asher was put in charge of that while Lisha agreed to make sure there was always fresh water in the vases. Jaxson said he would change out the newspaper as needed. With the new milkweed put into place and the various duties divided up the children went back outside to play.

Kate turned to Amber saying she almost hated to leave after such an interesting morning. Amber put her arm around her best friend and reminded her she never had to leave if she didn't want to.

"That's the kind of friendship we have, Kate. You know that," she said with a loving smile.

"I do know that," Kate smiled. "I absolutely love coming to spend time with you and the children. There's just so much fun and love in your home, Amber. I remember when you first got this place and let me tell you, you've made it into exactly what you dreamed of back then. I am so proud of the life you've made for yourself and the home you give these little ones."

"Thanks Kate, it is pretty special, isn't it? We're all so blessed to have each other, and I mean all of us. In case you don't realize it, you are a very important part of this family."

As the two women were hugging good-bye Amber reminded Kate to stop by often in the weeks ahead.

"The children will be going through the entire process of growing butterflies and setting them free," she said.

"Don't you worry," Kate answered. "I'll be here so often you'll want to kick me out. Your annual butterfly growing project makes this my favorite time of the year."

It can take as little as twenty-five days for a monarch butterfly to grow from an egg to a butterfly so everyone has to stay on top of things. More milkweed with caterpillars were added to the cages as they were found. The caterpillars grew and ate and ate and grew as each one continued making their way to the top of the cage. During the next fourteen days the process was for the caterpillar to attach itself to the netting so it hangs upside down in a J shape. It hangs as a J for about eighteen hours. The caterpillar then spins silk to form into a chrysalis and for the next ten days a continuous process of transformation takes place during which the old body parts turn into the beautiful body parts of what will soon emerge as an adult monarch butterfly.

The children watched closely over the next several weeks as the chrysalis became more and more transparent and the growing butterfly got closer and closer to emerging. It was soon to be free.

CHAPTER 13

So, you're guessing it's a girl butterfly?" Jaxson asked Lisha as he wrote her name in the girl column.

"Yes, definitely a girl!" Lisha answered.

As of this morning the chrysalis was completely transparent. It was getting awfully close to time for the butterfly to emerge. The children had been putting in their guesses for a boy or a girl all morning. The room was busy and loud and everyone was full of excitement.

"Okay, everyone," Ms. Amber called out, "let's quiet down now and gather around. Ms. Deb is here from the Nature Center to talk with us again about Monarchs. It's been a couple of years since she's been here and some of you weren't here when she came before so let's give her our full attention.

Ms. Amber and Kate stood to the back of the crowd watching the excitement. As the children gathered closely around her, Ms. Deb commended them on the wonderful job they'd done in providing a place for the monarchs to grow and getting the cages set up for them. As she was speaking, she kept a close eye on the chrysalis. When she saw it moving, she pointed out how the chrysalis was now jerking in short quick movements. Everyone stood watching as the butterfly inside the chrysalis continued moving quickly until the thin transparent layer began to open a tiny bit wider and wider. The butterfly's head popped out followed by its antenna which were immediately followed by the entire rest of the monarch's wings and body. This happens so fast, taking less than five minutes, that to actually witness it was a win/win for everyone.

"Is it a boy or a girl?" The children began to inquire competitively.

"We'll get to that very soon," Ms. Deb replied. "But for now, notice that it's still drying its wings, see? When they're dry it will open them up and we will easily be able to tell."

She continued teaching the children about the monarch. Everyone enjoyed learning while watching the beautiful creature settling into its new life as a butterfly.

Finally, Ms. Deb said, "Okay, children, who knows how to tell what this black, orange and white beauty is?"

Asher raised his hand just a fraction of a second faster than the other children so Ms. Deb called on him.

"Go ahead, Asher, and tell us how we can tell which we have here with us today - a male or a female."

"The male has two black dots on the bottom inside part of each wing and the female doesn't," Asher answered.

"That's correct," Ms. Deb nodded. "Okay then, which would you say this one is?"

Asher looked very closely at the butterfly. He waited for it to open its wings long enough for him to be able to tell.

"It's a boy!!" He suddenly shouted when the wings were fully opened. Everyone could now clearly see the black dots on the bottom inside of its wings.

"I knew it!! I knew we were going to get a boy," Asher said laughing with the other children.

"Well, you were right then." Ms. Deb said. "Did you also pick out a name for this little guy?"

"His name is Char," Asher said proudly.

"Alrighty then, we have our first butterfly and his name is Char. Tomorrow I'll come back and show you how to handle and release Char. Until then he will be fine. A new butterfly doesn't eat during its first twenty-four hours so waiting until tomorrow will give Char's wings more time to dry. They need at least five hours of drying time. This way he'll be ready to go by the time I arrive tomorrow."

Everyone thanked Ms. Deb and said good-bye.

Although Kate had been there several times in the past for the butterfly release, this was the first time she'd seen the process from the beginning.

She felt just like one of the children as she learned even more about growing butterflies.

The next day was the perfect day for a butterfly release. It's not good to release them if a storm is brewing and it was a beautiful Carolina day with no storm on the horizon. The children were excited for another fun day as Ms. Deb returned to teach them how to hold the new butterflies. Kate had returned as well and was every bit as excited as the children were. Ms. Amber's home was always full of activities and Kate loved joining the fun as often as possible.

Since it was easy to take the cage outside, reach in, catch the butterfly and then release it outside its cage that's what they would do. That way Char would be able to fly away instead of being accidently released inside the house and having to be caught and released again.

Once the cage was outside Ms. Deb reached in gently and pinched Char's wings between her first finger and her thumb. She asked Asher if he wanted to release Char. Since he did, she gently handed Char to Asher and told him what to do next.

You never know what to expect when releasing butterflies. Some fly away as soon as they're released while others take their time, just hanging around on nearby flowers or bushes before they fly away. Char was more than ready to go so as soon as Asher released him, off he went, over the house and on to new adventures only butterflies know about.

Three more butterflies had emerged between the time Ms. Deb was there the day before and the time of her return. Two were girls and the other was a boy. Three children named them and were the ones to release them. The girl butterfly Lisha named Madalyn decided to stay a while. To everyone's great enjoyment Madalyn flew over and alighted on the picnic table in the gazebo. She looked back at all of them for a few minutes before finally taking off.

By the end of the monarch growing season that year Ms. Amber, Kate and the children had released nineteen butterflies. The boys were the big winners with there being twelve boys to only seven girl butterflies. The girl's weren't worried about it though. They were determined that next year would be their year and were already picking out names and making a list.

CHAPTER 14

"I have no idea what I want to do when I grow up," Jaxson said to Matthew as he climbed up into the passenger's seat of the truck.

"Well, of course you don't," Matthew answered him. "You're all of what? Eleven years old? You've got time to figure this out. And if you don't know by the time you graduate high school, you won't be the first. I can assure you of that much."

"Yeah?" Jaxson asked. "When did you know what you wanted to do?"

"Me? I thought I had it figured out in High School but I was wrong. That's one of the funny things about life, kiddo, even when we think we know what we're doing it's fairly likely we really don't."

"Well, how am I ever supposed to know when I've got it figured out then?"

"You don't have to," Steven answered to Jaxson's surprise.

"You don't? What do you have to do then?"

"It's simple, kid, all you have to do is pray."

After realizing he was making this sound too easy Matthew went on to say, "Okay, well, that's not all you have to do but it's the main thing. I'm not saying you shouldn't give it thought and make your plans, just keep in mind that sometimes life has a way of changing everything. When that happens you just have to remind yourself that God's in on the plan so there's nothing to worry about. Nothing else really matters as long as you keep God in the mix.

"How do I do that?" Jaxson asked curiously.

"Just talk to Him," Matthew answered.

"Let me explain," he said. "Take today for example. We've got a list of things to pick up in town today. So, we've thought this through, we've made a list and now we're living out that plan. But any number of things could happen to change our plans today, right? I'm not telling you anything you don't already know. I mean, just think about it, life changes on a dime sometimes. What do you think could possibly happen that could change our plans?

Jaxson had been nodding in agreement as he listened. Now he said, "I don't know. Maybe the truck wouldn't start?"

"Exactly." Matthew agreed.

"Or even worse we could get in a car accident."

"That's true," Matthew said. "Remember last year when that riding-the-winds-of-the-hurricane storm came up and grounded us all for the day?"

"Oh, yeah, I sure do," Jaxson said wide eyed. "That was a bad one."

"For as far inland as we are, it sure was," Matthew commented while nodding in agreement. "We were waylaid a bit and didn't get the job done that day. Did it work out in the end?"

"Sure, it did," Jaxson said while looking out the truck window at the passing scenery. A few seconds later he added, "most things do."

"And therein lies the secret," Matthew told him. "What do you do when you're not sure what's going to happen? I'll tell you what I do. I pray thankful prayers."

"Okay, but what does that mean?" Jaxson asked, eager to learn.

"Well, take that day, for example, the day we had to shut everything down due to that storm coming in. Once I saw that we weren't going anywhere I started praying right away.

I probably said, 'Thank you God that you're going to watch over us out here today and keep us safe. Thank you that we're going to be okay without the things we were going to pick up today. Thank you that we'll figure out how to get along without 'em or you'll find another way to provide.' Do you see what I mean? When something scary or bad is happening I usually pray something like this, 'Thank you, father, that you always have good plans for us and even when hard times come you use them for our good.' In case you don't know this, Jaxson, the Bible says that in Romans. So that's what I mean when I talk about thankful prayers. Whenever I'm uncertain of what's gonna happen next, I remember that God isn't. He already knows what's gonna happen and since He has a good plan, He's gonna get me through it. Even when it doesn't seem like it, everything will work out in the end. I'm not saying nothing bad will ever happen or life won't have hard times. I'm just saying, we'll get through it and there's always joy on the other side.

I guess I pray thankful prayers for a couple of reasons. One is that it calms me down, another is that it reminds me to keep trusting God through everything.

One thing I've learned in my life is that no matter how much I may want to, I can't control what happens to me. I can only control what I do about it.

I'll tell you something else, once I accepted that fact life got easier. God's the only one who can control things and I'm not sure how much He even does that. Some folks may disagree but personally, I don't believe God makes things happen to us, I believe He lets things happen and then He uses them for good in our lives. Most of the time things that happen are just part of life on this earth - like the truck breaking down, getting in a car accident or getting sick. I do believe God works to answer our prayers though, mainly He works inside of us by giving us wisdom, courage and strength, things like that. I guess my praying thankful prayers is just another way for me to tell Him I know He's got my best in mind. Since I believe that I trust Him no matter what. That's the way I live my life anyway, and it's never failed me yet."

"Makes sense to me," Jaxson said as Matthew pulled the truck in at the hardware store.

Matthew reached out and tousled the boy's hair as they walked into the store. He was always on the lookout for teachable moments when they were together and Jaxson's worry about deciding what to do in the future seemed like a great one.

CHAPTER 15

It had been on his mind all through his work day and now, as he made the drive home, he felt a bit of uncertainty. Sadly, the anniversary of their baby girl's birth was never an easy day for them. He'd come to follow Marissa's lead on it.

That first year they'd sat quietly together, revisiting their happiness, then the terrible moments that followed. They got through the evening by talking, holding each other and praying together. They went to bed early and cried in each other's arms.

Then last year they talked it through, comforted each other and decided to revisit the search. Over the next several weeks they talked with the police in hopes of sparking a new interest in the case. While the detectives in charge took another look at things nothing new came to light and life simply went on.

As the day approached, they were both fully aware it was on the other's mind. Still, neither spoke of it until the actual day of their baby's birthday. Due to an early meeting, he was out of the house before Marissa was even up this morning. Now he wasn't sure what to expect when he got home.

As they were in the habit of doing, they greeted each other with a hug and quick kiss. Glancing through from the kitchen to the dining room he was very surprised to see that Marissa had bought a very small pink cake. She had placed a large number three candle in the center of the cake and set it on the dining room table. Seeing his expression, Marissa told him she had known he would be surprised. She then said the two of them needed to talk.

She took a few steps closer to him and stretched her hands out toward him. He reached out and took her hands into his. She said she wanted to talk about how they were going to move on even though they still had no idea where their little girl was. She told him she was tired of wallowing in her grief but she felt guilty for wanting to move forward.

Listening to her words and looking deeply into her eyes he felt relief slowly begin to flood throughout his body. As soon as she stopped talking, he told her he felt the exact same way.

Wordlessly, he took one step toward her and opened his arms. Without hesitation she stepped forward and leaned into him. The two of them simply hugged each other and cried.

They cried for every moment they had missed with their baby over the past three years. They cried for every moment they believed they would miss with her in the future. They cried for the guilt they felt for not being able to discover what had happened to her. They cried for the possibility that they might never know. They cried for the guilt of not being able to help her if she were alive somewhere right then and needed to be rescued. They cried until they simply had no cry left in them.

With their arms around one another they went to the couch and sat down together.

Finally, they promised each other that they would always tell each other the truth and share their thoughts and feelings. They agreed that having come this far together they were determined to make it the rest of the way. Still talking things through they decided they needed to come to some agreements and began to hash those out.

They agreed that they would never give up and they would never stop trying to find their missing daughter. They agreed to always talk to and listen to each other. They even chose a code word to say when they needed to talk and couldn't get started. They knew they were going to go through more hard moments but agreed it was time to allow themselves to have good times again.

They had been hanging in limbo, stuck somewhere beyond loss but not quite as far as death. It seemed to be an inescapable place but they agreed they had been there long enough and they needed to escape it now. Neither of them really knew how so they would learn together. Already knowing they couldn't get through it alone they promised to be there for each other no matter what. Just as they had done so far, when one needed to be held up the other one would do it. The rest of the time they would work toward having joy in their lives.

At the end of a long and emotional conversation they got up from the couch and Marissa led him back to the dining room table. As they stood there together looking at that small pink birthday cake, she turned to him and said, "I'm so thankful to be with you. I know I've been difficult these past three years. I've been stuck. I haven't known how to get through it but I've been trying. Your patience and love have been such a help to me. Of course, I would never want to go through what we've come through. But since it had to happen, I want you to know, there is no one I would rather have traveled this road with than you."

Tears welled up in his eyes as he took her hands into his again.

"Thank you for telling me that," he said simply.

"I'm so glad we've had this talk today," Marissa continued. "I'm so glad we're both ready to let ourselves heal. I want nothing more than to find new ways to move forward together. I guess I just needed to know you feel the same way. Knowing that now, I have something to tell you and I hope it will make you happy."

He looked at her curiously as she tugged on his hands pulling the two of them closer to the table. Pointing to the little cake she said, "as we cut this cake and enjoy it to remember our little girl, you need to know, we're also celebrating the coming of our next child."

At his look of confusion, she smiled the most genuine and beautiful smile he had seen on her face in a very long time. Happiness shone from her eyes as she said, "I see you're confused so let me clarify: yes, I am telling you you're going to be a father again."

His heart constricted as he put his arms around his wife and hugged her tightly.

He felt so happy.

"Being with you is more than enough, Marissa," he told her lovingly. "But having another baby is a wonderful blessing."

A few days later he was the one who wanted to talk. After reminding her of how much she loved the ocean and had always enjoyed their beach vacations he confessed his desire to relocate to South Carolina. Once she got over the surprise Marissa said it went right along with their need for a fresh start and she was all for it.

The following weekend they started packing and soon after they put their house up for sale.

Three months later Marissa followed in their car close behind him as he drove the U-Haul to a small town not far from the coastal Carolina shores where they made a new start.

CHAPTER 16

Ms. Amber was never about having the children feel as though they must try to convince people to choose to adopt them. She didn't even want them to see it as their job to impress people. She just wanted them to be themselves.

Of course, she made it a point to teach good manners, respect and kindness toward others. But that was all just a normal part of their upbringing. Beyond that, she just prayed for each of the children who came to live with her. She simply asked God to send the right adoptive family at the right time for each one. She constantly asked His help in being a good mother for as long as the child was with her.

To avoid unnecessary pressure or destructive feelings of rejection she never presented visits from prospective adoptive families in that light. They were simply a family who had gatherings with invited guests as part of the regular routine. In fact, Ms. Amber's parents and her best friend Kate often came along when prospective parents were visiting.

Of course, as they grew older and saw children go to live with some of the visitors, the children put it together on their own. And that was fine. Ms. Amber just didn't want them feeling pressure to be chosen and suffering great heartache if they weren't.

When people visited, the family simply interacted with each other and the visiting guests in the same natural and comfortable way they lived every day. In this way Ms. Amber helped them enjoy the company of others instead of striving to impress someone into choosing them. She always tried to handle these visits as just a chance to have fun and meet new people, never pushing anyone to dress in their best clothing or be on their best behavior. They were always clean and dressed nicely for whatever they were doing unless, of course, it was a work day or they were helping Matthew or Steven with a special project. Ms. Amber felt it was important for the adopting family to see the children in everyday circumstances as part of a family unit.

And so it was that the day had started out like any other day. But by its end it became the day Jaxson would never forget.

For as many times as Ma had talked with him about it, every time receiving his assurance that he understood, he had not truly understood. How could he have? How was a boy of twelve who had spent over three years caring for, protecting, playing with, teaching, loving and praying for the little sister he had taken into his arms ~ even more importantly ~ into his heart, supposed to understand watching her walk out of his life?

Ma had often cautioned Matthew, Steven and Jaxson that there was a possibility that when it happened it might happen suddenly. They had all agreed that if Jovie left them without notice, that was the way it was meant to be. They told themselves that though it would be really difficult it must be the best way for all of them.

That was the day which impacted his life like no other, there was no question about it. Nor was there any question that God had proven true to His promises, each and every one of them, just as Ma had always assured them all He would.

As she had said could happen, Ma got very short notice that a couple had chosen to be Jovie's new parents. Normally the child and the prospective parents met several times after the decision to adopt the child had been made and before the child's transfer to their new family took place. In this case the couple and their son had attended several family days at the Children's Home throughout the summer months. Their interactions with all of the children had been enjoyable during the first visit. During the second visit they again enjoyed interacting with all of the children, but most specifically, Jovie. During the third family visit they seemed to pay specific attention to Jovie; the mother even read her son's favorite book to him and Jovie at one point. Ms. Amber noted that the visit seemed natural and fun for all of them. Before leaving the parents commented on how adorable and smart Jovie was and Ms. Amber took notice of the positive connection between all of them.

A month later the adoption agency contacted her and asked if the couple could return for a family dinner to be with the children again. Of course, she agreed.

Steven and Matthew planned and put on a wonderful corn roast and cook-out for the entire family and the couple and their six-year-old son. Again, it was a very positive experience for everyone. Assuming this family to be interested in adopting Jovie Ms. Amber then did what she always did at that point. She asked for as much information as she was permitted to have on the adopting family. In this way Ms. Amber assured herself the child she had loved and given a home to would be safe, wanted and loved in their new home.

Ms. Amber had been a little surprised when nothing more came of it but could only assume they weren't ready or Jovie wasn't the child of their choosing after all. She didn't voice it to anyone but there was a bit of relief in knowing Jovie wasn't going to be leaving them. There was also a bit of sadness that a permanent home wasn't opening up for their precious girl.

In actuality, that had not been true at all. Unbeknownst to them the family was busy preparing a little girl's room in their home and completing all the legalities of adopting Jovie.

Ms. Amber should have been notified each step of the way but the adoption agency the family was working with neglected to do so. The couple, thought all along that Ms. Amber was preparing Jovie to go home with them.

It was most fortunate then that Ms. Amber had actually been preparing Jovie for such a possibility her entire life, just as she did with each of the children who came to live with her. It was a delicate balance trying to make sure each child felt loved and secure while also reminding them there was always the possibility of being adopted.

It was just a normal Sunday afternoon in the Delaney household when the final call came through. When the representative from the adoption agency realized Ms. Amber was totally clueless, she was very apologetic. She didn't know how this could've happened. She asked Ms. Amber if the transfer needed to be put off so Jovie and the others could be more prepared.

Due to the many discussions they'd all had regarding this day's arrival Ms. Amber decided to allow it to stand. In her mind she equated this to the simple, yet painful act of quickly ripping off a band-aid.

She felt confident this was the right thing to do for two reasons. First, it seemed best not to allow any postponement since the adopting family were surely very prepared and excited believing this to be the day Jovie would be going home with them. Stopping the process would be confusing and painful for them. Could it even possibly result in changing their minds? Probably not, but it wasn't a risk worth taking. Secondly, Jovie and the rest of the family were as well prepared as they could be. Letting this good-bye drag out overnight and into the next day would benefit no one.

Having made this decision Ms. Amber then did what she had to do.

First, she called Jaxson, Steven and Matthew together and told them what was about to happen. Once they'd had time to get over the initial shock everyone was on board to make this an exciting and happy day for Jovie.

Mama told Jaxson later when they talked about it that he had, once again, made her proud by asking to be with her when she gave Jovie the news. She had often wondered how she would handle it when the time came. Thinking it through she had asked God to guide her through it many times over the past three years. Having Jaxson step up to be there with her had helped her, when the actual moment arrived.

Mama asked Steven and Matthew to gather the rest of the family together to give them the news while she and Jaxson talked with Jovie.

As was always the case whenever one of the children in their home was going to be adopted the men presented the news to the other children as wonderful and happy news. Of course, they were sad Jovie would be leaving them. But they were also happy that she would now have a family of her own.

Those who had been through this before knew the family would talk about their own sadness together after Jovie had left. Until then those feelings and thoughts were to be set aside as they all helped Jovie celebrate going home with her new family. Everyone understood this to be what you did for someone you love.

CHAPTER 17

Ms. Amber and Jaxson gave each other a final hug and walked into the girls' room. They found Jovie busy playing with two baby dolls.

Hearing them enter, Jovie looked toward them and smiled brightly.

"Mama, Jaxson," she said smiling up at them, "play with me?"

"Not right now," Jaxson said. "We've got happy news."

Jovie looked a little confused but met their smiles with her own.

Ma and Jaxson had prayed together before entering the room. They knew Jovie would look to them for reassurance. She would gauge their expressions and they wanted her to see joy and happiness in their eyes. They had asked God to help them be genuinely happy for Jovie despite their own pain in letting her go.

Kneeling down to look Jovie in the eyes, Ms. Amber asked, "remember me telling you someday you may have parents of your very own?"

A look of uncertainty immediately crossed the little girl's face as she looked from one of them to the other.

"Today that's going to happen!' Jaxson said with a huge smile, "We are so happy for you, Jovie. You remember Mr. and Mrs. Jarvis and Tyler, don't you? The very nice people who came to our family gathering and the corn roast this summer. You liked them a whole lot."

"Yes," Jovie said. She did remember the nice people.

"That's good," Jaxson said. "They want you in their family. Tyler is your new big brother."

The little girls face lit up as she said, "You and Tyler!"

Jaxson's gaze faltered as he quickly glanced at Ma. She met his eyes lovingly before turning to answer Jovie.

"Yes, but Jaxson will stay here while you live with Tyler and Mr. and Mrs. Jarvis. You're going to be very happy with them, Jovie, and we will always love you, too," Ma kept the big smile on her face as she assured Jovie.

Again, Jovie seemed uncertain but their smiles and the happiness in their faces made her feel better.

"Uh huh," she said in her innocent little voice. "With a mama and a daddy."

"Yes, it's so exciting," Ms. Amber said.

"You're going to love having a daddy," Jaxson said, realizing that God was already answering their earlier prayer. Jaxson truly was happy that Jovie was going to have a complete family; a mother, father and a big brother. What more could he want for this little girl that he loved so very much?

"So now, let's get your things together so you'll be ready when your new family gets here."

"Yes," Ms. Amber said as she moved to Jovie's little dresser and began to gather her clothing. Jaxson walked into the hallway and picked up a small pink suitcase. Bringing it into the room he said, "here's your very own suitcase to take with you."

Getting caught up in the excitement Jovie rushed over to help him carry it. The three of them then proceeded to neatly pack her belongings.

"Now, Jovie," Ms. Amber said, "would you like to choose a baby doll or another toy to take with you?"

"Oh yes mama!" the child's excitement was contagious and Jaxson and Ms. Amber let it carry them away. Knowing they were the last they may ever have with this little angel, God had dropped into their lives, they were trying to enjoy each moment.

There was a knock on the door. When they looked up Matthew was peering in at them.

"May we join you now?" he asked quietly.

"Look Jovie," Jaxson said in a loud and happy voice. "The rest of the family has come to help you get ready."

With that everyone piled into the room. The adults stepped back and watched as the other children told Jovie how happy they were for her. They helped her choose which toy to take with her. This was always a part of the process when a child was adopted. The remaining children knew this so they never argued or cried over a toy being taken away. If another of the children favored it, Ms. Amber would replace it or get them a new toy. Once Jovie had chosen her favorite baby doll, Jaxson took her suitcase while Jovie carried the doll into the living room so they would be at the ready.

"Okay, then," Ms. Amber said in a cheerful but firm voice. "Everything seems to be ready so now we'll just go about our day until your new family arrives. I say we all go outside and enjoy this beautiful weather together."

"Yay!" the children shouted in unison and headed out the back door.

The three adults and Jaxson lingered behind.

"Okay now," Matthew said, looking from one to the other. "When we rescued her, we didn't know how long we'd have her. Well, now we do. I don't know about the rest of you but these have been three of the best years of my life."

"Yes," Ma said simply.

"Sure have," Steven agreed.

Jaxson moved toward them with his arms outstretched for a group hug. As they came together, he said simply, "it's not over yet."

Breaking away he turned toward the back door, "Come on, let's get a little more time with her before they get here."

An hour later Jovie's new brother placed her little pink suitcase into the trunk of the car and walked over to stand with his parents. One by one each member of the Delaney household stepped forward and gave Jovie a loving hug. It was done with such joy and excitement that the little girl sensed none of their sadness.

It took every bit of strength Jaxson possessed not to burst out crying when it was his turn.

"You be good, okay?" He said as he looked directly into her bright eyes.

"I will, Jaxson," Jovie answered him as she stepped forward and put her arms around him.

"I love you, little sister," he said into her hair.

"Love you," she said simply.

He couldn't help it, the moment she turned to hug Matthew he had to turn his face away. He didn't want her to see him trying to keep his emotions in check.

Jovie was still little enough that the enormity of this situation wasn't within her realm of understanding. She didn't realize she was never coming back to see these people again, let alone to be part of this household.

They were all being so brave and cheerful that she reflected their own attitudes back to them. When Jaxson looked again, it was to see Ma hugging Jovie. Immediately, he flashed back to the first night Jovie came to them, specifically the very moment he handed Jovie over to Ma. Looking at their mother now Jaxson was amazed at her strength, no one would know her heart was breaking inside her.

He knew though. He knew because his heart was breaking.

CHAPTER 18

After watching Jovie's new family drive away, they walked inside together. The adults encouraged the children to talk freely about what they were feeling. Several shared how much they loved Jovie and were going to miss her. Everyone truly wanted her happiness. Knowing she was moving in with a good family and her life had a promising future was helpful.

Honestly, Jaxson didn't remember much about it the next morning. The entire evening was a bit of a blur. Not long into the day he found himself alone at the back of the family property. It had taken every bit of strength inside him just to get through breakfast. After placing his dishes into the dishwasher, he told his Ma he was going to check on the canoe to be sure it was grounded safely and headed out the back door. It was all he could think of to get him out of the house and away from everyone else.

The second he was out of view he released the pent-up emotion he'd been holding in and tears flowed freely down his cheeks. He felt as if his heart was going to burst in his chest from heartache. It had been this way all night. Every time he closed his eyes, he re-lived those last few moments with Jovie.

All he could see was his little sister walking away hand-in-hand with her new parents. Just before her new father opened the car door for Jovie, she'd turned her head and looked back, her eyes seeking Jaxson's. He was ready with a smile and wave. Satisfied, Jovie willingly climbed into the back seat of the car and sat next to Tyler, her new brother. Mr. Jarvis shut the door and helped his wife into the front before walking around to get into the driver's seat. As soon as the car began to move Jovie turned to the window and began to wave goodbye to the family she was leaving behind. As the car passed them, she turned toward the back to continue waving out the rear window.

Everyone smiled and continued waving until she was out of sight. Jaxson's legs began to move seemingly without conscious thought. It wasn't until she was gone and he turned back that he realized he had run the entire length of the drive.

In his mind's eye he could still see her even now, smiling through the back window, waving enthusiastically as the car grew smaller and smaller in the distance. That scene was burned into his memory.

Once she was out of sight the tears had started. He wasn't the only one crying as the family went inside. After talking about how much they loved and were going to miss her they began to imagine the happy life Jovie would have. As the evening passed emotions calmed. Amazingly most of the children were already beginning to adjust to their new situation by the time they went to bed that night. It wasn't the first time this had happened in the Delaney household and it wouldn't be the last. Jaxson himself had seen many children come and go but none as dear to his heart as his little sister, Jovie.

And now, the very next morning, here he was, hiding out from the rest of the family. In this moment he was nothing but a twelve-year-old boy who couldn't stop crying. Afraid someone from the house would see him he stumbled toward the wooded area at the edge of their land and stepped inside. The next thing he knew he was sobbing, barely keeping himself under control. He couldn't stop crying and was afraid he never would.

How do people live through this kind of pain? He asked himself, bringing the back of his right hand up to his face and raking it across his eyes to wipe his tears on his sleeve.

'You've got to stop this,' he told himself as he sucked in his breath and tried to regain control. His crying began to subside but with thoughts of Jovie it started again. Desperately trying to calm himself he closed his eyes tightly. That was a mistake. Immediately he saw her walking away and getting into the car. Mentally watching it drive away all over again he sucked his breath in and tried to hold it. When he couldn't, a huge sob tore from his body.

Leaning over he wrapped his arms around himself and fell slightly backward. His back touched against a tree and he allowed himself to slowly slide to the ground. His body rocking as he held himself, he sat hunched over and leaning low. He stopped fighting the hurt and simply gave in to it. His cry was heart wrenching and tragic as he completely gave himself over to the pain. Rocking back and forth he let his tears fully flow.

After a few minutes he tried again to get control of his emotions. As soon as his pain started to subside, he'd think of his baby sister and everything would start all over again.

In desperation he began to call out to God between his sobs.

"God, please help me," he said, sobbing deeply.

"You have to help me," he sobbed, giving in to his pain.

A few moments later he said, "I don't know how to do this. I can't stand this pain, Lord. – My – heart - is breaking!" His cry was ragged as another huge sob escaped him. In deep despair he cried out, "Please help me God. I need you."

Almost as if that sob had taken everything out of him his crying began to subside and his breathing started to calm. Slowly he unwrapped his arms from around himself and again dragged his sleeve across his eyes to wipe away the tears. Feeling as if his self-control was returning, he began to stand up.

"You're going to be okay," he said aloud.

He was starting to feel better. As calm continued to wash over his body his mind began to clear. He missed Jovie so much. From the moment he'd watched that car take her away he'd felt such a void without her. But now, for the first time he somehow knew he was going to be okay.

Realizing the last thing he had said had been a desperate cry to God for help he suddenly knew that must be what was happening. God was answering his prayer. God was going to help him through this.

"Thank you, God," he said quietly, wiping the tears from his face one last time.

The emotional release he'd just been through had exhausted him but he was definitely feeling better. As he walked out of the woods, he saw the canoe at the edge of the lake and calmly went to do what he'd told Ma he was going to do.

As he checked to be sure the canoe was shored securely, he couldn't help wondering what he was going to do without his little sister in the days ahead. That's when he remembered what Matthew had once told him about praying thankful prayers when he didn't know what was going to happen next.

"Thank you, God," Jaxson said in a strong voice. "Thank you for helping me just now. I miss Jovie so much. I think I'll miss her every day for the rest of my life. But I still thank you for letting me be the one to help rescue her when she was just a baby. Thank you for making me her big brother these past three years. I wouldn't trade it for anything. Thank you that she knows we all love her. Thank you that you are with her right now and you're going to be with her every day for the rest of her life. Thank you that she's already learning to love her new family, her parents and her big brother. Thank you, God, that they want her and love her. Thank you for the happy life I know she's going to have.'

He had been walking up the hill toward the back of the house as he said these things. Reaching for the handle of the back door he finished his prayer.

"Thank you, Father, that you are already helping me get through this. Please comfort Ma. I know you're with us and you're going to be with us and help us every day just like you always have."

"Jaxson? Is that you?" Ma called out as soon as he stepped inside.

"It's me, Ma," he answered as he took his boots off by the back door. A glance at his watch told him he'd only been gone for twenty minutes. Knowing she had probably worried about him the whole time he went straight to his mother and wrapped his arms around her.

"I'm alright, Ma," he said calmly. "We're all going to be alright. God's gonna see us through this just like you've always said He would.

CHAPTER 19

Coming through!!!" the deep voice shouted in time to his pounding footfalls on the boards of the dock. With loud laughter the lanky, deeply-tanned teenage boy threw himself off the end. His long legs and arms flailed every which way as he flew through the air before plummeting into the water.

Seated at the end of the dock, Kate and Ms. Amber threw their arms up in a useless attempt to shield themselves from the splashes. Their laughter joined that of the children as several others clad in bathing suits raced past to hurl themselves into the water.

"We decided a dip in the lake was the perfect way to cool down on this scorching North Carolina day," Matthew's deep voice said, as he strolled up behind the two friends. "As soon as I made the suggestion, they raced to the house to get into their swimsuits."

"It's a great idea," Ms. Amber smiled up at him. "I assume you're going in with them?"

"I am!" he laughed heartily. "Why don't you two get suited up and join us?"

"We just might do that," she answered, looking toward her friend questioningly while pulling her dangling feet up out of the water.

"I'm all in," Kate answered, already half standing. "Sitting in the sunshine warmed me right up. A dip in the lake sounds like just the ticket."

"Okay, then. We'll be right back," Ms. Amber said.

Impromptu swimming was just another reason Amber loved this place. Being set on a peninsula in the middle of the three hundred eighty-eight-acre lake the house was surrounded by natural beauty.

The lake wasn't only good for cooling off from the summer heat, it was rich in history. Not long after Mount Tabor was founded it had become known as Spivey Millpond. Flanked by a rice field the grist mill was used to power the mill that ground rice and other grain as food for the people of the newly established town. It wasn't for some years, well after the mill had shut down, that the name was changed from Spivey Millpond to Spivey Lake.

The house and grounds, with the ample yard, large clearing behind it and dock in the front had won Amber's heart from her first visit. It was the perfect place for children to enjoy the outdoors.

The stately and yet homey, two-story house was more than suitable to house multiple children. Amber had immediately envisioned the two largest upstairs rooms being fitted with a good number of beds. One room for the boys and another for the girls. The large bathroom would easily convert to two smaller bathrooms. Two additional rooms downstairs could be used when a child reached teenage years and independence and privacy became more important. The huge kitchen was perfect for an oversized table, which Steven quickly custom made once the purchase of the home was secured.

It was very important to Amber that the family eat together. She definitely believed in home-cooked, well-conversed-over family meals.

The front of the house faced the tip of the peninsula where a long wooden dock stretched out into the lake. That dock, obviously great for running and jumping from, was especially inviting for lazy days of fishing.

The large gazebo some yards away was another great selling point. One of the first things Amber did after buying the place was to string lights around that gazebo making it, not only beautiful, but an inviting haven of rest even after dark. It soon became one of her favorite places for taking quiet time alone. With seating built in it was also a great spot for getting together with any number of the rest of the family. Before long she had a large picnic table placed in its center, after which, many impromptu picnics were enjoyed there. The gazebo was perfect for the steady Carolina downpours that often came up. Whenever a calm rain came through Amber, along with a child or two, could often be found there enjoying the sounds of the rain hitting its tin roof and watching the rain fall.

Shouts of approval rang out when the children saw the two women coming toward them in their swimsuits. They cheered loudly when their Ma allowed her inner child to take charge by following their earlier example. With shouts of 'coming through' she raced down the dock and threw herself into the water.

Not to be outdone Kate followed right behind doing a cannonball into the lake.

The happy family splashed and played in the water for the next hour until they each climbed up the wooden ladder and sprawled out on the hot deck one by one. As they lay drying in the sun, they talked about the fun of summer days and the soon approaching school year.

After reminding a few of the older children to keep watch over their younger siblings Ms. Amber, Kate and Matthew went inside. A short time later Matthew shouted, "come and get it!' as the three headed toward the gazebo. After tossing a cloth over the picnic table Ms. Amber set out paper plates and Kate began filling plastic cups with Hawaiian Punch. Matthew opened cans of sardines and set the saltine crackers out and the hungry children started eating.

"Nothing like sardines and crackers after a good swim in the lake," Jaxson announced while licking his lips contentedly.

"You said it," the boy who had started it all agreed. "Who'd have ever thought I'd love sardines?"

"Not me," one of the girls answered. "It took me forever to even try one, remember?"

"How could we forget?" Jaxson laughed. "You were so dramatic! Always telling us how gross they were and that you would never taste one, let alone eat one on top of a cracker."

"It's a good thing I can't resist a dare," she said, laughing at the memory. "If you two hadn't dared me I never would have tried one but now I love them!"

Seeing that the sardine cans were empty, Ms. Amber asked, "Who wants dessert?"

After a quick look around, she started to get up while commenting, "It looks like I forgot to bring out the fruit salad."

"I'll get it," one of the girls said, jumping up quickly and sprinting toward the house.

"Thanks," Ms. Amber shouted after her. "Grab some plastic spoons, too, would you?"

"I love your fruit salad, Ma," Jaxson said in anticipation.

"What don't you love?" one of his brothers teased. "I have yet to see you turn any food down."

Fifteen-year-old Jaxson tossed his wadded-up napkin across the table and both boys laughed loudly as its intended target successfully dodged it.

Watching the fun unfold Ms. Amber couldn't help but think that this was what life was all about. She was enjoying the company of her best friend, while her family's laughter echoed in her ears. How life could get any better she couldn't imagine, for in this moment she was as happy as anyone could possibly be.

CHAPTER 20

After getting Marissa comfortably settled and safely buckled into the front passenger seat, he shut the van door and headed for the driver's side. When he glanced through the front window to see his girls all buckled in and ready to head home it struck him what a bittersweet moment this was.

On the one hand he was happier than ever before. On the other hand, an intense sadness pulled at his heart. How could he possibly live through this moment without re-living the first time he had thought of and spoken the words 'his girls'.

Here they were, six years later, still with no idea where their missing daughter was. And yet, as it always does, life went on. He and Marissa made their new start in South Carolina, brought their baby boy home and continued to put one foot in front of the other. And as amazing as it now seemed they found happiness again. In fact, they were very happy, which just went to prove that even though hard, life goes on and God is good.

Simultaneous to automatically reaching for his seatbelt, stretching it across him, and listening for the click of it locking into place, he turned to smile at Marissa.

"Ready to roll, little mama?" he asked with a quick wink.

"I believe so daddy. These girls are snug in their car seats excited to go home and meet their big brother." Joy radiated from her face.

"Alrighty then, big brother has waited long enough. Let's get you girls home." He put the car in drive and pulled out of the hospital pick-up zone.

Fifteen minutes later as they approached their house the front door swung open and out came his and Marissa's parents with their three-year-old grandson. The new grandparents practically fell over themselves trying to help him and Marissa get the twins into the house.

A few minutes later amid lots of laughter and cooing sounds he and Marissa introduced little Ellie and her, younger-by-two-minutes sister, Marie to the entire family. Marissa had already embroidered their names inside the tiny hat's the hospital kept on their little heads. That would be helpful until everyone got to know them since the girls looked so much alike. As she'd done it the thought of embroidering their names onto lots of tiny clothing items in the years to come had Marissa smiling.

To say this was a joyous occasion would be a huge understatement.

After trying to prepare Ryan for the daunting task of becoming an instant big brother to not one, but two, baby sisters for several months no one knew exactly what to expect of the toddler. Everyone was thrilled when he rose to the occasion by sitting between the two car seats looking from one to the other with a huge smile on his face. The little boy seemed enamored as he gently rubbed the tiny arms and hands of his baby sisters.

All of the grandparents enjoyed meeting the girls and helping the new parents get settled in at home. Seeing that dad and big brother had things under control they left the little family on their own for their first night together.

It didn't take long, in the days ahead, for Ryan to start saying his sister's names as he hurried to bring blankies, diapers, bottles and whatever else their busy parents needed transported from place to place while parenting the little ones. When it was time for daddy to return to work Marissa's mother came to stay for a few days. From there on out it was a revolving door for the grandparents as they stepped in to help this quickly growing family get a new routine going.

What's that they say about it taking a village to raise a child? He and Marissa were blessed to have their family involved. When their first baby had gone missing both sets of parents had proven to be a huge support system to the grieving couple. In the years since, as their lives allowed for it, both the retired grandparent couples made the move to the Carolinas. Now everyone lived within an hour drive of one another. Not only was this helpful but it made for wonderful opportunities for family gatherings and happy times together. Having all four of their grandparents involved in their lives was a wonderful way for the children to grow up.

He knew how very blessed they were for having such a wonderful family and he didn't take that for granted. Yet there were times he still struggled with frustration and felt a heavy sadness from having lost their baby girl. He supposed he always would.

CHAPTER 21

While being placed into a children's home isn't the ideal situation for any child, Jaxson considered himself fortunate to be among those who found themselves as part of Ms. Amber's family.

The adults in that household; Ms. Amber, Matthew and Steven, were totally devoted to the children. They were patient, loving and kind. Each one, whether due to their own personal experience or just being blessed with empathy, was adept at understanding the needs of children.

Whenever a new child arrived, the adults quickly noted what they seemed to respond best to. They were well practiced at immediately showing comfort and love or keeping their distance - whichever was best in the situation. It didn't take children long to realize that in these three adults they had constant access to a listening ear, welcoming embrace, or gentle touch. They also knew that they would be given personal space when that was needed.

Ms. Amber regularly scheduled fun crafts and group activities into the structure of the family's life. Even if they were hesitant at first, with time, each child became willing to participate and eventually grew to anticipate the craft projects, athletic competitions, and many other team-building activities the family did together.

Jaxson specifically remembered the annual activity of building and painting bird houses. The results of which were hanging in the woods surrounding their home.

One of his favorite competitions was a yearly community miniature soap box derby race the family participated in every fall. Jaxson had wonderful memories of working together with his siblings on the designing, planning, building and painting of the soap box cars they entered in the race.

The overall environment of the household was of working as a team, doing things together, and simply having fun. Ms. Amber, Steven and Matthew did all they could to provide the children with the sense of having extended family as well. Ms. Amber's parents, her friend Kate and several of Steven and Matthew's friends were regularly at the house. They served as grandparents, aunt, uncles and wonderful sources of love for the children. With all of this extra support the children in the Delaney household were surrounded with plenty of love.

It didn't take newcomers long to realize Kate was more than just a friend of the family. She and Ms. Amber were the best of friends. The two often sat talking together, whether it be over coffee at the kitchen table, relaxing on the couch in the living room or outside in the gazebo on a beautiful North Carolina day. What they talked about was anyone's guess. Seeing them share laughter and tears left no question in anyone's mind that they were there for each other as the best of friends always are.

Since laundry is plentiful in a house full of children Kate often helped with that. The two women frequently cooked together and Kate had a regular seat at the table. She was invariably involved in whatever projects were underway and there through fun times and on work days.

One year Kate took a two-week vacation from her job and helped Ms. Amber with the task of painting the interior of the house one room, actually one wall, at a time. The older children took over caring for the younger children and the two friends could be heard talking, laughing and even singing together as they got the job done. Ma was often heard to say the test of true friendship was whether they jumped in to help or turned tail and ran the other way when there was a big job to do. There was no doubt those two women shared each other's burdens. Without question there was nothing one wouldn't do for the other. Through their own example they modeled what true friendship looked like for Jaxson, and for each and every child who spent time in the Delaney household.

Jaxson's memories encompassed all of Spivey Lake, not just the house and grounds but the entire lake as well. It really was a great place to grow up. The natural setting the lake provided was wonderful. It offered the fun experiences of swimming, fishing and boating along with special events throughout the summer months. The lake itself opened up into a whole new world with its alcoves of Cyprus trees draped in Spanish Moss sheltering

Egret, Heron, sunbathing turtles, alligators gently coasting through the water, and always the songs of frogs and crickets in the evenings. Jaxson had found peace in being surrounded by this natural wonderland.

While Spivey Lake housed private family homes, it was also open to the general public. All summer long families came to spend their days on the lake. Spivey Lake was definitely a daily hubbub of activity. Fishermen stopped at Dick's Trading Post, at the mouth of the turnoff into the lake, for their bait and tackle. Those not bringing their own, rented canoes or fishing boats, while most of the other visitors came to swim on the beach.

To the left of the long drive leading into Spivey Lake there were a few homes while the right was lined with huge pine trees. There were two small docks jutting out into the water and off to the right and about a quarter way around the lake a long pier led to a large pier house with a steep roof. Despite the disapproval of the grown-ups, many teenagers climbed up onto that roof to dive into the deep waters. For those growing up on the lake this was a right-of-passage of sorts.

Visitors took advantage of the small hut that housed vending machines for soda and snacks. Moms visited with each other as their younger children played on the playground.

Boaters used the three boat ramps straight ahead to launch their boats into the lake. At least four times each summer Spivey Lake hosted speed boat races. The Delaney family made a day of it on those occasions. At Ms. Amber's direction they spent the morning making sandwiches to pack into the picnic baskets along with chips and sliced veggies. Half an hour before the races began, they set up lawn chairs and spread blankets in the front yard facing the lake. Their front yard was the perfect location for watching the boat races!

As each child grew older Ms. Amber allowed them the freedom to go over to the public beach in the summer months. This gave them the opportunity to make friends from all over the country.

Some of Jaxson's fondest memories were of dancing to the jukebox tunes on the pier during the summers of his sixteenth and seventeenth years. He flirted with his share of cute girls while hanging out with a select group of friends. He was very proud when he finally mastered the climb and dive from the roof of the pier house. That was a monumental occasion for sure!

Living on Spivey Lake was awesome but that wouldn't have been true without a happy homelife. Ms. Amber had obtained her dream of creating a loving home and strong sense of family for the children living at the Delaney Home for Children. While that was the legal name of the residence there was no sign to that effect. The many visitors looking across the lake saw nothing but a house like all the others on the lake. And for those who lived there it was simply - home. Ms. Amber had done everything possible to keep the children from standing out or feeling different and for the most part her efforts were successful.

The family being happy and the children well-balanced, didn't change the fact that whenever a new child arrived or someone left, there was a bit of unrest. Since each circumstance was unique those adjustment periods varied. Tension often entered the house with new arrivals while having a child leave was bittersweet. With the guidance of the adults the children learned to maneuver through. Some children were only part of the family for a short time while others, like Jaxson, were permanent.

Ms. Amber rocked, cuddled and loved every baby. She read to, taught and played with every toddler. She was quick and natural with soft and loving touches for everyone on a daily basis. She and Steven and Matthew provided the needs of the home and worked together in parenting the children living there. As each child matured, they were there to listen and offer advice, especially during teen years and young adulthood. Dreams and goals for the future were encouraged and nurtured.

Ms. Amber worked with each child to help guide them in the direction of their chosen path. Everyone was shown love and support for the duration of their time in the household. As a result, many returned often for family visits once they'd come of age and set out on their own. Jaxson looked forward to doing the same when he grew up. Life in the Delaney Home for Children was all-in-all a well-rounded upbringing in a loving environment. Knowing first hand that some children don't get as much in their birth family, most of the children raised by Ms. Amber realized they were very blessed.

Sometimes Jaxon would find himself wondering what had become of one child or another who had come and gone. In most cases, he realized he would never know. And always his mind wondered and his heart ached after Jovie.

Each time she came to mind, he prayed for her. In those first few years after Jovie left them Jaxson made sure to assure Ma that he was doing alright. And he really was. God had been faithful to help him through the loss of his little sister.

There were often times the family would reminisce about their little Jovie, especially Matthew, Steven, Jaxson and Ma. They each believed she had been given to them as a special assignment from God. They often laughed together remembering her adorable little ways. They comforted each other over the void she had left when it was needed.

Sometimes, when he was alone, Jaxson allowed himself to dwell on the connection he had felt to Jovie, but in the end, he always gave her back to God. After all, God was trustworthy. He always had been, and Jaxson was certain He still was. Though he missed her deeply and wondered what her life was like and who she was now, Jaxson knew that God was watching over her. In the end that was all he really needed to know.

CHAPTER 22

During his Junior and Senior years of High School Jaxson talked about his dreams and plans for the future with his Ma quite often. Due to his love for children and his nurturing nature they both felt he would excel and find fulfillment in being a pediatrician. Being a big dream - it would require years of education. The two of them spent many evenings learning about scholarships and financial aid as he completed applications for colleges and assistance in his Senior year.

Things were coming together well and while Jaxson was excited to be heading off to college in the fall, he couldn't deny having a bit of anxiety over it. Ma told him that was normal. She explained that even when change is good it can be overwhelming. His feelings were only natural. She assured him that within two months at his new location he'd be feeling comfortable in his surroundings. They talked often about it and were both looking forward to his return home during the Thanksgiving and Christmas breaks.

During his last summer at the house Ma pushed Jaxson to have fun. He happily complied by spending lots of time with the other young people at the beach, even as he continued to work frequently with Matthew and Steven. He wanted to do all he could toward leaving the homestead in good shape since they'd be short one handy man once he went away to school.

While the number of children living at the Delaney Home for Children often varied there were only six that summer. The youngest child being four and the oldest eleven. Jaxson wasn't counting himself, since he'd turned eighteen on his birthday in July. He was now officially an adult.

Hurricane season in the Carolinas runs from June through November. Some years see little activity while others see too much. No one really knows why.

Hurricanes are a force of nature that belie explanation. One well established fact is that at their worst they're unbelievably strong, fierce and capable of doing tremendous damage and taking lives.

Business and home owners along the coast tend to stay updated on ocean activity. Keeping an eye on what's churning at sea is the best way to be prepared if a hurricane makes landfall.

The small North Carolina towns of Mount Tabor and Witville are just across the state border from Logan, South Carolina. Residents and business owners in those and other small communities lying well inland tend not to track hurricanes as closely since most hurricanes don't come far enough inland to do major damage. However, those areas do get strong rainfall, storms, flooding and even tornadoes sometimes. All as a result of being on the outside edge of a hurricane.

With hurricanes often churning at sea there had been quite a bit of activity that Hurricane season. Some had taken a turn away from land, some simply dissipated while a few continued in, made landfall and caused a bit of damage. In those cases, coastal residents had either followed evacuation procedures or boarded up their homes and waited it out depending on the intensity of the storm.

It's very difficult for news stations to make accurate predictions when it comes to hurricanes. They're totally unpredictable and can change course on a dime. It's frustrating for local residents. They find themselves either under preparing or over preparing. Depending on the person, long term residents either become skeptical and refuse to leave when they probably should or fearful tending to leave way before it's necessary. It's not an easy dilemma to be faced with repeatedly but it is part of coastal life.

Everyone was thankful to be nearing the end of hurricane season when another hurricane suddenly began to churn off the coast of Myrtle Beach. It grew in size and strength quickly but still wasn't expected to make landfall for a couple more days ~ if it did then.

CHAPTER 23

The day began like any other.

Over breakfast Matthew told Ms. Amber he and Steven and Jaxson were making a trip to the Lowes and Hardware Stores in Witville to get some supplies.

"Is there anything you need from the store while we're in town?" he asked.

"Since I just stocked up on groceries two days ago, I can't think of anything. It's too bad it's still raining. Y'all are going to get wet while loading and unloading the truck. But with that hurricane still churning near the coast it's likely to be raining all week."

"That's what the forecast is showing so we talked it over and decided to go ahead and get everything today. We've got a couple of big projects we want to finish while Jaxson's still here to help us out. No point in waiting."

"Okay, well, be careful and try to have fun with it."

"We always do," he smiled. "We'll be gone most of the day so we'll probably grab lunch at Joe's BBQ Barn. You know that's Jaxson's favorite place in Witville."

It wasn't long before the men headed out. Ms. Amber and the older children worked together clearing away the breakfast mess while the younger kids played. With the rain it was going to be another inside activity day.

Steven was in the habit of following the weather predictions and letting her know each morning what the current updates were. He had told her at breakfast there was nothing new to report on this hurricane. The meteorologists were still watching it closely but at this point it was holding steady where it was.

As the morning went on Ms. Amber noticed the sky looking darker but wasn't especially alarmed. Rainy, windy, dark days were common when a hurricane was close to the coast and it looked like this one might hang around for a bit. As she always did, she was praying it would dissipate or turn back out to sea without doing any damage. She was also asking God to watch over everyone in its path if it didn't.

Since Ms. Amber taught her children about God, prayer was just normal conversation in the Delaney family. The children learned from the example of the adults in the family that, just as they were, God was to be trusted in every circumstance. It didn't take long for them to learn that just as the love offered by the adults in the home was real and constant God's love is as well. Since many of the children came from difficult circumstances, they already knew full well that life is hard. Ms. Amber explained that God doesn't promise us an easy life. He only promises to be with us and give us what we need through difficult times. With God we are able to have joy regardless of circumstances. She was quick to point out that even on our worst days there are many things to be thankful for. She was constantly assuring the children that no matter what happened in their lives there are some things that will never change; God's love and good plans for them being at the top of that list. When a child was afraid, she freely admitted to being afraid sometimes, too. She helped them with what helped her. The assurances from God's word that He is always with us and we are never alone.

At about one o'clock there was a loud crash and the house shuddered. Startled, Ms. Amber rushed to the back of the house where the sound had come from. Looking out the back door window all she could see was tree limbs being blown fiercely. They were hitting against the house with the force of the wind. Since they completely obstructed her view either a tree had fallen or a large branch had broken off and landed against the house blocking the back door. Several of the children came running. They were scared and asking her what was going on.

"It's just a fallen tree branch. Nothing to worry about. The winds are really strong today. It looks like it's blocking the back door but that's okay. We're not planning to go outside anyway. The guys will take care of it after the storm is over." She had said all of this while inwardly thanking God the tree branch had not broken through the roof or wall where it hit the house.

Seeing the fear on their faces she added, "It's okay, remember that although the storm seems scary God is with us. He's with the guys, too. They're probably at Joe's BBQ Barn eating lunch. If it's storming like this in Witville, they'll just stay longer talking with everyone until the storm lets up. I bet they're going to eat way too much, don't you?" She had asked the question with a huge smile, still trying to calm their fears. It seemed to be helping as several of the children were smiling.

"I tell you what. Let's do some coloring and painting at the table. I'll put music on and we'll make an afternoon of it." She said before sending them to get the art supplies.

Ms. Amber quickly went to the front window to assess the storm. It looked very nasty and she began to feel alarmed as she watched the water swelling and crashing quite violently. This is the worst I've ever seen the lake, she thought and as always, turned to prayer.

"Lord, please watch over Matthew, Steven and Jaxson and keep them safe. Help them find a safe place to hold up if it's bad where they are. Please protect the children here with me. Help me keep them safe if this thing gets any worse," she hadn't realized she'd been praying out loud until Lisha, the oldest of the children interrupted her.

"I'm sorry mama, but no one's seen Carter for a bit. Do you know where he is?"

"What?" Ms. Amber said as her heartbeat quickened. "No. I haven't seen him since the little ones went off to play together while we were cleaning up the kitchen."

She rushed to the play room where the children were gathering art supplies. They again looked frightened because of the intensity of the storm.

"When did you see Carter last?" she asked them.

"When we were playing in here. He kept going to the window and talking about the rain," Sarah answered.

"Yeah. He said he liked hearing it hit the roof just like you! You like the Zebo in the rain," Robby spoke up, saying the word wrong.

Amber's heart leapt up into her throat. "You don't think he went outside in this, do you?" She tried to appear calm as she knelt down to look the little boy in the face.

"He said he was gonna. I told him it's scary out there."

"Oh, dear Lord," Ms. Amber said looking up at Lisha. "Go through the house and look for him," she said to the two older girls. "Call his name out loudly as you go! Check every room. Do it quickly!" Trying to calm herself but feeling very worried she urged them, "Do it now! If he's not here I'll have to go outside and find him."

Turning back to Sarah and Robby she asked, "what happened next?"

"Ummm, we got the building blocks out and me and Marcie started to build." Sarah offered.

"Robby?" Ms. Amber asked the little boy.

"I had to go to the bathroom," he said.

Suddenly, thunder cracked loudly and the power went out. The wind sounded fierce. It was still afternoon but due to the weather the outside lighting was that of about dusk on any other day. It made the house seem darker.

Scared, a few of the small children started to cry. Ms. Amber gathered them around her. "It's okay," she said with a calm she did not feel. "Come with me."

The children gathered closer to her as she led them to the bathroom that was near the center of the house. Along the way she had everyone grab throw pillows while she grabbed the actual couch cushions. Tossing those onto the floor she said, "We're going to play slumber-party in here until the storm calms down. Can you children make a bed out of these pillows while I get flashlights and your coloring books?"

They looked frightened but did what she'd asked as she ran through the house gathering things up. She met the two older girls in the hallway

"We can't find him," Lisha said, tears running down her face.

"Alright now. It's okay," Ms. Amber said, hugging them to herself. Looking at the younger of the two girls she said, "Take these and go to the bathroom and stay with the other children. I've got them playing slumber-party. They'll feel calmer if you can keep them pretending. Take some books so you and Lisha can read to them. Go on now."

Turning to Lisha she continued, talking quickly, "Now, listen to me closely. I'm sure this is just a bad storm like we've had many times before but these winds are strong and Carter cannot be outside in this. I'm going to have to go find him. I need you to keep the other children in that bathroom where you'll be together and safe until I get back. I can't be worrying about the rest of you right now. Do you understand? I don't care how long it takes me to get back. DO NOT come outside! You must stay inside and keep everyone together in the bathroom. Do you understand me?"

"Yes...." Lisha answered hesitantly though she was being as courageous as an eleven-year-old girl can manage in a frightening situation.

"Good! That's very good. You're being very brave and I'm so very proud of you, Lisha. You can do this! I'm counting on you to take care of the children until I get back. You'll do that for me, right?"

"Yes mama," Lisha answered, nodding her head.

"Okay, you've got this. Y'all will be fine. We're all going to be fine. God is with us. We are not alone! You remember that, okay? He never leaves us alone!" Ms. Amber hugged Lisha tightly for just a few seconds before gently pushing her toward the bathroom.

As soon as Lisha took off Ms. Amber flew to the back mudroom where she threw her mud boots on and grabbed her raincoat off its peg. Putting it on while running to the front door. When she pulled the door open the wind immediately grabbed her and threw her against the porch railing. Her raincoat whipped in every direction as rain pelted her. She peered toward the gazebo but it was impossible to see clearly through the bending trees and pouring rain.

CHAPTER 24

"CARTER!!!" Ms. Amber screamed at the top of her lungs.

The wind grabbed the name and flung it away as she rushed forward toward the gazebo.

"CARTER!!" She screamed again, searching the area with her eyes and moving as fast as she could through the relentless storm. She felt as if she were moving at a snail's pace but soon the gazebo came into view.

"CARTER!!" She continued to scream, lunging forward a step at a time. She thought she heard a faint cry. Grabbing the railing she pulled herself into the middle of the gazebo and saw him huddled beneath the picnic table. She rushed forward, getting to her knees as the small boy threw himself against her.

"Oh, Carter, thank God you're safe," she said as she grabbed him and began plastering kisses on top of his soaked head."

He was crying and trembling. Hugging him she continued to yell above the winds.

"We've got to get back to the house!"

The little boy looked up at her, feeling unsure.

"We'll go together," she shouted. "We're going to have to make a run for it." She grabbed his hand and held it up between them smiling at him bravely. "Hold my hand and we'll be okay," she yelled. "Hold on tight, but no matter what happens, you run to the front of the house and get in the door. Okay?"

Looking alarmed he cried out, "NO! You have to come with me!"

"I am coming with you! We are doing this together! Are you ready?"

His eyes sought hers and he nodded hesitantly.

"Okay! Here we go!" Ms. Amber pulled him closer to her as he crawled from under the picnic table and they lunged toward the railing of the gazebo side by side. She grabbed the railing to steady them while holding his hand tightly in her other hand. Looking down at him she screamed above the roar of the wind, "Okay, let's go!"

They stepped out onto the gazebo steps and moved forward still hunched together. They made it to the third step before the wind grabbed them. Ms. Amber could feel his hand slipping away as the wind threw her sideways and immediately pushed her backward. Her back slammed into the side of the gazebo with such force that her head jerked back and hit it with a loud crack. Pain shot through her as her vision blurred.

Laying in a crumpled heap she looked around desperately until she spotted Carter sprawled on the grass about four feet away. The wind jerked and pressed against him as he struggled to stand.

Hearing her yell his name he turned. She motioned for him to stay low. Understanding, he began to crawl in her direction making his way to her. An intense pain shot through her body when she reached for him and pulled him close.

"You are so brave!" She yelled as he cried in her arms.

She forced herself to push Carter away from her so she could look him in the eyes.

"Run to the house," she yelled as his eyes filled with fear. "You can do it! I'm hurt. I can't go but Matthew will be here soon." She was nodding her head up and down as she yelled. Trying her best to assure him. "I need you to check on the others. You can do that for me, can't you?"

He began to nod his little head.

"You're a very brave boy, Carter." She yelled. "You can do this! Just run in that front door. Are you ready?"

He looked at her with uncertainty but stood up. The wind was fierce and strong.

"GO!" She screamed.

His head snapped in her direction and he stared at her through terrified eyes as the rain pummeled him.

"GO!! she screamed again, lifting one arm weakly to point in the direction of the house.

He stood as though frozen in a trance. Feeling desperate she took a deep breath and tried one more time.

"CARTER!" His eyes cleared as he looked her dead in the eyes.

RUN HOME!!" Tearing his eyes from hers he turned away and began to run.

Dear God, she prayed. Please get him into the house. I'm hurt, Lord. I'm really hurt.

She wasn't sure what but she knew something had happened to her back and head when she hit the gazebo. Pain shot through her body with every movement and her head throbbed. There was no way she could make it to the house and she knew it.

Half of her was jammed against the gazebo and her body lay at an odd upward angle. The other half of her was dangling over the top two steps. Gritting her teeth, she threw herself upward and locked both hands onto the gazebo railing. She sucked air in and began to pull herself up. Feeling as if all but her arms were paralyzed, she was determined to drag herself up and into the gazebo where she would at least have a little shelter from the storm.

Worried about Carter she squinted her eyes tightly and looked toward the house all the while begging God to help him make it inside. Her view cleared and she saw the screen door fling open as Carter grabbed the storm door and ducked inside.

Thank you, God! She whispered before collapsing onto the gazebo floor.

"LISHA!!" Carter screamed as the wind knocked him further inside the front door and flung the storm door fully open again.

Lisha came running. Seeing the boy huddled in the floor she rushed forward and wrapped herself around him.

"Where's mama?"

The crying boy stammered 'hurt - she said - run home, Carter." She felt him pulled away from her as if to go back outside.

"Okay, it's okay," the girl said, pulling him further inside while pushing the wet hair from his eyes.

Standing up she left the screen door banging open, grabbed the storm door and slammed it shut before pressing her face to the window. She saw nothing but rain and the high water of the lake being tossed in every direction by the storm. It terrified her that mama was out there but she knew she had to stay with the children.

Turning away from the window she ran to Carter, wrapped her arms around him and they huddled on the floor crying together. After a few seconds, as if she could hear their mother's voice telling her what to do, she bravely wiped her tears on the back of her sleeve, smiled down at Carter and said, "Okay, that's enough. Come on, we're having a slumber party in the bathroom. The others are there waiting for us."

Ms. Amber would've been so very proud of Lisha. After getting Carter settled with the other children she hurried into the kitchen and rummaged through the cupboards to get graham crackers, chocolate bars and marshmallows. Unable to find everything she grabbed what she could and gave up. Hurrying back into the bathroom she smiled weakly at her siblings and said, "Let's pretend we have a campfire. Isn't it warm and pretty? I brought the marshmallows. Anybody want one?"

CHAPTER 25

The effort spent in convincing Carter to run to the house had exhausted her but he was safe now and that was all she needed to know. All of her children were safe inside the house and she trusted God that the men of the family were safe, too. She was thankful they had gone inland for their errands.

With everyone else accounted for it was time to take stock of her own situation. She was shocked and amazed at the intensity of the storm. She'd never seen the lake in this condition. Had the hurricane made landfall and come in this direction? She didn't know but with the size of the waves on the lake she was beginning to suspect that was what had happened. She had never seen a storm surge and this wasn't the ocean but what she was seeing looked like what she imagined a storm surge to be.

Whatever this was, it wasn't getting any better.

With the searing pain in her back, she thought it might have broken when she was thrown against the gazebo. Excruciating pain shot through her entire being with each movement. There was no question her body was badly injured and her focus was completely off.

She was beginning to wonder if she was going to survive this.

She'd been praying since the storm threw the tree against the back door. Thanking God that tree hadn't crashed through the roof and asking Him to continue to protect her family. God had helped her rescue Carter and she was grateful. She was hurt and alone and powerless against this storm but she was doing all she knew to do and asking God for wisdom and trusting in Him every moment.

With the storm raging on she had no choice but to stay where she was. She was too much of a mess to even attempt making it back to the house.

Needing to shelter in as best she could she scooted backward one agonizing inch at a time. Calling out to God with each movement until she was tucked underneath the seating built around the interior edge of the gazebo. Her entire body screamed in pain. As she continued being pelted by the rain and wind, she knew she was as sheltered as possible. She would stay put until the storm died or the men got home, whichever came first.

If they're driving in this, Lord, please keep them safe. Please keep the children safe and calm their fears. Her every breath was a prayer.

As if her situation wasn't dire enough, she was suddenly blinded by dirty lake water as an enormous wave rose up from the lake and poured completely over her. It left her choking and gasping for breath as the water fell away. Watching helplessly as another wave towered above her - she felt the full force of wind and water pulling at the gazebo. Above the winds she heard a creaking sound and felt the entire thing shift as it lifted from the ground and water washed over her again. Squeezing her hands tightly around the wooden leg of the seating she held on with all her strength as the gazebo rose and shifted with the wave. Gravity pushed her body downward and sideways as the gazebo rolled to its side. She screamed out in pain as the gazebo's movement threw her to her side and quickly onto her back.

Where she'd earlier been laying as close and flat as she could manage on the floor. She was now on her back against the gazebo and the pain in her body was unbelievable.

"Oh, dear Jesus", she cried out as the entire structure rose up out of the water on the force of the winds. It was thrown forward toward the opposite side of the house and property from where it had always stood. After literally flying through the air a short distance above the ground there was one final thrust and the gazebo landed just on this side of the dock. The entire upper end and roof was now under water and leaning at an angle. The lower end was sticking out, half on land and half in the lake. Finally finished with the gazebo the hurricane force wind continued to move forward. As it ripped through the dock it twisted the boards one after the other leaving the once long, flat structure no longer resembling a dock at all. It was now just a bunch of wood planks broken and jutting in and out of the water.

At long last, the gazebo lay still. Ms. Amber lay limp and silent. Her body was battered and broken from the abuse it had taken since she first left the house and headed into the storm not even an hour ago.

CHAPTER 26

"Ma's service was beautiful," Matthew said. "She would've been very pleased.

"She would have," Jaxson agreed. "The children did such a great job on their song. I could just see her smiling the whole time.

And the Eulogy Kate gave. Wow, what a testament to the friendship those two shared. As often as she was out here with ma, this is going to leave a huge void in her life. It's going to be very hard on Kate, that's for sure."

The others were nodding in agreement. The three men sat quietly, each of them lost in their own thoughts for a few minutes until Steven calmly spoke.

"As I recall it was just about a year after we first opened the Delaney Home for Children when Ms. Amber told me her story. It was around this time of day actually, just before dusk. We were sitting in this very spot drinking sweet tea, just like we're doing right now. We had just put the children to bed and were enjoying the evening when she quietly started talking about her life before we met.

Matthew's eyes met Jaxson's for a brief second before each man looked back at Steven. Neither wanted to miss a single word of this.

"We all know Ms. Amber had a happy childhood. Her parents are such loving, kind, good people. They've always been great stand-in grandparents to the children. I have no idea why they never had any other children but they didn't and Ms. Amber grew up wanting siblings. Despite her many playmates and friends being an only child left her wanting a large family.

She met Rand in Jr. high. By their freshman year they were sweethearts. They dated all through high school and married immediately after graduation. He was a really good man, she said. From the look in her eyes and love in her voice there was no question Rand was the love of her life.

He was a fireman with the County and she worked at the library. They'd been married almost two years when their little boy was born. He had black hair, deep brown eyes and a beautiful caramel complexion. Looked just like his daddy, she said, smiling in a way I hadn't seen before. She had a faraway look in her eyes that told me how happy they must've been together. He was a happy baby and they planned to have at least four maybe even six children together. They were both excited to have a large family.

She looked so happy telling me all about it, and then so sad telling me about the car accident that took Rand and little Randy a couple years later.

"I never knew any of this," Matthew said quietly.

"It wasn't something she talked about before or after that night. I guess losing them was so heartbreaking she just never could. I always suspected maybe she talked with Kate about it sometimes, but I don't really know. She did say Kate was there for her after the accident in every way a friend can be. Kate actually checked on Amber every day for the entire first year, either by stopping in or calling. That's a real friend, if you ask me."

Taking a long slow drink of his sweet tea he sat looking thoughtfully into the distance.

"You remember that necklace that was always around her neck?"

Both men nodded.

"It was a locket with their pictures inside. She showed me that night. I'm sure that's why her folks had them leave it on her for the burial. She would've wanted that.

Losing Rand and Randy was the hardest thing she ever faced. 'It almost broke me,' were her exact words. From the sound of it she drowned in her grief for a long while, just going through the motions of living, but not really going on with life. She told me she just couldn't snap out of it. Despite all the efforts Kate made with her she just couldn't get back to who she was before the tragedy happened.

His face was full of empathy as he looked from Matthew to Jaxson and said, "Knowing she's with them now makes losing her a little easier for me. Maybe that'll help you through this, too."

He gave a heavy sigh before continuing, "So, there she was just stuck in her grief for the longest time. Then one day one of Rand's buddies from the fire station came to see her. Explaining that he wouldn't need much of her time he invited her to step outside. He just wanted to tell her a baby girl had been left at the firehouse. She needed a home. Ms. Amber told him she was sorry for the baby but that wasn't something she could help him with.

He looked disappointed, she said, but told her he understood and turned to leave. That's when she heard a baby cry. He said he was sorry but he had to go and hurried to the driveway.

The baby was in his car. He leaned in the passenger side window and talked to the baby girl. Reaching in he tried to give her a bottle but she wouldn't take it. He opened the door and got her out. Even though he was holding her she cried harder. It was as if he had forgotten Amber was even there. He was just trying to help that little girl. That went on for a while.

Listening to that baby cry was tearing her up, she said. Finally, when she could take no more, she walked over and took the baby from his arms.

'Something happened the minute I held her,' she said with a twinkle in her eyes. 'Something good happened inside my heart. Oh, yes, and the baby stopped crying,' she laughed when she told me that."

The men smiled.

"And that little girl was the beginning of the Delaney Home for Children. She wanted to honor Rand and little Randy so she used their last name instead of her first in the legal title of the place." Steven finished.

"Wow! I never knew any of that," Jaxson said. "Ma was quite a woman, wasn't she? Just look how many children she gave a loving home to after that. Me included."

"And me, even before you came along," Matthew said. "Looks like there was a lot we didn't know about our Ma."

"I guess so," Jaxson said as a sad look crossed his face.

"That's true. But we all knew what matters." Steven said smiling directly at Jaxson. "And we still do. We know how very much she loved us. We know she would want us to go on building good lives for ourselves, loving and serving God, loving others and being happy," he paused for a moment and the three of them just sat there together looking out over Spivey Lake.

"As you fellas know I've been helping out at the children's home over in Myrtle Beach whenever they've needed an extra hand for a few years now. Since they've taken the children from the Delaney home in, I've asked if I can come around more often. I thought it might help the children as they adjust to living there, you know?

They said they'd do me one better and asked me to come on until I figure out what I'm going to do next. They say I can stay on there if I want to. They're even offering in-house living, like I had here. I'm going to take them up on it, at least until we see what's going to happen with this place. I really want to keep doing what I've been doing all these years and I think Ms. Amber would want me to. I'll be taking care of the house and grounds over there. I think she'd be very pleased they're getting me, don't you?"

"Absolutely!" Jaxson answered, slapping his thigh loudly. "That's wonderful news, Steven! It's perfect really. And you're right, it's going to help the children so much having you living there with them. I'm sure it'll help you, too. This is absolutely great!"

"Jaxson's right. It couldn't have worked out any better! I love it!" Matthew said. He then turned to Jaxson and asked, "What about you, Jaxson. What do you plan to do now?"

"I've been thinking about that a lot," Jaxson answered as he looked from one man to the other. "I'm not sure there's any other choice really. What can I do but to go ahead with the plans we made together? Ma and I talked this all through. We did all the research and filled out all the applications. She was so happy when I got accepted and the funding came through. Nothing's really changed except that she's not here so I'm going to go to college just like we planned. I don't know what I'll do during breaks yet but I'll figure that out. I want to honor Ma by following her example. It's in a different way but I'll still be taking care of children for the rest of my life. Being a pediatrician is what I want to do and it's what she wanted for me."

"That's awesome," Steven told him, "And you have a place to go during school breaks. You will always have a place to go as long as I'm around. There's plenty of space where I'll be staying. We're still family, you know. We'll always be family."

Jaxson was relieved by Steven's invitation.

"You're right Jaxson. That's exactly what Ma would want for you. I'm really proud of you and I know she is, too," Matthew said. "And just for the record I'm with Steven, the three of us are family and that's never going to change!"

"That's right!" Steven said, placing a hand on Jaxson's shoulder.

"As for what I'll be doing," Matthew continued with a smile much bigger than either of the other two men had seen on his face in quite a while. "You two don't know this yet, but I'm happy to say Ma did. I confided in her just two weeks before the hurricane."

Looking sheepishly from one to the other he practically gushed, "Ruby has agreed to marry me!! We designed our wedding rings together and they're being made now. We were just waiting to tell you when she could show you her engagement ring. We're getting married next spring."

"What??" both men exclaimed standing to their feet with huge smiles on their faces.

"I could not be happier for you, Matthew! This is wonderful news," Steven said as he moved in for a hug.

"Yes, it is," Jaxson said, turning it into a group hug. "I bet Ma was so excited for you."

"You're right, she was," Matthew answered. "She really was."

CHAPTER 27

Marissa sat the plate of fried chicken in the center of side dishes spread out on the dinner table and sat down. Letting out a satisfied sigh she smiled and turned to her husband, "It looks like we're ready, babe. You wanna say the blessing?"

"Sure do," he answered and reached his right hand out for hers and his left hand toward their thirteen-year-old son, Aiden. Taking his father's hand Aiden, in turn, took his fifteen-year-old sister Ellie's hand and she took her twin sister Marie's hand. The circle was completed when Marie took her mother's hand. It was a tradition in this household to hold hands during the dinnertime prayer. Their oldest son, Ryan, wasn't there. He would be in a few days since it was his habit to have Sunday dinner with the family. A fact that gave his mother another reason to love Sundays.

Ryan got involved at the local fire station on a volunteer basis during his last year of High School. After graduation he immediately attended a nine-week fire-fighting training course offered by Emcare to meet the educational requirements of the job. Currently he was completing four months of training. He would then begin taking exams in an effort to be promoted as he continued in his career.

He shared an apartment with a few other fellows across town.

"Thank you, Lord, for this meal we've all worked together to get onto the table today. Thank you, for the money to buy it, the good health to enjoy it and each other to share it with. Thank you for all you've seen us through and all that you bless us with each and every day. Thank you for giving us joy despite life's sorrow. We are grateful and we love you, Father. Amen."

The chain of hands released as each began to fill their plates.

"Oh, dad," Ellie said excitedly "you should've seen Aiden's hit in the game today! It was awesome. Tell him about that play, Aiden. It was unbelievable!"

"It was insane, dad. I guarantee you've never seen anything like it."

"It really was crazy," Marissa added. "I mean, even as we watched it unfold, I couldn't believe what was happening."

Aiden went on to describe the details of the play.

It wasn't often that he couldn't get out of a work meeting but that was the case today so his family was filling him in on what he'd missed. He smiled into the face of first one and then the other as he turned to whoever was speaking, making just the right comment here and there until the exciting story was all told.

Happy conversation continued until the meal was finished and the children were excused to do their homework.

Their parents stayed in the kitchen cleaning up together. As he watched his wife filling the sink with hot sudsy water and dropping the dinner dishes into it, he was struck again with how lovely she was. Her strawberry blond hair hung in loose layers around her face and light freckles could be seen just beneath her pale skin. When she blew upward trying to blow away the few stray strands of hair that were tickling her nose he reached out and tucked them behind her ear for her.

"Thank you," she said, smiling in his direction. "That's a little hard to do when your hands are sudsy."

"I guess so," he laughed.

He found his thoughts going back in time to the small apartment they rented when they were first married. Before the children there was a lot less clean up to do but even then, they had done it together. And now here they were twenty years later with the happy life and beautiful family they had looked forward to back then.

The only thing missing was their oldest daughter.

True to His promises God had given them the daily doses of strength needed to survive that loss. True to their promise to each other they never lost hope of one day finding their sweet baby girl or at least learning what had happened to her.

Through the years he had followed even the slightest lead in hopes of finding her. Always to no avail. They told their other children about their older sister and the family never stopped praying for her.

And still they hoped. Still, they wondered, as they undoubtedly always would, where she was now and whether they would ever know the answers.

CHAPTER 28

'I miss you something awful, Ma," Jaxson said under his breath while hurrying across campus.

At twenty-four years of age, he was exactly halfway through his medical program. He was definitely feeling the pressure.

These past four years without Ma's loving support had been more difficult than he could've anticipated. He knew going in it was going to take determination to get through such an extensive process. He just hadn't expected it to wear on him this much. Not having Ma to talk to was taking a toll. She had been there for him all of his life, always so supportive of his dreams and endeavors. It was very hard without her sometimes.

But for Steven, Matthew and Ruby it would've felt to Jaxson as if he had no family at all. Those three had sure stepped up for him.

When his first college break rolled around Jaxson stayed with Steven at the Myrtle Beach Children's Home where he worked and lived. Everyone made him feel welcome. It was great to help Steven with the many projects on the house and grounds. It was almost like old times.

Steven was the closest thing Jaxson had to a father and Matthew had always felt like his older brother. Matthew and Ruby invited Steven and Jaxson over to their home for every Holiday and they all got together often in between. If it weren't for the love and support of those three in his life, Jaxson wouldn't have made it through that first couple of years without Ma. With them on his side he was doing quite well. Thank you, God for blessing my life with Steven, Matthew and Ruby he thought as he quite often did. We may not be blood relation but we're family through and through.

After hurrying across campus Jaxson dodged into the building his next class was in. Taking the stairs to the lower floor two at a time he sprinted down the hallway hoping against hope to get to class on time. He hated walking in late. Some professors would call a late student out for the express purpose of embarrassment. Thankfully this one didn't do that.

Finally, he ducked into the last doorway on the left and grabbed the first open seat he came to. Not even two seconds later the professor stood up to address the students.

Whew, I made it by the skin of my teeth, he told Ma silently, wondering how long he'd been talking to her. After giving it a few moments thought he had to admit he had never really stopped.

No, he wasn't delusional. He knew she was gone. How could he not know that? Life as he knew it had changed in an instant the day of the storm. It would never be the same again.

Though he missed Ma terribly, college was a great distraction for him that first year. Seeing it as the exciting new adventure they had talked and dreamed of together he was determined to enjoy it for the both of them.

Although Ma's death was a huge loss and his grief was heavy, he did well most of the time. Starting right into college that fall had not been easy. There were times he could've drowned under the weight of grief if he'd let himself. When his grief was especially deep, he would drive out to Spivey Lake, park his car and walk out to the pier house. Sitting at the end of the pier looking across the lake at what was once his home was helpful in the beginning.

As time passed, he began to focus more on the wreckage than on his happy memories. The broken gazebo looked out of place where it had been up-righted by the damaged dock. With its wooden boards jutting at odd angles out of the water, the dock now served to remind him of the hurricane's path. He wanted instead, to remember having run its length to jump gleefully into the lake.

With the passage of time the place took on the look of a forgotten home. Instead of remembering her watching the rainfall beneath the gazebo lights, he found himself thinking of Ma's last moments, as she lay broken and battered. The joy of his childhood became lost in the tragedy of the storm which had taken his mother's life.

On the evening of the storm the men of the family talked extensively with the children about what they had all been through that day. Lisha and Sara told how scared they were while waiting for Ma to come inside or the men to return. Young Carter felt responsible for Ms. Amber's death since she went out into the storm to rescue him. Everyone assured him it wasn't his fault. It was just the way things happened. Ma loved him very much and he had nothing to feel badly about.

Carter told them about him and Ma holding hands as they started back to the house together. The little boy cried as he talked about the wind tearing them apart and throwing her backward into the gazebo. He cried harder saying she couldn't move after that. He sobbed while sharing that she told him to leave her and shouted for him to run home. Everyone praised him for obeying her. They hugged him saying they were so glad he was there to tell them the story.

Jaxson, Matthew and Steven agreed they would continue to assure Carter there was nothing he could've done to change the outcome on that day. Assuring him that God knows the date, time and circumstances when each one of us will enter into eternity they shared from the Bible. King David said in Psalm 139:16 "All the days ordained for me were written in your book before one of them came to be."

God already knows how long each of us will live and what day our earthly lives will end. Ms. Amber died on the day that was appointed for her. They reminded Carter their mother knew God and trusted in Him. God loved her dearly and was with her every moment right up to her last breath.

She was the one who had taught them they were never alone. Didn't she tell them often that God is always with us? Carter couldn't deny that. Being reminded his Ma was not alone when he left her outside seemed to comfort him. Steven assured him God was with her then just as He was with all of them in their heartbreak over losing her.

Jaxson often wondered about the last hour of Ma's life. After three years had passed, while in his second year of college, he told Steven and Matthew he wanted to know exactly what she had gone through.

Actually, all of them wanted to know.

Through her doctor they were able to obtain a copy of the medical examiner's report. From it they learned Ms. Amber suffered a grade three concussion and her back was broken. She also had several cracked ribs. The complications from all her injuries were simply more than she could survive.

True to how she had lived, Ma had given her life for the sake of her children. It made him think of a Bible passage she had read to them in John chapter fifteen and verse thirteen. It says "Greater love has no one than this, than to lay down one's life for his friends". No one loved their children more than his ma. It was no surprise she would risk her own life to save one of them. Jaxson felt very proud of her.

Being fairly young at the time of her death Ms. Amber had yet to take care of the details of a will. The house and property went into probate and remained locked down in that process. As a result, their upkeep was neglected - a situation that caused Jaxson great sadness whenever he looked across Lake Spivey at his childhood home.

These were his thoughts as he hurried across campus. Having made it to class on time and settled in Jaxson pulled out a notepad and got busy taking notes. His last two classes were just across the hall. After the second class he would be done for the weekend. He was more than ready for a few days of downtime.

CHAPTER 29

"Don't forget we've got the girls gymnastic competition this evening and all day tomorrow," Marissa said to her husband as he grabbed his briefcase and headed toward the back door.

Suddenly stopping in his tracks, he turned around and hurried toward her. Pulling her close he planted a quick kiss on her lips. He then took a few seconds to enjoy the moment as she smiled up at him

"It's the Myrtle Beach Sports Complex this time, right?" he asked as he released her and turned away to head for the back door again. Hearing her quick 'yes', he called out, "I'll get there as soon as I can after work. Don't wait for me. I'll find you."

Marissa laughed softly as she went back to cleaning the kitchen. She loved cooking a big breakfast for her busy family only to watch them devour it hurriedly and rush out the door one by one every weekday morning.

Her goal was to get them all together for at least one meal most days. The determining factor as to which meal that might be was which season of the year it was. Breakfast seemed to work best during the school year and winter months while supper worked in the summer.

When Ellie and Marie were little Marissa enrolled them in ballet, tap dance and gymnastics classes, in that order. It was gymnastics that held their interest. Not only did they continue to enjoy the classes, their confidence grew as they improved until each of the girls began to aspire to place in competitions.

The sport was good for them individually while also giving them a strong understanding of teamwork. Best of all, the girls often helped one another. Marie was strong on the vault and uneven bars and Ellie excelled on the balance beam and floor exercises. Though they were twins and looked alike, each girl had her own unique personality which came across in her chosen fashion, accessories, choice of music and favored school subjects. No doubt they would end up pursuing very different careers as their lives unfolded. While they did share many similarities - they were very distinct individuals. As is true with most twins her daughters were very close friends.

Their gymnastics coach, JJ, was awesome. The girls loved her. The whole family did really. She'd grown up in the area, even attending the same school the girls were in now. The two families even went to the same church.

Like the twins, JJ had been involved in gymnastics most of her life. After graduating she began to assist the coach on a volunteer basis which led to her becoming a coach in her own right when she was twenty. She was now twenty-one and this was her first full year as head coach. She was still young enough to have fun with her students but mature enough to seriously strive to give them a successful year of competition. She invited her students input on decisions that affected the entire team and the twins loved that. She even welcomed and considered their opinions on which uniforms the team would purchase.

Marissa was happy to have JJ coaching their daughters and her husband agreed. It was comforting to have their girls spend time with someone they'd known for most of her life and were fond of.

Although it wasn't something they talked about openly it was never far from their minds how easily a child can slip away. Losing their first daughter had left them extremely overprotective and they knew it. After Ryan's birth they battled the demons that haunt all parents of a missing child.

The constant fear of history repeating itself is especially difficult to overcome. Even all these years later neither of them had completely overcome it but they'd worked hard, both alone and as a team, not to let it be the governing emotion in their life.

Ryan was three when the twins were born. As is often true they were able to relax a little more with each addition to the family. It's just a fact that breathing a bit easier comes more naturally the longer you go without a tragedy. And so it was that by the time Aiden was born, two years later, each of them was feeling more comfortable.

That's not to say there weren't extreme moments of fear and panic on those rare occasion's life throws at every parent. When you momentarily lose sight of your child in a busy store, or when your child runs ahead of you at a public park. There had definitely been moments when one or the other had been called upon to calm and comfort their partner after such an incident. But thankfully here they now were with four healthy and happy offspring so many years after the loss of their first child.

By staying true to their long ago promises to always talk to and tell each other the truth they made it through every scare along the way. Still, those random panic moments had almost always prompted them to revisit the search for their missing daughter. Unfortunately, the ache in their hearts remained as they continued to come up empty-handed.

CHAPTER 30

"Twenty years!" Thatcher Foreman shouted as he angrily reversed direction to pace back toward the concrete block wall. For almost an hour he had been pacing the small prison cell ranting about the injustice of his current situation. Raising both arms above his head in exasperation, he dramatically let them drop. They hung loosely downward a few seconds until he turned quickly again and slapped both palms flat on the wall.

For the first time in over an hour he fell silent. He stayed there, his upper body leaning toward the wall as his lower half stretched back just a bit to where he'd planted his feet flat on the floor.

Moments passed and there he remained, palms flat against the concrete, face held high staring at the block wall. Into the silence the man quietly said, "I've spent over twenty years here." His head dropped and he stared at the floor. Again, he remained in place, head hanging downward between his outstretched arms and slumped shoulders.

He looked totally defeated.

Thirty seconds passed before he finally raised his head and slowly turned to face his totally unimpressed cellmate. The man was used to Thatcher's dramatics.

"Been that long, huh?" his cellmate said unsympathetically. "For you and eighty percent of everyone else inside, I imagine. I don't know what you want from me. We've all got a sob story. I'm sorry ol' pal but you are not unique."

Immediately, Thatcher said, "Oh, but I am."

As though his fire had been reignited, he declared, "I've made him pay! That despicable detective who put me in here suffers daily right along with me. I made that happen! I did!! The rest of that eighty percent you just threw out at me didn't do that to their tormentors, did they?"

He's got me there, his weary cellmate thought.

The despondent Thatcher of mere moments ago was completely gone now.

"Thanks," he said, nodding his head slightly in the direction of his cellmate. "I needed that reminder. I am where I am. I can't change that fact. But I'd wager he's in a worse place. And that's thanks to me. See? It's all good. As good as it's gonna get, anyway. The only thing better would be if he knew I was the cause of his misery. Maybe someday I'll tell him, 'til then this is good enough. I'm the winner. That's right Mr. big detective man, I'm the real winner here!"

And he's off, the cellmate thought, knowing Thatcher would now tell the same story he'd been telling since they got locked up together; how he'd suffered that first two years of his incarceration, being eaten up inside from knowing the detective felt proud, victorious even, while spending his days celebrating Thatcher's conviction. How he'd known all the while he was going to make that man pay, he just didn't know how - until he suddenly did. Thatcher always laughed at this point in his rantings. It had taken him a bit to put it all together. But eventually he had come to realize that without him even knowing it, fate had smiled on him. That had been an exciting moment in Thatcher's life, for sure.

Thatcher's previous cellmate had a sister who regularly visited. Missing female companionship Thatcher made it a point to meet her. He then made sure to be present when she came to see her brother. Like most women she was needy and boring. Not his type. In fact, he didn't even think she was pretty. He didn't really even like her. He was just bored and she was the only woman he could interact with. It was for his own entertainment, at first, that he showed her any notice at all.

She was easy, only wanting someone to pay attention to her. All women want attention. Tell them they're pretty, special, you're falling in love with them and they'll do whatever you want.

He wasn't sure, in the beginning, how he was going to use her since he was locked up. He just figured it would pay off later. There would come a day he'd need someone on the outside.

To get her on his side he started telling her how he'd been wronged. He was innocent. That detective was just out to get him. Had framed him, no less. She bought it all, stupid girl.

Meanwhile Thatcher was always keeping an eye on the detective's personal life, watching for something he could use against him; a way to hurt him.

Finally, after two years the answer came.

She was talking about herself again. The same old boring stuff he'd heard before. How she loved to travel, where all she'd gone, what all she'd seen. Being a traveling nurse was a great way to get to see the country. Anywhere she wanted to go she just applied for a temporary job there, got hired, and saw the sights during her off hours. When she was ready to move on, she did. He had to agree when she said it was a sweet set-up. There had been a few times he'd wondered if that was something he could use in his plan. He just wasn't sure.

It was then he learned the detective's wife was expecting a baby. What better way to make a man pay for your suffering than to make him suffer? What better way to make a man suffer than to take away his firstborn child?

CHAPTER 31

Seeing her husband entering the gymnasium in which today's competition was taking place Marissa stood and began waving her arms above her head.

His face lit up, he waved in return and headed in her direction. Despite the slight greying of his dark hair and a bit of wrinkling around his eyes she still found him to be quite handsome. Watching as he climbed up the bleacher steps and turned to work his way through the other spectator's she found herself feeling thankful he was still hers.

"Hey, buddy!" he said to Aiden before tousling their teen-aged son's hair as if he were still five years old. Aiden laughed and swatted at his father's hand before quickly trying to put his hair back in place.

"How's it going?" her handsome man asked as his arm slid around her waist to pull her just a little closer while settling in beside her.

"You haven't missed anything. They're still getting set up and the teams have been practicing. I've been looking at the competition though. See that tall girl on the red team?" she asked, pointing to the left side of the gym. "She's going to give Ellie a run for her money in the floor exercises. Her routine is fun and energetic and she's excellent. I haven't seen her slip up even once while practicing."

"Okay, well, Ellie's got her routine down good. I guess, we'll see what happens when the time comes."

He turned his attention to the team in green uniforms currently practicing their routines on the vault.

"How were the girls feeling when you talked to them?"

"We were able to chat with them for just a few minutes as soon as we got here. They're okay. Pre-competition nerves, as usual, but they're both feeling good about their routines."

"That's good," his eyes had been scanning the floor trying to catch one of his daughters glancing his way ever since his arrival. Suddenly his smile broadened and he waved. "Well, Ellie knows I'm here, at least. Now to watch for Marie to look this way."

Marissa's heart constricted as she looked from her husband's face to Ellie's. She loved the connection he had with each of their children. Despite the fact that the demands of his job kept him from making it to every one of their events the children knew they were important to him.

He was always there when he could be but law enforcement positions usually don't give way to family activities. She'd had to learn that early in their marriage and had worked hard to help the children understand when he wasn't able to make it to their events. It seemed to her now as though they had achieved their joint goal of creating a loving family despite his demanding career.

We have so much to be thankful for, Marissa thought as she looked over at her husband and son. They were huddled together talking as they watched the activity on the floor.

"Mom," Aiden suddenly said, leaning around his father to catch her attention. "It looks like Marie's braid is coming apart. I think she wants you to go down there and fix it for her."

"Where is she?" Marissa asked her eyes searching the floor. "Oh, never mind. I found her. Yeah, you're right she's pulling it the rest of the way out and motioning for me. I'll be right back you two."

Marissa jumped up, worked her way past them and hurried down the bleachers.

Locating JJ, she rushed over to the coach. "Hey JJ, I'm so sorry to interrupt. It looks like Marie's braid came loose. Is it okay if I go over and re-do it for her?"

"Oh geez," JJ answered, looking around for the judges. "Okay, they're still getting things organized so that's fine. Just do it as quickly as you can. We'll be lining up for competitions to begin as soon as they're ready. Thanks for checking with me first. And as always, thanks for being here!"

"Of course," Marissa answered. "Thank you for everything you do for the girls! They're an awesome team and you're doing a great job!"

Mere seconds after Marissa finished the new braid an announcement was made for the teams to line up.

She barely made it back to her spot with the guys before the audience stood and the teams turned their attention to the flag for the playing of the National Anthem. As the applause died down the teams spread out on the various matts across the gymnasium for the judging of events to begin.

It was an exciting evening. Both Ellie and Marie did well in their events. The overall performance of the team was good which kept them in the tournament for the next day's competition.

CHAPTER 32

Hearing the overhead page Dr. Jaxson Delaney immediately raced toward the Emergency Room. Taking the last three steps in a bound his palm hit the stairway exit door as he flew through it and rounded the next corner. He literally ran down the last hallway, shoved the ER doors open, rushed to the second cubicle and jerked the curtain aside. There on the bed was his patient, five-year-old Emily in obvious distress.

Visibly assessing her condition as he rushed to her side, he was shouting orders to the attending nurses. As quickly as possible he injected the medication the child needed to avert her current crises. Within seconds she began to rally and in less than three minutes she was coming back around.

"Hey there, Emily. It's Dr. Jaxson. Do you see me, sweetheart? Hey, would you look at this? I'm wearing my Bugs Bunny tie today. It's your favorite, right?"

As he spoke the child's eyes searched his face. Then, not only hearing his words but beginning to comprehend them her eyes began to avert toward his tie. This was exactly what he was watching for.

"I'm with you, Emily. I'd rather see Bugs Bunny than Mickey or Minnie Mouse any day," he said, still watching her closely.

With her vision and comprehension becoming clearer each passing second her eyes finally alighted on his brightly colored tie.

"No," the child said weakly as she tried to smile.

This was a game the two of them had played many times before.

"No?" the doctor asked in a teasing voice.

"Are you sure Bugs Bunny isn't your favorite?" He knew full well she was absolutely crazy over Minnie Mouse.

"Oh, yes. That's right," he now said, giving a huge smile as the little girl actually tried to raise her upper body up off the bed. "Minnie's the one you like."

"You don't have to sit up, Emily," he said gently. "You don't want to see my silly ol' Bugs Bunny tie anyway."

"Yes, Minnie," the little girl said, smiling weakly.

"That's my girl," the doctor said, leaning down to look her directly in the eyes and pat her head gently.

"Now you just rest a minute while I talk to your mommy. Let the nurses take care of you now. You're okay sweet girl. You're going to be just fine."

Turning to the nurses Dr. Delaney, who was more commonly known to patients and staff as Dr. Jaxson, thanked them for their quick reactions.

"We got her through that one," he said with great relief while reaching out to gently pat those closest to him. As he turned away and started out of the room he continued, "I'm admitting her for the night. You know what to do so I'll leave you to it while I talk with her mother. Good job everyone."

Those who knew and worked with Dr. Jaxson knew that on those occasions when he barked out orders it was only because of the intensity of the situation at hand. He treated everyone with the utmost respect and appreciation. Unlike some at his professional level, and still others who wore the doctor title, he was respected and well-loved. He had an impeccable reputation both for medical knowledge and a gentle bedside manner.

Most everyone in his circle of colleagues would have been surprised to learn of his traumatic childhood circumstances. Jaxson had been rescued from a chaotic, abusive and extremely violent family situation at only six years old. Being placed in the children's home run by Ms. Amber Delaney was really the first bit of good fortune he'd ever had. Jaxson lived, and was loved there, for the rest of his childhood. At the age of nineteen, after the tragic death of the woman who had not given birth to him but had been his mother in every way that really mattered, he made the decision to have his last name legally changed to hers.

Although Ma wasn't there to see it, Steven, Matthew and Ruby were, along with Lisha, Asher, Carter and several other family members from his childhood. It was a proud day and a true honor for him to wear her name as he crossed the stage, received his medical degree and walked away as Pediatrician Jaxson Delaney.

CHAPTER 33

Vonda Graham sat sipping her coffee and rocking gently in the rocking chair on the back patio of her home. She lazily looked out over the new houses that had been built one by one to the side and back of her property. It was hard to believe this entire area had been a field of wildflowers when she first moved in. Eighteen homes had gone up over the past five years, most of which had brought, not only new neighbors, but new friends into her life.

Logan, South Carolina, the town she lived in, was continuously growing. It was said that within the next ten years there would be little to no open land between the small communities of Logan and Stokesbury and their neighboring large city; Myrtle Beach. While Vonda hoped that wasn't true, she couldn't deny how quickly things were changing.

Only time will tell for sure, she thought as a chilly breeze suddenly blew through. It picked up a few tendrils of her brown-beginning-to-turn-silver hair and gently laid them back across her shoulder.

Vonda had now lived in Logan for just short of six years. She had moved there with her late husband Stanley just a year before his passing. This community had come to feel like home since then.

Realizing she had been momentarily distracted, Vonda's eyes returned to the book she was reading. She was hoping to finish it today as her monthly book club meeting was fast approaching.

With only five ladies in the group, they took turns choosing the monthly selection. Whoever chose the book was always the hostess for the next meeting and in charge of making its plans. Since it was such a small group, they usually did something special rather than just meet and talk books.

This month's selection was a cozy mystery. In keeping with that theme Monica, their hostess, had decided it would be fun to go to a local theatrical production of a play entitled "The Butler Did It".

They would meet for lunch first and discuss the book. Vonda was looking forward to the occasion but she needed to finish reading it first.

Her cell phone rang. She saw on the screen that it was her fiancé. Her relationship with Marshall had started as an unexpected friendship after they literally bumped into each other at the local ball park during a little league ball game. They then shared a growing friendship for several years. The relationship had recently deepened and just three months ago Marshall proposed marriage from the pitcher's mound of the ballfield where they first met.

"Hello Marshall," Vonda spoke cheerfully into the phone.

"Are you having a good day?" he asked.

"I am now. I'm in my rocking chair finishing up that book I was telling you about a few days ago. It's really been good."

"I'm not surprised. From what you told me it sounded like it. And I know that rocker is just about your favorite place in the entire world."

"You got that right."

"I wanted to check on Lilly," Marshall said, asking about Vonda's beautiful, white, long-haired cat. "Is she doing any better?"

"Yes, thankfully she is. I took her to the vet this morning. It's definitely arthritis, which as you know, is what I was suspecting. Poor old girl, I really feel for her. I guess the two of us are just in sync with one another. It looks like we're going to go through the perils of aging together."

As her chuckling ended, she continued, "He gave her a shot to relieve the inflammation and I've got some pills to give her. If they relieve her pain, I'll be getting a bottle. We agreed it would be best to try them first just to be sure they'll help. Apparently, there are several kinds we can try.

You know how she hates going to the vet though. My poor girl yelled at me all the way home. She was not happy I can tell you that! As soon as I let her out of her carrier she went straight to her room and curled up on her favorite pillow. She's been recuperating from her traumatic morning ever since. I'm going to check on her as soon as I finish this book. I've only got three chapters left and I'm anxious to find out if I'm right about who done it."

Marshall could hear the smile in her voice.

"I'm just glad it's nothing worse and there are options for keeping the pain at bay. I don't want either of you girls unhappy," he said with a smile before asking what she wanted to do for dinner.

They were in the daily habit of eating together. It was just a matter of where. Since they hadn't specified a certain plan for this evening, he'd gone straight home from work and cleaned up. About to head her direction they discussed the various eateries on the way. After deciding where he would stop by for their take-out dinner, they ended the call and Vonda went to set the table for their meal.

CHAPTER 34

Dr. Jaxson knocked gently on the hospital room door and waited for the patient to answer.

"Yes? If that's you Dr. Jaxson you can come on in." He gently pushed the already-slightly-ajar door further open and entered the room.

Smiling in his direction the baby's mother began, "The nurses said you'd be coming by to do the first examination on our new little one. It's nice to finally meet you." She then introducing herself and her husband.

"We aren't usually anxious to get a new doctor but we're so happy to actually need a baby doctor that we've been excited to meet you. It's been quite a wait for us. Truthfully, we didn't know if this day would ever come." She then lifted the baby girl from where she'd been comfortably resting between her parents and offered her to the doctor.

As he reached out to take her Jaxson noticed she was tightly bundled in a light green baby blanket. He found himself suddenly overcome by a sense of familiarity and there he was, a nine-year-old boy on a fully moonlit night.

It wasn't the first time such a thing had happened. He shook his head ever so slightly to break the hold of the memory. A few seconds later as he looked into the tiny little face in the center of the tightly wound blanket, he found himself immediately transported back in time again.

What's gotten into me? He asked himself silently as he did another quick head shake and proceeded to give the new parents a brief summary of the examination process.

Dr. Jaxson was a popular pediatrician in the area, especially with other doctors within the same health care system. They liked keeping it all in the family, so to speak, and he'd been a pediatrician with Columbus County Healthcare for a number of years now.

"If you don't have any questions, I'll just take your daughter down the hall to the examination room for the newborn exam. It won't take very long. We have no reason to suspect she's not in good health, this is standard procedure so please don't be concerned. Every newborn must be thoroughly examined before being released to go home. Since she's just recently made her appearance, we're getting it in a little early is all. After my examination I'll return her to you and you'll continue your brief stay until you're both ready to be released."

"Thank you, doctor," the child's father said.

"It's my pleasure," Dr. Jaxson answered and turned to go.

Just before he was to leave the room he turned back toward the new parents. "One thing before I go, I haven't looked in her chart yet so please tell me what name you've given this little beauty?"

"Jolee," her mother said. "She's named after an author my mom admired when I was a child. Mom read all of her books. I have, as well. I just always liked the name. Mom's going to love it when she finds out that's what we've named her. It's a round-about way to honor my mother, I guess."

"That's great," Dr. Jaxson said as he turned away again and stepped out into the hall.

Carrying little Jolee toward the examination room he couldn't help noticing yet another similarity as he allowed his memories to pull him into the past.

The memory of the night he, Matthew, Steven and Ma gave Jovie her name tugged at Jaxson's emotions causing him to reach up and wipe a tear from his own cheek.

The baby before him was taking her first official medical exam in stride. Little Jolee wasn't crying as some newborns did. Her bright little eyes seemed to be taking it all in as the doctor turned her in different directions and manipulated her little limbs.

"You're being a very good little girl, Jolee," Dr. Jaxson told her in a soothing voice. "From the moment I first saw you today you've been reminding me of my little sister. Your names are even similar, did you know that?"

The baby girl seemed to grin just then and Dr. Jackson laughed out loud saying, "That's right! Your name is Jolee and hers is Jovie. Did you know that?"

The baby girl's eyes followed his face as he spoke to her. "Of course, you didn't," Jaxson said as he finished the examination.

"I'm happy to report that you're in very good health, Jolee. You seem like a happy little baby, too. Your mommy and daddy love you very much. Apparently, they've waited for you for a very long time. That's another thing you have in common with my little sister. Her adoptive parents had to wait a long time for her, too. They were so happy the day they came to take her home with them. Seeing their joy helped me a lot that day. It was a difficult time - that's for sure. Some days haven't been easy for me since then either but that's okay. God is good and He has always helped me through."

He was talking in the soothing, cheerful voice he used with all of his young patients. Since they were alone together, he spoke from his heart to little Jolee. It was calming for both of them. Having finished her examination, he was now carrying Jolee back down the hallway to her parent's room.

Handing her back to her mother in just a few moments would be a lot easier than watching Jovie leave with her new parents so many years before. While watching them drive away his vision had blurred with tears as he begged God to keep her safe and give her a happy life.

In his role as the big brother in Ms. Amber's Home for Children Jaxson had seen many children come and go through the years. No other leaving had ever tugged at his heart the way Jovie's did.

She had been assigned to him. He had been the keeper of the treasure the night she arrived and he could never see her differently after that. She was the one who had started his lifelong pattern of praying for a child's future. At the young age of nine he had started praying for her. From then on - he had done what he was doing right now.

Walking that long hospital corridor, he was praying as he went. After having said good-bye to Jolee's parents, as he'd done so many times for Jovie through all these many years, he was now asking God to watch over little Jolee.

'Please God, keep her safe and give her happiness, bless her parents and help them as they raise her to be the person you created her to be.' As often happened all down through the years he drifted naturally from praying for this current baby to praying for Jovie.

117

'My little sister is a grown woman now, God. I don't know where she is or what her life is like. But you do. You've been with her every moment I haven't through all these years. I know you have and that's comforted me through all this time. Please continue to watch over her and keep her safe now. Please assure her she is loved - by her family and by you – and if it's at all possible, please remind her she's also loved by me. I don't know if she remembers me. It was just six months after her third birthday party that she hugged me so tightly while promising to be a good girl and said good-bye.

Even though Ma explained that she was going to her new home that day she had no idea she was never coming back to us. She was too little to comprehend. All she knew was what we had always told her, that someday she would go to her new home and that was going to be a wonderful day. There's no way she could've understood that we weren't going to be together anymore.'

He swallowed the emotion that rose up in his throat as he remembered the boy he had once been. That boy hadn't understood that knowing something beforehand is entirely different from comprehending it. That was something he had learned the hard way. He remembered the exact moment in time when he came to realize that understanding and comprehending are two entirely different things. It was the moment of his first heartbreak.

CHAPTER 35

Vonda carried another box out of the backyard shed and sat it on the picnic table. Opening it she picked up a pair of work gloves and smiled.

Immediately, in her mind's eye she remembered her late husband, Stanley, wearing those gloves as he used the weed-eater to trim the stray weeds from the edge of the house and patio. She saw herself step out of the back sliders with his go-to drink, Mountain Dew, in her hand. She carried it over to him and he took a long and appreciative swig. They spent a moment chatting together and he thanked her as he handed it back to her. She took it over to the small table on the patio and placed it next to her own glass of southern sweet tea.

After he finished the trimming the two of them sat in their matching rocking chairs on the back patio and admired his work. They chuckled about Lilly sitting inside looking longingly out at them through the sliders. They talked about the vacant lots behind and beside their house, lamenting the fact that someday new homes would be constructed all around them. The view they were enjoying would be gone.

Having shared a long and happy marriage Vonda and Stanley were finally at a low-stress, comfortable time in their life. Being new to the small town of Logan they looked forward to getting to know people in the community and embarking on their older years there together.

Vonda felt as if she'd pressed the fast forward button as she came back to the present. It was almost unbelievable to her when she realized it had been five years since Stanley had so unexpectedly been called home to heaven. The year following her husband's death was just a blur. Honestly, there were lots of things she didn't remember about that time at all. She had since learned that is common during grief. She was certain it was God's way of helping her through the pain and loss.

Standing here now, with those work gloves in her hands, the memory seemed of only a few days ago. At the same time, it strangely felt as if it were another lifetime altogether.

After all this time of living here alone – well, almost alone – since she had Lilly, her sweet feline companion; it felt surreal to be clearing out Stanley's shed. While some might see this as a finality, a closing of that part of her life, Vonda didn't see it that way at all.

The life she'd shared with Stanley would always be a part of her - beautiful memories of a life and love shared. While this was the closing of one door and the opening of another, it wasn't like she could never visit her cherished memories again.

She would be moving to Stokesbury as soon as she and Marshall were married. She was beginning a new life with this wonderful man she loved. But Marshall had never made her feel as if she had to abandon the life she'd shared with Stanley. That was just another of the many reasons she had grown to love him so deeply.

Vonda met and became friends with Marshall Davidson about a year after losing Stanley. Their friendship steadily grew stronger over the next couple of years. It had taken first one and then the other by surprise as each of them began to recognize they were in love.

Since their recent engagement the couple had been making many life-changing decisions. Vonda was ready to soon leave the home she and Stanley had chosen together. The day was fast approaching when she and Lilly would be moving on.

While she loved her life in Logan, she also loved the life she knew she and Marshall would have together. Marshall had a beautiful home and ran his construction business out of Stokesbury. Vonda was excited to begin her new life there with him.

Actually, the timing seemed perfect since Vonda's neighborhood was changing. She was certain the house she had loved so much would make a wonderful home for a family with growing children. She loved the idea of a young father keeping his yard tools and sports equipment in Stanley's shed. She knew Stanley would love that, too. The thought of a family living within the walls of this house brought her joy and she was ready to let that happen.

With these thoughts in mind, she continued the work of going through the boxes in the shed. As she sorted through Stanley's possessions, she welcomed the memories that flooded in. She divided his belongings into sections; one which she and Marshall would take to the local men's shelter or other donation centers, another of items for her children to look through as she thought those items may have some special meaning for them, and yet another of items to take with her.

Vonda chuckled when she looked over at the sliders and saw Lilly sitting on the inside looking out at her. Some things never change, she thought with a smile.

It would be good to have this job completed at the end of the day. This coming weekend everything would be delivered to its new location and another item in preparation of her move would be checked off of her list.

She and Marshall were still discussing the details of their coming wedding and the reception to follow. They wanted it to be somewhere beautiful and meaningful, somewhere that represented new life in more ways than just being their wedding day. As of yet they had no idea where that would be or even what exactly was going to make such a place obvious to them. They weren't stressed as the actual wedding wasn't going to be a huge event. It would simply be a joyous gathering of their immediate family and friends so they could pull it together in a short amount of time.

There was still a bit to be done with Vonda deciding what to take with her and what to part with. Meanwhile Marshall was doing a bit of condensing in his home in preparation of his wife joining him there.

Marshall loved Vonda's homey decorating style and had invited her to make whatever changes she wanted in his house. The two of them were having a wonderful time talking things through as she did exactly that. It was a happy time for both of them and they were each content to enjoy this time of transition before the actual wedding took place, whenever and wherever that was going to happen. At this point it was anyone's guess and the happy couple was having fun keeping everyone, including themselves, in suspense.

CHAPTER 36

Aiden had already said goodnight and gone to his room. As the credits rolled at the end of the television show, they'd been watching Ellie and Marie stood up and went from one of their parents to the other giving each one a hug. The girls called out their good-nights as they headed upstairs to their bedrooms.

He winked and moved closer to Marissa stretching his arm out and slightly upward to issue a silent invitation for her to snuggle up with him. Without hesitation she slid closer to take her favorite place in all the world. He gently tightened his arm around her shoulder, looked into her eyes and said, "You are such a good mother, Marissa."

The warmth in her heart spread along with her smile, "Aww, thank you for saying that, may I ask what prompted it?"

"Sure, I've just been enjoying our life all evening. It's hard to do that without taking note of all you do to make our house a home and bring this family together. You just have a way of keeping everything moving smoothly. I love that you love caring for us the way you do. Supper was delicious, as usual, and then sitting here with our children talking and watching our show together. I don't know, I guess it was listening to them talking about their activities that got me to thinking. Do you realize this weekend will be the last gymnastics tournament our girls will ever be in?"

"Oh no, stop!" Marissa said as she playfully punched him. "Now you're just going to make me sad."

"No, now, I'm not trying to do that. I guess I've just kind of been taking a stroll down memory lane since they'll soon be moving onto other things. It's hard to think back over it all without noting that if you weren't such a good mother, you wouldn't have enrolled them in ballet, tap, and gymnastics when they were just tiny little girls," he smiled at that thought. "But you did, and through gymnastics they've learned so much that will be helpful in their lives overall. Really Marissa, don't you think there's been so much good that's come from it? We've had fun as a family. We've had some pretty proud moments as their parents. The same is true with Aiden and his pursuits. Our children are blessed to have you, and so am I."

He leaned toward her uplifted face to plant a soft kiss on her lips.

"Well, thank you for saying all of that," she said as she snuggled into the crook of his arm a little closer. "When they were little, I just wanted to dress them up in their little ballet tutu's and watch them have fun, really. They're the ones who chose gymnastics. Looking back though, I'm really glad they both liked the same sport. Can you imagine if they'd chosen two separate activities. As if we weren't busy enough!" She laughed out loud and he quickly joined her.

A little sadness crept into her voice as she went on.

"To tell the truth I've purposely avoided thinking about this being their last tournament. I'm not sure I'm ready to let them go. It's a good thing for me that God doles out strength when the need arises. But yes, I totally agree that good has come from it all.

Our girls have done very well with their gymnastics, especially this year. Actually, the entire team is doing great this year. It won't surprise me at all if they take first place this weekend. In fact, I'm kind of expecting them to."

"I am, too," he agreed before changing the subject to ask about their schedule for the next day.

Three days later the family piled into the SUV and headed toward the Sports Complex for the final competition. Ellie was stressing over her routine while Aiden and Marie assured her it would be flawless. Once the vehicle was parked the girls ran ahead to join their team. Fifteen minutes later when the rest of the family entered the gymnasium, they saw the team huddled together while JJ gave them a pep-talk.

"She's an excellent coach," Marissa said. "I'm so glad the girls are on her team."

Her husband and son nodded in agreement. "She's the best gymnastic coach they have in this division," Aiden said just as the huddle broke up.

Watching from his place in the bleachers their father saw JJ smile above Ellie's head as she released her and turned to hug the next girl in the circle. It wasn't the first time JJ's one dimple had caught his attention. Whenever she smiled there was a deep indentation in her left cheek but none in her right. He focused on it for a brief few seconds assuming, as he had before, that it caught his attention because his beautiful Marissa's smile was the same way. Though it was also in the left cheek, Marissa's dimple wasn't as prominent as JJ's. It must be a pretty common phenomenon, he supposed. His attention diverted to the other teams which were lining up at the mats for the National Anthem. The tournament was about to begin.

Just as they had anticipated JJ's team of girls took the lead in the competition early in the day. As the day progressed, they continued to advance and won first place. What an exciting end to Ellie and Marie's gymnastics career!

He and Marissa took lots of pictures of the closing ceremony as first place medals were placed around the neck of each girl on the team. He rushed forward and got the team to line up with JJ in the center for several poses. JJ asked if he'd be sure to get the pictures to her so she could print them out for all the girls' parents. Of course, he agreed, saying he'd send them to Marissa's phone and she would text them to JJ within the next day or two.

As he and Marissa had earlier discussed, he told JJ they'd like to host a victory party at the house. She accepted the offer, thanking him and saying the team would be really excited. He told her they would leave soon and have things ready for the team whenever they were finished.

As he and Marissa stood watching the girls hugging each other and their much-loved coach, he couldn't help thinking that his oldest daughter would be close to JJ's age now. As he sometimes found himself doing, he wondered what she might be like as a young adult woman. He was beginning to despair of ever knowing.

On their way back to the house he, Marissa and Aiden decided a pizza party was in order since this was now a victory celebration. Marissa placed the order and they swung by to pick the food up on the way home. Marissa made popcorn and Aiden set out the sweet tea and sodas. Everything was ready by the time JJ and the girls arrived.

It was a fun celebration for everyone over the next several hours.

"You two are the absolute best!" JJ told them later just before heading out to drop several of the team members off at their various homes.

"I have loved coaching your daughters! I've already told them this but I'm really going to miss them. Not only that, I'm going to miss seeing you and Aiden and Ryan at these events. You all are such a special family."

"Aww, well thank you, JJ," Marissa said giving the young woman a tight hug. "We think you're pretty special, too. And so is your family. Thankfully, it's not like we're never going to see each other again."

"Yeah, since we all go to the same church," Aiden piped in as he and his dad gave JJ a quick hug as well.

"That's true," JJ laughed. "Now I just feel silly. You're right, of course! We'll see each other Sunday."

"No need to feel silly," Marissa said. "It's not the same! But I'm glad we'll still see each other sometimes."

"Me, too!" JJ said, waving as she followed the last of the girls out the front door.

CHAPTER 37

"Well, this looks interesting," Vonda said as she strolled through Dianne's kitchen looking at the various baskets containing prepackaged foods.

"We've got pop-tarts, granola bars, protein-power bag mixes with candy, nuts, and granola."

"That's a pretty arrangement of cheese, meats and crackers on the wooden tray there," Deb said, pointing it out to Stacey who'd just entered the dining room.

"Oh, wait!" Lynda exclaimed. "I see what's going on here! Dianne set out all the foods Alan carried in his backpack while he was on his cross-country trek. What a great idea!"

Laughing Dianne said, "that's also why we'll be eating outside around the campfire. With camping wherever he could, Alan often took his meals by the campfire on his walk so we're going to do it for our meeting today."

"Oh, I love that idea!" Monica said.

"I knew you would," Dianne replied. "Since you have campfires in your backyard quite often, I'm counting on you to help get the fire started. What do you say to that?"

"I'm on it!" Monica replied with a smile.

Dianne was the one who had chosen the book series The Walk which the book club group had just finished reading. In it the main character walks across the country. The book relays stories of the places he sees and the people he meets along the way. He eats packaged food he buys enroute and keeps in his backpack when he's not eating at small diners. He sleeps wherever he can, sometimes in a small cabin or hotel, sometimes in the tent he carried on his back.

Dianne was the hostess of the meeting since she had picked the book. In that role she'd chosen to provide them the same foods Richard Paul Evans had his character eat in his series, namely all the foods on display.

Dianne had gone above and beyond by also putting together a taco bar. She wanted her friends to have more to eat than just snack foods and would encourage them to take those with them when they left later.

Monica was already outside getting the fire going when they started filling their plates. She actually passed Vonda coming out with her plate full as she was heading back in to get her own. Once they had all made it outside and were seated around the fire ring Dianne said, "You did a great job with this fire, Monica. Thank you so much!"

"She sure did," Stacey agreed before asking the entire group, "So, who did you think was the most interesting character Alan met on The Walk?"

And that was all it took to get the discussion going.

Deb, Dianne, Stacey and Lynda were the original members of this book club. Those four initially knew one another because they all attended church together. After being in a few church classes with each other Deb and Dianne realized they shared a love of reading. From then on it wasn't unusual for them to be overheard talking about the contents of the various books they'd read. It wasn't long before they were loaning books back and forth. When returning a book, one would ask the other for their opinion. They had some great book conversations together. Once they began to talk about forming a book club group Stacey, Lynda and Monica's names came up as readers.

Those five formed the book club. They'd been meeting for about a year when they jointly agreed to invite Kate. Several of them had gone to High School with her and knew her best friend had passed away some years before. They felt for her in her loss. Remembering her to be a reader they decided to invite her to a book club meeting. She fit right in and had been coming ever since.

Later that year Stacey became friends with Vonda through Mason, Stacey's husband. His brother Marshall and Vonda were new friends which put the two women together with the brothers fairly often. It didn't take long for Stacey to realize they were having regular discussions of the books they were reading. When she learned that Vonda had recently read their book club selection for that month Stacey invited her to the monthly meeting. The other ladies enjoyed her input and Vonda soon became a regular part of the club.

While all of the ladies were friends who cared deeply about each other and enjoyed each other's company Vonda and Kate were beginning to share a deeper connection. They often chatted between themselves before or after the meetings and sometimes got together outside of book club. The same was true of Monica and Deb.

Since The Walk is a series of five books, they hadn't met for their usual monthly meeting. It had now been six weeks and just as had been suspected their discussion of the series carried them through the entire meal. The group then sat comfortably around the fire ring talking about life in general as friends so easily do.

When Deb asked Vonda how the wedding plans were coming, she confessed that she and Marshall were on the lookout for the perfect place to have their ceremony. This sparked a discussion of possible venues in the area along with more questions as to colors and themes for the big day.

After a bit Monica put another log in the fire and Dianne broke out the graham crackers, chocolate bars and marshmallows for s'mores. An hour later when their gathering broke up everyone headed home feeling full and happy.

CHAPTER 38

"You've been awfully quiet these past few days," Marissa said to her husband with a bit of concern in her voice. "Something on your mind?"

He looked at her sideways trying to appear unconcerned as he turned away and answered, "I'm okay."

"Clearly, you're not," she said, calling him out. "Have you forgotten our promises? I'm sure you haven't. I know it's not always easy to talk about what's on your mind, especially when it's something troubling but we promised never to keep anything from each other so spill it, mister."

He looked her in the eyes but still hesitated.

Finally, he began, "It's not like it's anything new. We've been talking about the same thing for over twenty-three years now."

She got up from her place in the easy chair and walked across the room to join him on the couch. "Our daughter, our sweet, missing daughter," she said with a weak smile. "What is it you're thinking?"

"I just can't stop wondering if I've done everything possible to find her, you know? I mean I was a police investigator when she went missing. I've steadily advanced in my career all these many years since she's been gone. I've looked at her case, I hate even calling it that, but that's what it is. It's our daughter's missing person case. I've looked at it from every angle and I've had my colleagues look at it repeatedly all through the years. How is it possible I haven't been able to crack this case wide open? I guess, I'm just not as good at what I do as I thought I was."

"No! You are not going to do that," Marissa said firmly. "I'm not going to sit here and let you blame yourself that this case hasn't been solved. As you've just said yourself you are not the only detective who has looked at it. You've had multiple people study her case and no one has seen anything new. This is not your fault. You are great at what you do or you never would have been promoted. You were specifically chosen to be on an FBI Task Force for heaven's sake. You have to be good to accomplish that. How can you even question your abilities? I'm very proud of you and I don't ever want to hear you doubt yourself again, do you hear me? You are the best FBI agent they've got Jeremy Alan! Do you hear me?"

Though her words were stern her touch was gentle as she reached out and laid her hands on the arms he had tightly folded across his chest. At her touch he crumbled into her, leaning forward 'til his forehead rested against hers. She lifted her long, slender arms and placed them around him pulling him into her for a deep and loving hug.

"Thank you for that, Marissa. I know you believe it but it's really hard to live with myself when she's still out there and her case remains unsolved."

"Okay, I get that," she said quietly. "What can we do to help you? I'm willing to do whatever you think would be good to do. You haven't been yourself for weeks now. What have you been thinking? Do you have any new ideas at all?"

She wasn't sure what it was, but something told her he did. "You do, don't you?" When she looked up at him their eyes met and she went on, "tell me. Tell me what it is, Jeremy. What are you thinking?"

He backed out of her embrace to look her fully in the face. "It's a long shot so I don't want you to get your hopes up but I have been thinking of trying something we haven't tried before."

"Okay," she said hesitantly. "What is it?"

"I keep thinking about the FBI Task Force you just mentioned."

"You had a great experience with that team. You said it was the best team you've ever worked with."

"The team was great, that's certainly true, but the team leader is who I keep thinking about. Leanza Williams is the best missing persons advocate I've ever met and her reputation backs that up. She put together a top-notch team, kept us on point, worked right down in the trenches with us and led us to victory. It's making me crazy that we're coming up on twenty-five years since our baby went missing, Marissa. I don't think I can go for the rest of my life without at least finding out what happened to her. If there's even a chance that she's still alive we need to find her. I mean look at us. We're almost through raising her siblings, we're getting older every day. Our lives are passing us by and if she's alive out there somewhere we're losing precious time with her."

"I can't argue. You're right, Jeremy. You're absolutely right. So, what are you thinking? You want to form a Task Force to look for her?"

"No, I'm not saying that. I'm not sure what I'm saying. I just keep thinking about Leanza and the exemplary work she does. I don't know. What do you think? I guess, I'm wondering if I should at least tell her about our baby. Maybe just ask her if she's willing to look into the case for us."

"Yes, absolutely. Let's do it! We've paid private investigators in the past. Why not pay a missing person's advocate? Especially one you know and trust. I think it's a great idea, Jeremy. Like you said, she's the best there is. What's the worst that can happen? She finds nothing new. But what if she does find something? We've got nothing to lose here and everything to gain."

"Yeah?" Jeremy looked at his wife for assurance.

"Yes!" Marissa said. "Absolutely yes! I think you should call her."

CHAPTER 39

"Good-night Dr. Jaxson," several of the nurses said as they passed him in the hospital hallway.

"Good-night ladies, keep up the good work," he replied with a quick wave as he headed out the lobby doors.

"He's so good looking," one of the nurses cooed to the agreeing nods of her colleagues.

"Don't even think about it. He's married to his job," a nurse who'd been there a good number of years remarked.

"That's the way it is with these doctors you know," another nurse chimed in. "They're either already happily married or they're flirting with every one of us while ignoring their own wife. The rest are married to the job and won't give a glance in our direction. Take my word for it, we're better off finding a man outside the medical profession."

"That's true," another said. "That's the secret of a happy life for a nurse. Just look at me and James. We're going on fifteen years together. Happy years at that."

"You're one of the lucky ones," the comment brought agreeing nods as they went on their way.

Those nurses were the furthest thing from Dr. Jaxson's mind. It had been a long day and he was tired. Along with keeping a full schedule at his office each week he served on the hospital Emergency Room rotation once a month. This was that weekend. Where he'd once dreamed of being the pediatrician for his mother's Home for Children, he did this instead. But he wouldn't always do it. He hoped to settle down with a wife and have a family of his own now that the time-consuming process of getting his medical education was behind him.

He had a circle of good friends he enjoyed spending time with and there was one particular young lady he could possibly see himself with. He just hadn't had time up to this point to focus on finding out if she was interested.

They chatted when they got the chance but she was been busy building her career, too. Their friendship was progressing well so that gave him hope. Only time would tell what would happen next.

It was early Sunday evening and he was ready to relax at home before starting a new week. Turning onto Ten Mile Road his thoughts revisited his decision to buy a house on the back side of Spivey Lake instead of at the front on Lakeside Drive.

Any home in the Spivey Lake community was equally as beautiful as the others. That had never been a factor in his choice. The view or more accurately, lack thereof, had driven his decision.

Every home on Lakeside Drive had at least a partial view of Ms. Amber's home, the house in which Jaxson had spent his childhood. Running along the back side of Spivey Lake, Ten Mile Road led to Spivey Lake Road and Wildlife Club Road. Wildlife Club Road led directly to the backyard of Ms. Amber's home. A little way into house-hunting Jaxson realized there was only one road on which a person could buy a house and not see any of the property at the front or back of Ms. Amber's home. That was Spivey Lake Road, and therein lay his answer.

Jaxson loved life on Spivey Lake and wanted it as part of his life forever but seeing the neglected condition of Ms. Amber's home saddened him. By purchasing a house on Spivey Lake Road, he was able to continue enjoying lake life without revisiting the sad sight of his childhood home every time he went somewhere. That had been the deciding factor when he made his purchase.

There were occasions now in which he couldn't help wondering if he should have just bought Ma's house himself. What better way to ensure life and happiness would live within its walls again? On those occasions he always came to the same conclusion. He just hadn't been ready.

With the passage of time, he had come a long way in his grief over losing Ma. The days of not being able to pass by her house were gone now. He often took his kayak out on the lake and gently drifted by the place. Those times always brought to mind happy memories of kite-flying, ball playing, swimming and chats with Ma at the picnic table inside the gazebo.

He enjoyed attending the speed boat races throughout the summer, along with many of his friends, including Steven, Matthew, Ruby and their little ones.

Sometimes he sat at the end of the dock under the pier house roof with his feet up on the railing just watching the sun set. He always felt glad he could now look over at the house, smile and enjoy his happy memories. Always, he thanked God for the blessing of landing at the Delaney Home for Children. The neglect of the place did still tug at his heartstrings a bit from knowing Ma would be sad to see it this way.

Someone had bought it pretty quickly once it cleared probate. From what he'd heard it was a small company wanting to make some sort of retreat center for young people out of it. Apparently, they bit off more than they could chew financially and ended up going bankrupt. The house had been sitting there ever since.

Jaxson held onto the hope that someone would come along, fall in love with it and be willing to invest the finances needed to make the repairs. He would like nothing better than to see children run the length of a newly repaired dock to hurl themselves into the lake on a hot summer day. A smile tugged at the corners of his lips at that thought.

"Let it be, dear Lord," he heard himself say aloud as he unlocked his front door. If he wasn't so dog-tired, he would call Steven and Matthew and get the whole family out for a cook-out. Liking that idea, he decided to call shortly and invite them for the following Saturday instead.

Feeling weary at the end of this long work stretch, he grabbed an ice tea from the fridge and headed straight to the master bathroom with only one thought in mind, a relaxing hot shower followed by a good meal. Later this evening he'd be watching the sun set over his own little section of Spivey Lake. Perhaps Ma would get a little glimpse of that and smile down on him from heaven. That thought left him feeling happy.

CHAPTER 40

"This dinner is outstanding," Marshall said, smiling across the table at Vonda.

"Well, thank you, good sir," she replied, obviously pleased by his praise.

"I'll have to join a gym after we're married if you're going to prepare meals like this several times a day. My bachelor lifestyle leaves more and more to be desired the longer I know you, lady," he laughed while dishing a second helping of cheesy potatoes onto his plate.

Having finished eating, the two sat at the table a while longer updating each other on the goings on of life over a cup of coffee. Marshall filled Vonda in on the latest projects his company, Davidson Construction Inc. was working on. He reminded her the Old Timer's baseball games would be starting back up on Thursday evenings soon. Vonda didn't need to assure him she would be walking to the ball field to cheer the fellows on. She had faithfully done that since the first year Marshall got the teams together. Being where the two of them met, where their friendship grew and where Marshall proposed, the ball field would always hold a special place in their hearts.

Vonda filled Marshall in on the latest news from her children and grandchildren. She also shared a little about the book she was currently reading and who would hostess the next book club meeting. The ladies in that group were Vonda's closest friends.

When they finally got up from the table Vonda went about putting left overs into containers for the fridge. Marshall loaded the dishwasher and washed up the pans as they continued chatting.

"I heard from Leanza a few days ago," Vonda said as Marshall handed her the pan he'd just finished washing and drying so she could put it away.

"Oh, that's good. It's been a little while since you two have chatted, hasn't it? How's she doing these days? Still working with the FBI on the same case or is she back in Virginia?"

"Her most recent FBI case ended two weeks ago. She's back home in Norfolk and hoping to be there a while. She's currently working backward on a few cold cases.

It's always so interesting hearing about her work.

I'm so amazed every time a cold case gets solved. I just can't believe the type of things that get overlooked or fall through the cracks when those cases are active. It's a shame really. Thankfully some get reopened years later. With the advancements in DNA evidence some of those old cases are resolved from that alone. Hearing they've been solved after so much time makes me happy every time. I can't imagine what it must be like for the victim's families to finally get answers after years of not knowing what became of their loved one."

"What a bittersweet feeling that must be," Marshall observed. "It doesn't bring them back but there's something to be said for finally getting closure, I'm sure,"

"Yes, Leanza says the families are always grateful to finally know what actually happened. Well, she herself knows what that feels like. I still thank God sometimes for the way things finally fell into place for her family. Learning what happened to her father after all those years has given her a sense of peace. She told me she and her brother Wade, hadn't even realized how much it weighed on them until the case was finally solved.

I'll tell you one thing, that young lady could not be in a better line of work. Who could be more empathetic to the families of those missing than she is? She lived with her father's disappearance for over twenty years."

"What amazes me is how young she was when her mother knew she was going to end up being an advocate for missing people," Marshall said.

"Megan says she saw it coming when Leanza was only eight years old, can you imagine?"

"I couldn't if it were anyone else. Since we're talking about Leanza I really can. She's an outstanding person; super intelligent, detail-oriented and diligent to a fault. She's perfect for the work she does.

Leanza Williams is the best example I've ever seen of someone who has bloomed into the person God created them to be. That's how I see her anyway, both professionally and personally, especially since Christyan's part of the mix. There's been such a peace and contentment about her ever since they met. They're perfectly suited for one another. It makes me so happy to see good things happening in her life."

"Kinda like with us, you mean?" Marshall asked pulling her close for a quick kiss.

"Exactly," she answered, smiling up at him.

CHAPTER 41

Arriving right on time at the Seafood Restaurant in Mount Tabor Vonda pulled the door open, rushed inside and walked to where she could see the dining room. Spotting several of the book club ladies getting settled at a table near the back she waved to the waitress and headed in that direction. The waitress nodded her understanding and went back to work.

Vonda saw the small glass jars filled with sand and tiny seashells near each person's napkin when she got closer. Smiling, she called out, "Of course! I knew Lynda would come up with a clever way to tie our lunch in with Where the Crawdads Sing. This looks great! How creative!"

In the center of the table was a line of large conch, cockle and calico scallop shells along with a few strategically placed feathers.

"You think so?" Lynda asked. "I'm so glad. It was all I could come up with."

"These decorations tie in with a seafood lunch perfectly, Lynda," Monica said as Vonda pulled out a chair and got seated. "Not to mention the book itself."

Looking around the group Vonda asked, "Deb's not here yet? I was sure I'd be the last to arrive."

"She's on her way," Monica answered. "She sent a text earlier letting me know she was stopping to get a friend she's bringing with her today."

"Oh, that's fun," Vonda responded as she picked up a menu and began perusing the choices. "I never know what to get when I come here. I like so much of what they offer!"

"I have the same problem," Stacey answered.

"Oh, good! They're here," Kate said pointing toward the entry as Deb and her friend came into view."

"Hey, girls!" Deb called out while approaching the table. "This is my friend Jovie. When we were talking about books a few days ago I found out she's read this month's selection. We had such a good discussion about it that I invited her along."

"That's great," Dianne said, as Deb went into making introductions. The ladies took the time to study the menus and make their lunch choices. Having placed their order, they began to discuss the book.

The general consensus was that in this her debut Novel, the author, Della Owens, did a great job with her descriptions of the various wildlife living in the marsh as well as the actual story of Kya's life there. The group also shared their personal suspicions as to what had actually happened and who did what in regard to the mystery contained within the story.

While eating lunch they continued to talk about the challenges Kya faced as a young girl living alone in the marsh.

"In a way, it's unbelievable. But then we all know people who've overcome incredible odds to survive so anything is possible, if you ask me," Kate said.

"It makes for a great story anyway," Jovie agreed before adding, "and whether they're as dramatic as Kya's or not we all have our own story, right?"

"That's very true," Monica said. "We're all relatively new friends here. I mean, sure we've had this book club going for what?" She looked around the table questioningly before going on, "almost three years? I joined about a year after the rest of you so when did it start exactly? Does anyone remember"

"It was in July, wasn't it?" Lynda asked. "For some reason I'm thinking July. But yes, you're right Monica, it was three summers ago. Then when you joined you got us to read the Bishop Murder book. We loved it and went on to read that whole series."

"That's right!" Dianne jumped in. "They were all set in the Amish community so we went to that Amish store in Myrtle Beach that September, remember?"

Heads were nodding in agreement as they figured it all out.

"But you're absolutely right, Jovie," Monica said, revisiting her comment. "Even though the rest of us have known each other for several years we still have a lot to learn about each other's stories. What about you two?"

Turning toward Deb and Jovie she asked the next question, "How did you ladies meet?"

"Oh, well, actually I watched Jovie grow up," Deb said with a huge smile. "Her family lives right down the street from me and Bob."

"That's true," Jovie said. "We've waved at each other all my life! But their kids were a bit older than my brother and me so we weren't in the same classes or sports or anything like that. Actually, our love of books is what brought the two of us together. Here's what happened; my mom decided to have a yard sale and I had this vast book collection so I went through it and put a bunch of my books out on a table...."

"And that's where I come in," Deb interrupted with a laugh. "I walked down our street to check out the sale and we got caught up talking about which books Jovie liked or didn't like and why. Every time she recommended one of her books, I'd set it aside. I had quite a pile and we were still talking so I had to put a stop to our conversation!"

Both women were laughing at this point in Deb's story.

"She walked home with an arm load of books that day. It was hilarious!" Jovie said as everyone joined in on the laughter.

"And that was the beginning of a beautiful friendship," Deb smiled warmly at her younger friend. "Every time we saw each other coming and going we'd stop and compare notes as I read through her books. One day I asked if she wanted to have lunch sometime. She did and we've been getting together ever since. How old were you when I bought those books, Jovie? About seventeen? You were going to the vocational school taking early childhood development classes back then as I recall."

Turning to the rest of the group Deb said, "Since then she's gotten her social work degree and is working full-time. We're still getting together. We talk about a lot more than books now days, don't we, friend?"

"We sure do," Jovie answered with a happy smile. Turning to the other's she added, "Deb's become a very important person in my life. She's so supportive and such a great friend. I've always been so glad she came to mom's yard sale that day!"

"What a great story!" Kate said as the other ladies made agreeing comments. "It just goes to show we never know where we're going to find a new friend. I hope you'll keep coming to our book club Jovie."

"If you'll all have me, I would absolutely love to!" She answered.

"It's all settled then," Stacey announced. "We'll work you into our rotation and have a new schedule next month so you'll know when it'll be your turn to make a book selection. I look forward to seeing what you come up with."

CHAPTER 42

"It's great to see you again, Leanza," Jeremy said. "Marissa will be joining us shortly. She's talking with our youngest son at the moment."

"No, I'm not," Marissa said, coming across the room to join her husband at the dining room table where he sat facing the open laptop directly in front of him. "Hey Leanza! Thanks so much for working us into your schedule this evening," she said with a wave.

"Are you kidding? I've missed you both! It's been quite a while since we've talked. I'm glad you got ahold of me. We've definitely got some catching up to do."

"Actually," Jeremy said with a serious expression, "this is more than just a social call."

"Oh?" Leanza's voice held a question.

Jeremy began talking with Marissa occasionally interjecting here and there. When they finished sharing their story Leanza sat silently staring at the couple through the computer screen.

She seemed stunned.

Finally, she spoke, "I'm really sorry you two. To be honest, I'm kind of in shock here. I mean, Jeremy, we've known each other quite a while now. I chose you to serve on my team and we met a month later. We then worked together almost eight months. It's been what? Another six months since we parted ways.

I'm just a little shocked that this is the first time I'm hearing your story. Being that we served on a task force to locate missing persons it feels ironic that the rest of us never knew your own daughter was in that very category.

More than anything else I'm so very sorry your daughter disappeared and has never been found. This is every parent's nightmare and you've been living it for almost a quarter of a century. Not to mention you're in a business that solves this type of case. I am just so sorry."

"Thank you," Jeremy and Marissa said in unison.

"It really does help when people care," Marissa finished quietly.

"I understand your surprise, Leanza. We met by working together on a team whose express purpose was finding missing people. If I was ever going to tell anyone about our missing baby, you'd think those would be the people I'd tell. I don't know what to say except that I just couldn't bring myself to do it. For one thing I didn't want to change the team's focus.

If you and the team had known my story you would've seen it every time you looked at me. That wouldn't have served the purpose we were there for."

"Yes, you're absolutely right Jeremy," she jumped in. "You were on that team to do a job and you did it. Quite well, I might add. I do understand. There were plenty of people I never told that my father was missing in all those years. I really do get it, Jeremy. The news was just shocking since I know you so well.

You've told me now so let's get into some of the particulars of the case. I'm all over it. You don't even have to ask. You both know that, right? Without question, I'll be looking into this. I'll promise you one thing. If she's out there we're going to find her."

The couple spent the next half an hour giving Leanza any and all information. They covered where the baby was when she went missing, and every effort made to locate her.

By the time they hung up Leanza was like a bloodhound on a scent. There would be no stopping her now.

Looking at her husband Marissa said softly, "I've got the strangest feeling, Jeremy. I know you said not to get my hopes up but I can't help it. If anyone can locate our girl it's Leanza.

"You're right," he said, and a smile began to spread across his face.

He took her into his arms and she turned her face to the side and rested it on his chest. He leaned his chin onto the top of her head and just stood there holding her.

After a moment he said in a voice that was just above a whisper, "are we finally going to find her? Let it be, Lord. Please, let it be."

"Amen." Marissa said.

CHAPTER 43

Putting the last of the four grocery bags into her cart she smiled brightly at the cashier and cheerfully called out "thanks again". She gave a quick wave and left the store.

Walking across the parking lot she popped the trunk on her car, loaded the bags into it and walked the cart over to the cart corral. Smiling and waving at those nearby she showed no sign of how she was really feeling deep inside.

A few minutes later as she headed toward home she breathed deeply in and let out a heavy sigh.

Guilt was pulling at her soul.

It didn't happen as often as it used to but sometimes the guilt still settled in on her. She hated how it tore at her mind and hurt her heart but she didn't know how to stop it. On days like this she always ended up paying a visit to the past, questioning her actions and condemning herself all over again.

How could she have done such a terrible thing? Why did she do it? What kind of person was she anyway?

How she was even able to live with herself, knowing her actions had changed lives and brought lasting pain and sorrow was beyond her.

"How can you even look yourself in the eyes?" She asked her reflection in the rear-view mirror.

Letting Thatcher deceive and manipulate her was the biggest regret of her life. And only those two knew the scope of what she'd been a party to. By some unexplainable miracle she hadn't been seen, hadn't gotten caught and had yet to face even one consequence for her part in his terrible plan.

That's not entirely true, her mind said to her. Your guilt is your consequence and I'm here to remind you of it. You may have the rest of the world fooled but you know who you really are and I'll never let you forget.

Sitting at a stop light now she hung her head low in shame and self-condemnation; tears falling from her eyes.

At the time she had believed Thatcher to be innocent. She had believed her actions to be noble. She was helping a man who had been unjustly set-up, found guilty and incarcerated; the man she was falling in love with.

How could you have even entertained love for that man? she now asked herself in disgust. It just goes to show how far loneliness can push a person she thought. Not that she was making excuses. There was no excuse for what she had done and she knew it.

The blast of a car horn pulled her from her thoughts. Her head jerked up and her eyes riveted to the rear-view mirror. The light had changed and the driver behind her was impatient to get going. She pushed on the gas pedal and her car lurched forward.

Again, for the thousandths time she asked herself what she could do to correct the situation now. It was too late.

It was far too late now.

That little baby was now a grown woman. If she had any idea who and where she was, she could go to her and tell her the truth. Maybe help find her birth parents and bring them back together. But she had no way of knowing where the baby ended up. Oh, how she hoped her life had been a good one. If so, at least she didn't bear the blame for giving the child a bad life. The only thing she could even consider doing now would be to turn herself in, confessing to her part of it all. But how would that help anything?

This is where I always end up, she thought sadly. I'm so sorry for my actions but turning myself in cannot fix it. Nothing will ever fix it. The sadness and pain I've caused can never be undone.

Without that I'm not willing to suffer in jail for the rest of my life even though I surely deserve to.

If she were a praying woman, she would have asked God for help. Those who knew her probably thought she was a praying woman but she couldn't pray. Why would God ever give her the time of day? He was good. He was holy, and she was far from that. There was nothing she could do to make recompense for her sins.

No, God wasn't there for people like her.

CHAPTER 44

Deb took a left turn at the dilapidated old building. Following the slight curve, she drove past the long white structure which, years ago, had replaced the huge pine trees that once lined this road. It had been built as an event venue but now served as Mount Tabor's Senior Center. Having arrived at their destination Deb turned in and parked facing the picnic pavilion. Spivey Lake spread out beyond it.

"This is lovely," Jovie said looking out at the lake as she stepped out of the passenger's seat. "I don't know what I was expecting but this far surpasses it.

Deb smiled brightly as the two fell in step heading toward the pier dock as if it were calling their names.

"It really is beautiful out here," she agreed, adding quickly, "we better pick up the pace. Looks like we've got the same idea in wanting to look out over the water before joining the others. Neither of us even looked around for them."

The two ladies giggled quietly while hurrying up the dock.

"Oh, I guess we're having our meeting here," Jovie said pointing toward the long table in the center of the pier house.

"I guess so," came Deb's surprised response.

"I see you found our table," Monica called out as she and several other book club members followed from behind them. "Since we're discussing *Stranger in the Lake* we decided to set up where we've got a good view of the water beneath us.

The group broke out in laughter causing Deb and Jovie to look at them questioningly.

"Sorry! Just before you arrived, we had the most hilarious conversation," Lynda told them. "Kate said we should've made a dummy - you know like you see sitting around during Halloween. We could've put it face down in the water under the pier and waited to see which one of you spotted it first."

They all burst out laughing again.

"Oh, my," Deb said with an awkward chuckle. "That might be taking this setting-the-scene of our meetings to match the books a bit too far!"

"That's what we decided," Dianne answered. "But not until after imagining your reactions if you'd casually looked down to see what you thought was an actual body floating - just like in the book."

"I'm glad you didn't think of that before today's meeting, Kate! At least there wasn't enough time for you to actually do it," Jovie said. "I like being part of this book club but finding a body during our meeting would definitely run me off!"

The ladies doubled over laughing as they imagined that.

Once their laughter died down, they covered the table and divvied out the contents of the picnic basket. When everyone had table service and the food was spread out, they began their meeting.

As always it was interesting to hear who had thought what in the reading of the story. Everyone agreed the author, Kimberley Belle, had done a good job casting suspicion on the husband. She kept them guessing as to the story of the man hiding in the woods, as well.

As was common after their book discussions the topics of conversation drifted to other things as the friends sat enjoying themselves.

Jovie commented again on how beautiful the lake setting was.

"This would be a great place for a wedding," Stacey said while gently nudging her soon to be sister-in-law, Vonda, with her elbow.

"Oh, it would!" Kate said enthusiastically. "It really would be, Vonda. What a great idea! You should definitely give that some thought. You could get married in the beach area with the guests seated all around you. Didn't you say it's going to be a small group? You could even have the ceremony right here in the pier house."

"That could actually work," Lynda agreed. "It could even be cool to have the guest standing along the dock between here and the shore if you needed to."

"Okay, okay now, that's enough," Vonda said, laughing as she made a downward motion with her hands. "Let's take it down a notch, you're getting too excited about this. You're right and this lake would be a beautiful setting for a wedding. Let me mention it to Marshall and see where we go from there."

Deb couldn't help noticing, despite the lively conversation, that Jovie seemed distant. She had been very quiet ever since their earlier arrival. She seemed to be studying their surroundings and kept looking across the lake.

A few minutes later the topic of conversation changed again. Still seeming distracted, Jovie got up and walked quietly to the railing. Leaning forward to rest her arms on the rail, she stood staring at the abandoned house that sat on the peninsula directly across from their location.

When there was a pause in conversation Deb asked, "Jovie, Are you alright?"

Everyone turned to look at Jovie. A few seconds went by. Realizing their chatter had stopped Jovie's head slowly turned back in the direction of the other women. Seeing them all looking at her she said, "Oh, I'm sorry. What is it?"

"I was just asking if you're alright." Deb said, "You've been awfully quiet today. It seems as if you're not quite here."

"I'm so sorry. I'm not sure what's going on. I feel... I'm sorry, I don't know how I feel. I'm sure I've never been here before and yet this..." she made a sweeping gesture with her arms that encompassed their entire surroundings and continued with "all feels very familiar to me. Actually, Deb, I noticed it the moment you turned by that broken down old building."

"You mean Dick's Trading Post?" Monica asked. "Oh, I'm sorry, you wouldn't know that, would you? That building used to be a bait and tackle shop back in the day. It was called Dick's Trading Post. Everyone stopped there on their way to the lake to buy bait, tackle and snack food. Dick and his wife ran it. Everyone loved them."

"Oh," Jovie answered, looking back in the direction of the drive into Spivey Lake. Her eyes drifted across the beach, parking area, picnic pavilion and boat dock. "I don't know why but this entire place feels very familiar to me. It's like I've been here before. Actually, it's more than that. It's almost like I've spent time here but I'm positive I haven't. It's weird, I know. I just have a really strong sense of déjà vu' right now."

CHAPTER 45

"Your mother's been excited all week about having you and TJ home at the same time," her father said. Putting his arm around her shoulder he pulled her close to give her a tight squeeze. "I have, too," he added with a quick wink.

"I'm thrilled to be here," Jovie said. "Still, it shouldn't be this hard getting only four people together at the same time."

"No, it shouldn't, but it is," her brother said as he came up behind them.

"TJ!" Jovie shouted, turning to give her big brother a tight hug. "How long are you staying?"

"He's never leaving again if I have any say in it," their mother said from the doorway.

"It's a good thing you're not in charge, mom," Jovie said with a laugh. "None of us would ever be allowed to leave this house if you were."

"That's not true," their mother said with a twinkle in her eye. "You'd all be allowed to go into the back yard for a cook-out and singing around the campfire anytime. You just couldn't go any further."

Everyone laughed, obviously happy to be together again.

The family went into the kitchen. They talked and laughed as they carried the plates, flatware and variety of delicious dishes their mother had prepared and set them all on the table. Once everything was ready their father stood up and said a beautiful prayer in which he thanked God for his many blessings; especially the blessing of this reunion.

After supper the men went out back and got a fire going in the fire ring. Once the ladies finished cleaning the kitchen, they went to join them. Everyone got settled comfortably to enjoy the fire. TJ picked up his guitar and sat strumming softly as they continued to get caught up with the happenings of life.

"I've missed this," Jovie said after a while. Looking at TJ she continued. "Some of my best childhood memories took place right here around this campfire with you and dad strumming your guitars."

"Those are my best memories, too," her brother said. "You got me my first guitar when I was only eight, remember dad?"

Their father picked his guitar up as he answered, "I was eight when my dad started teaching me to play. Music was a heritage I always wanted to pass on to my own son. My daughter, too," he winked at Jovie.

"Yeah, I'm sorry that didn't work out for you, dad," she said laughing. "For whatever reason I wasn't blessed with natural musical ability. Let's face it, I can barely carry a tune."

"Not all of us are," her father said simply "and you carry your own when it comes to singing."

"It's all good, sis," TJ said with a smirk on his face. "After all, God only said to make a joyful noise and you can do that with the best of them."

Jovie made like she was throwing punches in her brother's direction as he laughed wholeheartedly.

It's good to have them home, Lord. Their mother thought as she sat smiling and watching their childish antics.

After the campfire fun the family moved inside and played board games at the dining room table. They eventually ended up in the living room relaxing together.

Though Jovie's apartment was within a reasonable driving distance she usually stayed over whenever TJ made it back for a visit. It made their parents happy and she enjoyed being there. It also gave her and TJ the chance to spend time together.

There wasn't anything stressful she needed to get away from in her own life. It just felt good to go home again, even if only for a few days at a time.

She was glad her parents had never sold her childhood home and moved as many of her friend's folks had done once all of their children were raised. There was something about this house that made Jovie feel safe and loved. She supposed it was because this was the first real home she could remember.

Though she had no clear memory of it her family had told her about the day she came to live with them. They had spent a month getting her bedroom ready. After painting it pink, they bought a white canopy bed with matching furniture. The three of them then turned an ordinary bedroom into a haven for the little girl they were adopting. They wanted her to feel loved and welcomed from the moment she set foot inside it.

Jovie didn't remember how she'd felt that first moment. She had no memory of the day she'd come home with them or her life before that day. What she did know was that growing up in that room she had felt exactly the way they had hoped she would. Jovie had always felt loved and wanted in this family. She supposed that was why she never had a strong desire to seek out her birth parents.

Owen and Myla Jarvis were the only parents Jovie had ever known. They adopted her from a home for children. All they were told about Jovie's past was that she'd come to the children's home at less than a week old. The couple had planned to have more children but Myla experienced complications and was unable to carry another child so they decided to adopt.

Jovie loved her parents and big brother and was happy in the life they shared. She never felt anything was missing nor did she have a driving desire to learn about her life before she became Jovie Jarvis.

After a lengthy conversation in which TJ updated them on the happenings in his life, he asked Jovie what was new with her.

'Nothing's ever new with me," she said with a laugh. A strange look crossed her face and she added, "actually, there is something new. It's not terribly exciting but I've recently joined a book club."

"A book club, huh? "How did you fall into that?"

Jovie answered JT's question with a question. "Oh, well, you know I've been talking about books with the neighbor lady, Deb, for years, right?"

"The one who lives about five houses from here?" TJ asked. Seeing her nod in agreement he went on, "for sure, you two even go out to eat together sometimes, don't you?"

"Right, we've been doing that for a couple of years now. So, anyway, a couple of months ago we realized I'd just finished reading her book clubs choice of book that month. She invited me to attend the meeting to discuss it. It was so much fun. I've been going ever since."

"That's right up your alley," her father said.

"That's cool," TJ commented.

"What book are you reading this month?" their mother asked curiously.

"I don't know yet. Since we just had our meeting, I'll be finding out in the next couple of days. You know what, I'm glad we're talking about this because I had a strange experience that day."

"Really? What was that?" her father asked.

"I had the strongest sense of déjà vu I've ever had. You know, when you feel like you've been there or done that? The feeling actually hit me before I even got out of the car. It was uncanny, really. Usually, I enjoy just sitting and talking with the other women. Not this time. Even though I knew I hadn't, I spent the entire couple of hours trying to shake the overwhelming feeling that I'd been there before."

"That is strange," her brother said.

"Whose house was the meeting being held in?" her mother asked.

"Oh, we don't meet in each other's houses. That's what makes this such a fun club. We always try to recreate something from the book we're discussing. We'll meet somewhere similar to a scene in the book and we'll eat foods that are mentioned in the story. It's really fun and it gets pretty interesting sometimes. The book we just finished, "A Stranger in the Lake" was centered around a body that was discovered floating in a lake just under a dock so we met at a lake.

"What lake was it?" TJ asked.

"It's in Mount Tabor, North Carolina. That's how I know I've never been there. The place is called Spivey Lake."

CHAPTER 46

Ma was alive again; beautiful and full of life and laughter. Jovie was his little sister again; sweet, innocent and happy. The sun was peeking in and out of the lazy clouds as they drifted on a baby blue blanket that was the summer sky. Tree tops swayed as the wind swept through them, rustling the leaves and playing in his hair on their journey to wherever winds go on their many travels. Children chased one another in the yard in a robust game of tag, laughing and happy. Jaxson's heart was light with not a care in all the world.

Time had slipped backward, taking with it the realities of life; the hurt, loss, grief, and responsibilities that come with being an adult.

Such is the way of dreams.

Jaxson lay perfectly content in this place somewhere between the unconsciousness of his current dream-state and the consciousness of daily life. He wanted to stay, feeling the joy of being with his family again. He had missed them all so very much; Ma, Jovie, Sarah, Carter, Lisha, Asher and so many others. Along with Steven and Matthew, they were his childhood.

In the weird way of dreamland everything suddenly changed. It was late afternoon now and Ma was sitting in the gazebo. The picture of relaxation she sat alone just looking out across the lake, watching the ripples on the surface of the water. He watched himself, as a child, come out of the house and walk across the lawn to join her at the picnic table. He sat down across from her as he had so often done in the past. A spirit of contentment, peace and love surrounded them.

A monarch butterfly fluttered over and circled around them. Even in this dream-state he remembered monarchs having been his mother's favorite butterfly. Ma looked at him and smiled. Instantly Jaxson changed from the boy he had been to the man he now was.

"You've become such a good man, Jaxson," Ma said with a loving smile. "Just as I always knew you would. I'm so very proud of you."

The monarch was still fluttering around them.

"I wanted you to be part of a great adventure," laughing lightly she pressed her hands together touched her fingertips to her chin, smiled brightly and finished with, "and you were!"

"You were so young when I assigned you to be the keeper of the treasure. If I had realized what I was doing I wouldn't have done it. I never meant to place a man's responsibility on a boy. When I saw that's what had happened it troubled me. I didn't give in to worry though. I prayed instead.

I prayed so many prayers for you, Jaxson. I was always asking God to help you when it was time to release our treasure back to Him. In His great goodness He answered those prayers. You've carried that burden well, even so, the cost has been great."

The monarch gently came to rest on Ma's shoulder. Giving it a slight glance, she smiled again.

"I'm glad you have such a good life, son. I see your joy, your worship of God, all of your accomplishments. Just as I knew you would be, Dr. Jaxson," her smile spread with the use of his professional title, "you are so loving and gentle with the children in your care."

Her maternal pride filled his heart with joy.

"I am so pleased you're happy and content, even though she's still in your heart; in your thoughts. I know that void has never been filled."

He watched himself begin to speak but Ma put her finger to her lips in a shushing gesture.

"Wait," she said ever so softly. "Wait upon the Lord."

The monarch lifted from her shoulder, fluttering between them briefly and alighting on Jaxson's hands which lay at rest, one folded over the other, between them on the table. His mother reached out and pushed the hair on his forehead gently to the side. She let her hand slide softly down the side of his face in a loving, motherly gesture.

"The day is coming," she said. "Rest now my son, the void will soon be filled."

Stirring slightly Jaxson reached up and placed his hand on the side of his face. It was almost as though he had felt his mother's touch in his sleep.

CHAPTER 47

"So. what you're saying is - I've not only been there before - but I actually lived there for the first several years of my life?"

"Yes," Jovie's mother answered softly, wondering it this new information would upset her daughter.

"How did I not know this before now?" Jovie asked, leaving her family to wonder if her furrowed brow was a sign of confusion or anger.

"It didn't seem important," her father said. "You became our daughter. We were your family. There seemed no point in telling you about the time you spent there since you were too young to actually remember it. It was only natural that those memories fade away with the passage of time. Your relationship with those who lived there ended the day we brought you home so we saw no sense in telling you about them. We don't live far from Mount Tabor but we had no cause to return there. It was part of your past, nothing more. It never seemed necessary to talk with you about it."

"I can see that," Jovie said with a smile. "That makes perfect sense. "You were right, or course. That part of my life didn't need to continue."

"It's interesting that you felt the way you did when you were there last week though," her brother said, leaning forward in his chair with great interest.

Jovie met his eyes, "that's for sure. I can't tell you how strange it was to feel that way. It almost makes me want to learn more."

"Maybe you should," her mother said thoughtfully.

"Really? Do you think so, mom?"

"I'm not sure. You're the only one who can decide that, Jovie. All I know is that you were well cared for, happy and obviously loved during the time you lived there."

"That's certainly true," her father agreed. "It wasn't easy watching all of them say good-bye to you the day we brought you home with us."

"Really?" Jovie asked, her interest definitely piqued.

"Oh yeah," TJ said. "As young as I was at the time, I still remember that. It almost felt like we were doing something wrong by taking you."

"Do you remember talking to me about that later, TJ?" their father asked, turning to look at his son. "After we got Jovie settled in her room that night, when I was tucking you into bed you said that exact thing to me. You asked me if we had done something bad by taking Jovie away from those people. I explained that a children's home was meant to be a temporary place until a child was taken in by a family that wanted them. We were that family."

"I do remember that," TJ answered. "It made me feel better. It wasn't long before I forgot all about it because I loved my new sister and we were all so happy together."

Jovie shot a smile across the room to her big brother.

"What do you want to do, sis?" He asked her. "You want to go back there and take a better look around? You want us all to go together? We could tell you what we remember about the day we picked you up."

"I don't know," Jovie answered, looking from one to the other of this family she loved and was so blessed to be a part of. "I'm not sure what to do. I don't know that there's any point in all of us going there together. I don't even know where the children's home is. One of the ladies in the book club takes her canoe out on the Spivey Lake sometimes. The one who hosted our meeting goes with her husband to eat on the picnic tables sometimes. She thought it would be a good idea to have our meeting there, that's all.

Deb took a public access road to the lake and parked in a parking area near the beach. Our meeting was in the pier house at the end of the dock. Does any of that sound familiar to you? Do you know where the children's home is from there? Did you get to it through the Spivey Lake entrance?"

"We never went to the Lake, did we, dear?" her mother asked, looking at her husband questioningly.

"No," he answered. "We always drove past the public access road. There was a back road we took to get to the children's home. The children's home isn't there anymore. It shut down years ago after a tragic storm took the life of the house mother. I remember reading about it when it happened. I have no idea what happened to the house after that. I would assume someone bought it and lives in it now, if it's even still there.

We were just grateful God brought you into our life, Jovie. As I said before, there was never a reason to stay in touch with the people there or tell you anything about it. None of that had anything to do with your future. I hope you understand that."

"Your fathers right," her mother added. "You're not upset with us, are you?"

"Oh, no, mom. I'm not upset at all. You and dad have always handled all of this wonderfully. You've always been honest with me and answered any questions I've ever asked. You have never made me feel awkward about being adopted. Maybe that's why I've never been drawn to search for information about my birth parents. I'm not planning to do that now either. I guess I'm just curious about living there because of the way I felt when I was there last week. I can't even explain it. It was just such an overwhelming sense of familiarity."

"That makes sense to me," TJ commented thoughtfully. "Like mom said, you were obviously well cared for, happy and loved when you lived there. Maybe that's why you felt so drawn to the place last week. If your experience had been bad, I would think you would have felt bad about it. Now that we're talking about all of this, I do remember you asking about your other big brother when you first came to live with us."

"You do?" Jovie asked.

"That's true," her mother admitted. "You asked after him for quite some time, actually. You talked about the house mother and some of the other children as well. I remember wondering if you would remember them when you got older. But it didn't happen that way. The more comfortable you were with us and the more time that went by the less you asked after them until you just never mentioned them again."

"Wow," Jovie said, realizing this was a part of her life she remembered nothing about.

CHAPTER 48

Vonda had been watching out the window off and on for over an hour when she finally saw a vehicle pulling into her driveway. Rushing to the front door she pulled it open and hurried out to greet her friend.

"Leanza! I thought you'd never get here! How was your flight?"

Meeting halfway up Vonda's front walkway the two friends embraced tightly before walking back to the car for Leanza to get her luggage.

"It was good," Leanza answered. "But still, I'm glad it's over. Getting through the rental car process always takes a bit of time but it went smoothly."

"I'm glad to hear it. I'm so excited about our visit. It'll be nice to talk in person instead of seeing each other through the computer," Vonda said, quickly adding, "although I'm thankful we can do that. It's good to see each other while talking long distance, but nothing beats being together."

"That's for sure. It feels like it's been forever."

Dropping her things onto the bed in the guest room Leanza reached out to pet Lilly who was curled up where she'd been sleeping. "Hey Lilly, it's good to see you again, old girl," Leanza cooed before turning back to Vonda, "That's good enough for now. Let's get this visit started!"

"Sounds great! Follow me," Vonda led the way as Leanza and Lilly followed close behind her. She motioned toward the living room for Leanza to go get settled as she went into the kitchen to pour them each a warm apple cider.

Lilly pounced into her lap as soon as Leanza sat down in the overstuffed easy chair at the end of the couch.

"Thanks so much for letting me crash with you, Vonda," Leanza said, running her hand up and down Lilly's long white fur. "I got excited to see you again when I realized my new case was bringing me back here."

Absolutely!" Vonda said, happiness oozing from her voice. "You would have offended me and Lilly big-time if you had gotten a hotel room. You're like family to us and welcome here anytime. I'm looking forward to getting caught up and hearing about your new case. If your work leaves you any time to spare, maybe we can do a few fun things before you have to head back."

"For sure. I was hoping to see Marshall tonight but with my flight getting in so late I figured he'd have to head home by the time I got here. I'm looking forward to walking to a couple of ball games over the next couple of weeks. It'll be good to see the guys and their families again."

"Marshall went home earlier than usual. His company is finishing up a pretty big project so he wanted to go over his notes before the meeting tomorrow. He asked me to tell you he'll see you tomorrow evening. We have supper together every evening."

"That's great Vonda. I'm still so happy for you two. Chrystian and I are looking forward to your wedding but I'm here now and it's so good to see you! Even though it's a work trip we're going to take advantage of the opportunity. We'll definitely get some fun in. I have to admit to feeling a bit nostalgic on the drive out here. I may have only lived here for eight months but this place will always feel like home. Outside of solving our missing person cases and giving those families closure, having you for a neighbor is the best thing to come from that assignment. Well, that and meeting Chrystian!" Leanza's smile spoke volumes. "It's hard to believe it's been over a year already. Time goes by so fast!"

"Yes, it does. Take it from me, you're going to find that the older you get the faster time goes." Looking fondly at her friend Vonda went on, "I'm so glad your work has sent you back to us. I've missed you, Leanza. It hasn't been the same around here without you."

"I've missed you, too," Leanza answered as Lilly settled more comfortably in her lap and went to purring loudly. Leanza looked and felt right at home. She was settled deeply in the cushions of her chair as she gently stroked her furry friend.

Her curiosity getting the best of her Vonda said, "I know you just got here but I'm wondering if this new case is one you can talk with me about. I hope you won't need to keep it confidential."

"Normally, I protect my client's identity by talking in general terms if I share information at all. This case is a private hire. In other words, it's not an assignment from my department or the FBI. I've been hired by an individual client to look into a missing relative so that's a little different. Since you actually know the client who hired me, I've specifically asked if I'm at liberty to share details."

"Really?" Vonda's voice dripped with interest, her curiosity at an all-time high. "Who would that be?"

She could think of no one in her realm of acquaintances and friends with a missing relative. No one she knew had even hinted at such a thing and she said as much to Leanza.

"Actually, I was a bit shocked to hear it myself," her friend admitted. "Especially since we've known each other going on two years and worked closely together."

Vonda's mind immediately went to the FBI Task Force – Leanza's most recent long-term assignment. If she worked with this person and had known them for less than two years they had to have been on that team. Realizing she had gotten to know everyone on the team, Vonda's mind was now searching her memory for even one clue of who Leanza may be referring to.

"You just said you asked if you're at liberty to share information with me. What was the answer?"

"Jeremy loves you, Vonda. What's more, he trusts you. He and Marissa didn't hesitate in the least when telling me I'm free to share with you."

Vonda's heart constricted as soon as she heard Jeremy's name. In her mind's eye she could clearly see the handsome young man she'd grown so fond of while getting acquainted with the Task Force team Leanza had worked with.

Jeremy was one of the most diligent, devoted, hard-working members of the team. On a personal level he was warm and fun to be with. Through her friendship with Leanza; her mother, Megan and her brother, Wade and his dear family Vonda had seen firsthand the turmoil having a missing loved one can cause in a family. She was deeply concerned to learn Jeremy and his family were faced with that same turmoil.

Leanza went about updating Vonda on what Jeremy and Marissa had shared with her about their newborn daughter being taken from the hospital nursery just two days after her birth some twenty-three years earlier.

It was an unbelievable story that broke Vonda's heart. Both Leanza and Vonda were deeply saddened knowing their wonderful friend and his dear wife had learned nothing in all these years about what happened to their beautiful, healthy, baby girl. Of course, Leanza was determined to do everything humanly possible to solve this mystery and possibly find their daughter for them. She had already made some great strides in that direction and went on to share her progress with Vonda.

"The first thing I did was fly to Austin Texas for a visit with the police department originally handling the case. I looked through everything in the casefile and spoke directly with everyone working the case at the time. It never ceases to amaze me, when looking into a cold case, how much was overlooked in the original investigation. Every case I take leaves me hoping police departments are being more thorough these days.

The advancement in technology in the years between is very helpful. We've made huge strides in DNA and forensic science so I truly hope there are less unsolved cases now. But I'm getting sidetracked. One thing I realized was that the only hospital personnel that were interviewed back then were those on the maternity ward floor on the night the baby went missing. In my humble opinion that was the investigating department's first mistake. So, of course, I went to the hospital and began the process of learning what other staff was on duty the night of the disappearance and where they are now. From there I began the painstaking process of locating and speaking with each person."

"Wow, that's a lot of back tracking," Vonda said while refilling their mugs and bringing out the pumpkin scones she'd made that afternoon. "Did you find anything interesting?"

"I did," and that's what brings me here. "During my interview with one of the janitorial staff on duty that night I learned he saw something interesting. He came across a staff member in the stairwell when he was on his way out at the end of his shift. While it wasn't odd for the person to be there, he did notice something odd about her."

"Really? Go on...." Vonda said, perching on the edge of her seat.

"This particular staff member was a traveling nurse. I've since learned she had hired on well over a month before so it wasn't that unusual for her to be seen by other staff, which is exactly what the janitor said.

The thing is these traveling nurses often carry a large canvas bag with their personal belongings in them. It would make sense for those to be carried in the first day or two of them being hired as they sometimes stay in the hospital staff area until a temporary apartment comes available for them. This nurse had been on staff for well over a month which begs the question; why did she need her bag that night? What's more, she wasn't simply seen carrying her bag, she was carrying it in an odd way. Instead of it being flung over her shoulder she was carrying it in her arms.

The janitor remembers thinking perhaps it was full of medical books. He assumed she was studying for a medical licensing test. When I asked him to demonstrate it was easy to see one carrying the bag in that manner if there was a baby inside it. Of course, this has raised my suspicions. I'm very interested in speaking with this traveling nurse."

"I should think so! It's been over twenty-three years since that baby was taken though, have you had any luck finding out where she is now?"

"I have. In fact, that's the reason I'm here. She lives about ten miles from where we're sitting right now."

CHAPTER 49

"Hey, friends," Jovie said as she got into the back seat of Deb's vehicle. "I didn't know you were coming with us today, Vonda."

"Well, Deb and I are working on a church project together. We decided to meet earlier for that so it just made sense to go together." Vonda answered with a smile.

"Gotcha. Well, thanks for giving me a ride, Deb. You don't have to do this every time we have a book club meeting, you know."

"I know, but it's just as easy to go together as long as you don't mind getting picked up at your folks house."

"Not at all, it gives me the chance to visit them either before or after our meeting. Dad took mom to her doctor appointment this morning. They're going out to lunch afterward. I imagine they'll be getting back about the same time we do so I'll visit with them before I head home. Today's meeting is at Kate's place, right?"

"That's right." Deb answered. "She's the one who chose our book, *The Butterfly's Daughter*, so she's our hostess today. She lives on the backside of Spivey Lake so we'll be getting a different view of the lake than we had at our last meeting."

"That should be interesting," Jovie said to herself more than anyone else.

The three chatted pleasantly during the drive.

Not quite ten minutes later Deb drove past the turn off for Spivey Lake and took a left turn onto the next road. Jovie took note that nothing felt familiar as Deb drove passed the next street and took another left turn onto Club House Road. She drove almost to the end of the street before turning into the driveway of a very nice, smaller, brick home.

"The GPS says this is the one," Deb said, putting the car in park and turning it off." Looks like we're the first to arrive."

"Not by much, that's Stacey pulling in now and it looks like everyone else is with her."

Everyone got out and were heading toward the house when Kate opened the front door and called out a welcome.

"Did you ladies carpool on the way here?" Kate asked as they came through her front door single file one after the other.

"We did not," Deb answered. "I guess it was just good timing."

"I'd say so, since you've all arrived at once," Kate answered.

"Oh, what a cute idea." Stacey said, when she saw the monarch butterfly placemats underneath the place settings at the table.

"With napkins to match," Dianne pointed out.

"And look, girls, Kate's got decorations anyone could use in a Day of the Dead celebration," Monica pointed to the skull flower holder filled with Marigolds.

"And just like what would be at those celebrations we've got skull cookies. I'm certain those are used since they even give out sugar skulls as gifts. Skulls are very popular at the Day of the Dead. Well done, Kate. You nailed it." Stacey said as the others agreed with her.

"Well, thank you. I'm glad you all like my choices. Full disclosure here; I didn't make the cookies," Kate said with a laugh. "I ordered them from that new bakery that just came in on Main Street."

"I don't care if this is what they eat at those celebrations that would be the day I'd ever order skull cookies," Monica said, shaking her head in disbelief. "I bet they're delicious though."

"I'm sure they are," Vonda chimed in. "I've had several things from that bakery already and it's all been wonderful."

"I wasn't sure everyone would want to eat skull cookies, so I do have another sweet treat available," Kate said while pointing toward a round cake covered in beautiful flowers made from, what was sure to be, a delicious icing. "Monarchs eat flower nectar for the sugar it contains. That's what gives them their seemingly ceaseless energy for the long trek when they migrate to Mexico. I figured we could all use some sugar energy."

Everyone nodded agreeably as they looked forward to the sweet desserts.

The book discussion went well. They delved into the belief of Mexican people that the spirits of the recently departed inhabit monarch butterflies on their migration trek. They also talked about what part of the journey in the story was their favorite.

Deb, Jovie and Vonda weren't ready to go when the others said their good-byes. Kate was pleased they wanted to stay a bit longer.

After Kate explained how to tell a boy monarch from a girl Jovie asked, "How did you come to know so much about Monarchs anyway?"

"I was wondering that myself," Deb chimed in. "You know a lot more than what was covered in the book.

"She sure does," Vonda agreed.

"Do you really want to know?" Kate asked. Seeing their affirming nods she smiled and said, "If you're all up for a little walk, I'll be happy to show you, but first let me show you my monarch farm. It's right here on my back porch."

They got up from the table and Kate led them out her back door and onto her porch. Everyone was fascinated with what they saw as Kate explained how she had put everything together to provide a place for the monarch eggs to grow into a chrysalis and later hatch as monarchs. There were several eggs of various sizes on milkweed stems, a few hanging Js attached to the netted enclosures and some chrysalis' well on their way to being ready to hatch. While studying the tomato cages with the milkweed stems standing in vases of water Jovie had a vague sense of déjà vu. She didn't remember ever having learned about any of this in school but none of it felt new to her either.

After answering their various questions Kate led them across her backyard and they entered into the woods. While there wasn't a distinct pathway it was obvious Kate had taken this walk many times. In a few moments they came to the edge of the woods and stepped out into an overgrown clearing. There again part of the overgrowth was more cleared away than the rest, having obviously been used as a pathway. After following it for a few feet Deb, Vonda and Jovie were all surprised to see it open up into an area that was very well taken care of.

As Kate continued leading them forward and to the left Jovie sensed the same feeling of familiarity she'd experienced before. When Kate took a slight turn Jovie continued looking straight ahead. In the distance behind a covering of overgrown trees she saw what appeared to be the backside of a tired old two-story house.

Suddenly she heard the slamming of a screen door. The sound was immediately followed by echoes of children laughing. She watched as a group of children came running toward the clearing. Just as quickly as the mental image had come it left her.

Shaking her head in confusion she turned slightly to her right. This time she saw a very pretty brunette woman with a clothes basket against her hip heading toward the house. Directly behind her Jovie could see clothing clipped to a clothesline and flapping in the wind. Again, the image quickly dissipated.

Jovie shook her head trying to understand what was happening to her.

"Hold on tight," the boy's voice seemed so close to her ear that she turned to look for him.

"Don't let go, Jovie," a little girl's voice called out from somewhere beside her.

"Don't let go," the boy's voice said again just before he laughed loudly. She had the sensation of being carried in his arms as he ran. An overwhelming sense of happiness seeped over Jovie and in the faintest whisper she heard herself say, "Okay, Jaxson, I won't"

In the distant sky Jovie saw a large orange butterfly kite flutter against the baby blue sky for just a few seconds before it vanished taking the voices and childish laughter with it.

"Are you alright, Jovie," she heard Deb's voice ask from somewhere behind her. Turning slowly, as if in a trance, Jovie looked into the bewildered eyes of her friends.

"What's the matter?" Kate asked with a look of concern. "We were almost to the field when we realized you weren't following anymore. We called out to you but you didn't seem to hear."

"Are you okay?" Vonda asked.

"I'm sorry. I felt a little lost there for a minute. It's okay though. I'm fine. I'm sorry I worried you. Yes, of course. I'm fine." Looking directly at Kate now Jovie asked, "What was it you wanted to show us?"

"Come this way," Kate answered motioning in the direction she'd headed earlier. "It's a milkweed garden."

Everyone followed Kate to an area that was very well attended. The women were pleasantly surprised by how nice it looked considering all the thistles and weeds they'd just walked though.

Seeing their expressions of surprise Kate said, "The woman who used to live here planted this milkweed specifically for the purpose of raising monarch butterflies each year. She taught me everything I know so when we lost her - quite a few years back - I just didn't have the heart to let her milkweed garden be neglected. She meant a great deal to me, to everyone who knew her really. Tending this garden, that meant so very much to her, has become my way of honoring her memory these many years."

Another vision danced into Jovie's head. In it she was one of a group of children gathered around the woman she'd earlier seen with the clothes basket. They were all hovering around a milkweed garden studying the stems. Just as before the vision lasted only a few seconds.

"I really enjoy having a small part in raising those beautiful monarchs every year and I learn something new each time I do it," Kate said before turning back toward the wooded area. "We probably need to head back so you ladies can get home. Are you ready?"

"Wait," Jovie said turning to point toward the tired old house. "What is this place?"

"It's nothing anymore," Kate said sadly, "but once upon a time it was a very happy place called The Delaney Home for Children."

And with those words Jovie realized the visions she'd been having weren't visions at all, they were memories.

CHAPTER 50

"Are we ready to roll then?" Jeremy called from the driver's seat of the SUV as he turned to wink at Marissa who was seated beside him up front.

"We're all here and accounted for," Ellie said, laughing at the phrase she'd pulled up from when they were little.

Their father used to say he had to be sure everyone was 'here and accounted for' before putting the car in drive. Their mostly-grown-now children liked to tease him by using it again on the rare occasion when they were all together again.

"Okay, good! Let's get this show on the road," Jeremy said, making everyone laugh by using another phrase he was known for.

As he put the car in gear and backed out of the driveway Marissa looked into the mirror on the back of her sun visor. Seeing her three youngest children packed closely together in the back seat made her smile. When did they all grow up, her mind questioned. She was feeling sentimental. With the girls in their first year at college they weren't all at home at the same time much anymore. Even less often were they all in the car going somewhere together.

Her mama heart felt happy.

"This is going to be so much fun," Marie said. "Does JJ know we're coming?"

"We haven't told her. She won't be surprised to see us - it's just you girls she won't be expecting. We've been to several gymnastic events this year. I have no idea why, but your brother has wanted to come," their mother said in a teasing voice since the girl Aiden was currently dating was on the gymnastics team.

"We probably would've gone to a few anyway," Jeremy spoke up. "Just because you girls aren't on the team anymore doesn't mean we can't enjoy these competitions. We've always liked to show school support."

"I can't wait to see JJ," Ellie said. "I want to tell her I've been using the equipment at school to keep up with some of my balance routines."

"We've actually gone to some of the college level competitions on campus, too," Marie told them.

"JJ will be happy to hear about that. You girls know how it was when you were on the team though. She'll be focused on coaching this event so you'll need to pick the right time to talk with her, you may even have to wait until it's over, which is fine. We're not in a hurry to leave, are we?" Marissa asked, turning to look at her husband.

"Not at all. I was actually thinking of offering to host another pizza party celebration if they win this thing today. What do all of you think of that idea?"

"That would be super!" Marie said and Ellie's declared, "Awesome!"

All Aiden did was give his dad a huge smile.

They arrived at the Myrtle Beach Sports Complex, got parked, went through the line and headed into the gymnasium.

"There they are!" Ellie said excitedly pointing the team out to her twin as soon as she spotted them. "Can you believe it's been a year since we were out there with them, Marie?"

"That can't be!" Marie answered leading the way toward their old team as they were warming up on the mat.

"Are you sure you don't want to go with them, Aiden?" Marissa asked.

"No, mother," Her son answered, not sure if she was being playful or actually meant it. He decided to clarify just in case she was being serious, "Just for the record, guys do not go out on the mat to talk to their girlfriends."

"Oh, okay then," his mother said, sincerely. "I'm sure she'll spot you in the stands and know you're here."

"I'd wager she already knows he's here," Jeremy said grinning at his son. "Women have a way of keeping track of their man. Either that or he sent a text to her phone as soon as we pulled into the Complex."

Aiden shot them both a look they couldn't interpret before heading up the bleachers to take a seat.

It was fun watching the reaction of their daughter's younger teammates when they spotted Marie and Ellie; there was lots of jumping up, running and hugging. Clipboard in hand JJ was conferring with some of the officials and missed out on the team reunion. It took her only a few seconds to realize there were a couple of extras in the circle when she came back. A huge smile broke out across her face as she rushed to enfold both girls in a hug before the rest of the team turned it into a group hug.

JJ had to ban the sisters to the bleachers as soon as things got started though.

Marissa and Jeremy enjoyed the experience of having the girls in the stands with them throughout the tournament. That wasn't something they were used to and it was interesting to hear their commentary on how their old teammates were doing. They were pretty accurate on their guesses of what scores each girl would earn from the judges. Just like last year JJ's team took the win for a very exciting conclusion after a long day of competition.

The family hung around a bit while the team's parents took pictures. JJ took them up on their victory pizza party offer so Marissa, Jeremy and Aiden headed home to get things ready. Marissa placed the order from the parking lot and they swung by and picked it up when they got to town.

Marissa made popcorn and she and Aiden had everything set up and the sweet tea and soda were ready by the time the team arrived.

The house was filled with fun and laughter for the next several hours. All too soon it was time for the team to pile into JJ's van to be dropped off at each of their homes. But first JJ made sure the girls filed through saying thank you to their hosts.

The family stood smiling at JJ as she looked from Marissa to Jeremy and said, "You have no idea what it means to have people like you supporting our team. I mean, your girls aren't even on the team anymore and look what you're doing! You've always been such a special family."

"Surely you realize how special you are to all of us, JJ? It was wonderful having you coach our girls, but you were important to us even before that. I mean, we've been attending the same church as your family since you were just a little girl. That gave us the chance to watch you grow up first, you know," Marissa said.

"That's right," her husband chimed in. "We watched you in the children's Christmas plays, and saw you sing specials with the youth group. You've been part of our church family since way before you started working with the girls at gymnastics. And since then, we celebrated your High School and College graduations with your folks."

"Absolutely," Marissa spoke up again moving in for an end-of-the-evening hug. "You'll always be special to our family JJ!"

Aiden, the girls and their father moved in for a group hug as JJ said again "Y'all are so great!"

The group hug broke up and the individual hugs started as the team said their goodbyes and filed out the door.

"That was awesome!!" Ellie said. She, Marie and Aiden stood in the front yard waving good-bye 'til the van disappeared from sight.

"That was so awesome!" Ellie said again as the siblings came in the front door.

"It was great!" Marie said. "Thanks dad."

"Yeah, thanks," Aiden added.

"It wasn't all my doing,' Jeremy said nodding toward his wife.

"Thanks mom!" all three of their children said together.

"It was your father's idea. A great one at that! And you're very welcome!" Marissa replied happily.

CHAPTER 51

"Hello Ms. Reynolds. Thank you for coming in today. I'm Leanza Williams. It's nice to meet you. As I mentioned when we spoke on the phone yesterday, I'm a cold case investigator and I think you may be able to help me."

"I really can't imagine how but as I said when you called, I'm willing to try. I just have no idea what kind of cold case you could be looking into that I would know anything about," she replied, calmly playing ignorant.

"Walk with me, would you? They've been gracious enough to offer me a room here at the station since I don't work in this precinct," Leanza explained, leading the way to the interrogation room of the Mount Tabor police department.

In a very friendly voice, she continued, "I sure appreciate you being willing to talk with me, especially since I haven't given you much information. The main reason I hoped to speak with you is you being a traveling nurse."

"Oh," Ms. Reynolds said in obvious relief. "I haven't been a traveling nurse for many years but I can give you whatever information you may need about that. I've actually held a full-time position at the Witville Regional Hospital for almost twenty-five years now."

"That sounds wonderful. You like working there, I suppose?" Leanza smiled with feigned interest. "If you could explain to me how it works to be a traveling nurse that may be very helpful."

Reaching the interrogation room Leanza opened the door and flashed the woman a huge smile while motioning toward the table in the center of the room.

174

As Ms. Reynolds took a seat Leanza nonchalantly placed the file folder she'd been carrying onto the table. She quickly adjusted her ear pierce and gave an unnoticed glance at the two-way mirror on the wall to silently acknowledge Jeremy on the other side. Taking a seat Leanza leaned forward and rested her chin in the palm of her hand in a relaxed yet interested pose before nodding slightly for Ms. Reynolds to continue.

"Oh, of course. Well, let's see. As a traveling nurse you actually work through an agency. The agency has a list of hospitals, clinics and offices in need of extra nursing staff for temporary assignments. You can see where those facilities are located and how long the assignment is and choose which position to apply for.

It actually provides wonderful traveling opportunities which is the reason I chose to do it for many years. I wanted to see this beautiful country of ours and was able to look for work opportunities in the specific locations I was interested in. The agency pays your travel expenses. It also either provides an apartment or a stipend with which you can locate and pay for your own. It's a wonderful program really."

"Why yes, I can certainly see how. That sounds lovely. So, you chose the locations you wanted? Tell me a little about that. Where did you choose to go and why?

Before you share, would you like a cup of coffee, I believe I would. Or a soda perhaps? What can I get you, Ms. Reynolds?"

This was Leanza's attempt at putting her suspect perfectly at ease. She wanted this conversation to feel like nothing more than just a visit between new friends.

"Thank you so much," the woman replied. Nervousness had left her mouth dry. Now that she was feeling less stressed, she said, "I'd absolutely love a Cheerwine if they happen to have one."

"Certainly. You just relax a moment while I round that up for us," Leanza stepped out and passed the request on to an officer she'd spoken with earlier. She rejoined Ms. Reynolds to pick up where they'd left off.

A few minutes later the officer came in and gave the ladies their drinks.

"Thank you so much, officer," Leanza said, her voice dripping with sweetness. Turning back to Ms. Reynolds she went on, "They are just so kind here. Everyone's being so helpful, you included, of course. I just can't tell you how much I appreciate it.

So where were we? Oh, yes, you worked in Colorado because you'd always wanted to go snow skiing and you worked in Washington DC because you wanted to visit the state house and the monuments. What a wonderful idea."

"As I said earlier, I would never have been able to visit so many beautiful tourist attractions but for my job as a traveling nurse. It worked out great for me."

"I see, and what was it that you wanted to see in Austin, Texas?"

The question took her by surprise.

"What? Oh, well, yes," thrown off balance she looked down at her hands for a few seconds. "Yes, you're right. I did work in Austin for a time. Austin is most well-known for its live music opportunities," she added trying to appear composed.

"So, you were interested in performing live music? I had no idea you are a singer," Leanza said evenly.

"What? Oh, no. I didn't say that. No, I don't sing or perform live music," her face grew flushed. "I was just saying, well, I meant that I enjoyed going to live performances. Yes, that was why I wanted to work and live there."

She's a quick thinker Leanza thought as she sat up straighter and looked directly across the table to meet the other woman's eyes.

"I see. So, it had nothing to do with the fact that a certain police detective's wife would be delivering his baby in that hospital?" There was no friendliness in Leanza's demeanor now.

"What? No. I mean, what? I don't know what you're talking about."

"You don't? So, you're not aware a baby went missing from the nursery of the very hospital you worked in while you were working in Austin? Really? That's a bit hard to believe. This missing baby was very well publicized at the time. It wasn't just known throughout the hospital. It was all over the news. It was a major case at the time. The media coverage lasted for weeks. Are you seriously telling me you know nothing about that?"

"Yes. No. That's not what I'm saying at all. Of course, I remember that," The woman was trying to maintain control at this point. "Yes, as you said, talk of that was all over the hospital, of course I heard about it. All I'm saying is that I know nothing about it personally."

"Really? Oh, okay then. Let's talk about what you do know. Since you remember the case, what were you doing when the baby went missing. Did you work at the hospital that day?"

In a feeble attempt to appear as if she were trying to remember, the suspect answered, "Let's see, that was a long time ago. I haven't thought about that situation in years. What day of the week was it again?" This was a stall tactic. She was trying to give herself time to decide how to play things.

"It was a Tuesday evening," Leanza answered immediately relaying the time frame in which the baby went missing.

"Oh, yes, I remember now. I did work that day. I was in ICU on day shift. You asked what I was doing when the baby went missing, didn't you? I would've gone home hours before. I'm not sure what I would've been doing at that exact time but most likely I was watching TV if I hadn't fallen asleep by then.

We worked twelve-hour shifts at that hospital, I do remember that. Those shifts are exhausting. I generally fell asleep early and made up for the lack of sleep on my days off. I'm sure I was home sleeping on the couch when it happened.

I didn't hear about the missing baby until the next day. One of the nurses called and told me about it. I wasn't on the schedule 'til the day after that. Everyone was still talking about the Code Pink and the police being there when I went in. Everything was in an up-roar. There was a lot of police presence at the hospital over the next several days. I remember feeling so badly for that baby girl's parents."

"Do you now?" Leanza said coldly.

She could feel Jeremy's eyes through the two-way mirror and her heart went out to him.

CHAPTER 52

"So, to be sure I'm understanding you correctly here, Ms. Reynolds. What you want me to believe is that you were at home, most likely sleeping on your couch at the time the baby went missing that night. Is that right?"

The woman had been repeatedly rubbing her hands together for some time now. She kept her eyes on her hands and softly said, "that's right."

"That's correct?" Leanza asked again leaning in and tilting her head slightly downward in an effort to meet the woman's eyes.

"Yes, that's correct," Ms. Reynolds answered a little louder.

Leanza slammed her hand onto the table and shouted, "Why don't I believe you then?" Startled the woman's head jerked upward. She stared wide-eyed as Leanza scooted back from the table, her chair scraping against the floor loudly. Snatching up the file she had earlier laid aside Leanza leaned back in her chair. She was changing tactics in an effort to break her suspect. Slowly flipping the file open Leanza calmly looked the woman dead in the eyes.

"Let's just see if we can't get to the truth now, shall we? It says here – well look at that, you're right." Her voice softened ever so slightly as she went on, "You did work the day shift in ICU that day. It says here - your shift ended at six o'clock p.m. Well, isn't that interesting? Maybe you are telling me the truth."

This was just another tactic to confuse and throw the suspect off balance.

"I suppose you could've gone home and fell asleep on your couch just like you said. Maybe you just needed to take a little rest before coming back to the hospital. That would make sense. I mean, after all, you were going to need to have your wits about you in order to kidnap a baby."

"No," the word was spoken softly.

"No?" Leanza asked almost kindly just before leaning forward to pose her next question more directly. Raising her voice slightly Leanza asked again, "No?" Watching the woman's face closely she continued, "Then why does it say right here that you were seen in the stairwell at precisely 10:15 p.m. that night? That's right and not just any stairwell, the stairwell directly adjacent to the maternity ward."

The woman's eyes widened. Her head slowly began to shake from side to side. She was staring vacantly ahead continually repeating the word 'no' over and over.

"It's true, isn't it?" Leanza's tone was matter-of-fact now. "I can see it in your eyes."

Leanza closed the file. Leaning forward she laid it on the table between them. "I can see where your confusion is coming from though," she said, her tone of voice soothing. "None of this came out in the original investigation. That's right. And all these many years you've been wondering how you got so lucky. Why was it that night-janitor never mentioned seeing you in the stairwell?

You remember that moment like it was yesterday, don't you? He looked you right in the face, didn't he? You can probably still see his eyes as clear as you see mine right now."

Unbidden, a tear slipped out of the woman's eye and slid slowly down her cheek.

Leanza had her and she knew it. It wasn't the first time this had happened in a cold case. Keeping secrets year after year takes a toll on a person. If there's any good in them at all they can't hold up under the pressure of guilt and time.

Leanza reached out and gently laid her hand over the woman's hands causing them to still. "Tell me what happened," she said softly. "Why did you take the baby that night? Come on now, Ms. Reynolds I know you want to tell me."

"No," she whispered almost illegibly before taking a deep breath. In one last-ditch-effort to be convincing she met Leanza's eyes, tears still welling up in her own. "I didn't. I could never. I did not do this terrible thing," she said feebly, her eyes begging Leanza's to believe the lie.

But Leanza's patience was at its breaking point. Jeremy's pain was in her mind and heart. She had no compassion for this woman if she wasn't going to confess. Leanza would have no part in helping her sooth her own guilty conscious.

Jerking her hand away sharply Leanza slammed it down on the table again. "We know you took that baby!" she shouted. "You were seen by the janitor in the stairwell. He told us it wasn't unusual to see you traveling nurses with your duffle bags since you sometimes stayed at the hospital a day or two. The reason he noticed you that night was that instead of it being slung over your shoulder as usual you were carrying your duffle bag in your arms.

You hid a baby in that bag and stole it that night, didn't you Kate? We know you did. And you are not leaving this room until you tell me why!!"

CHAPTER 53

Leanza Williams was correct about one thing, if nothing else; carrying a secret year after year will eventually destroy a person.

The pressure of her secret guilt had built up in Kate Reynolds for almost a quarter of a century. Only two things were needed to push her to the point of confessing; being interrogated by the best of the best and finally being confronted with the truth.

Unable to take the lies anymore Kate finally broke down crying and confessed to everything. Once the dam broke, she was filled with remorse. It soon became obvious the woman had been sorry for years.

Jeremy stayed behind the two-way mirror hearing everything and asking all the right question through the wire Leanza wore. By working together, they were able to get all the answers they needed.

Kate explained how it had all played out. By the time she was twenty-five, through nursing school and a practicing nurse, her only brother was incarcerated. Being a good sister, she faithfully visited him in prison. When she became a traveling nurse, she continued to visit her brother as often as possible.

Her traveling job made it difficult to date. Meeting someone special was even harder. Kate was still unattached when she turned twenty-six. She met her brother's cellmate shortly after that. He made her feel special by making the effort to be involved whenever she visited. Against her brother's wishes she began to have an ongoing relationship with him. Looking back on it all later she could see how her loneliness and low self-esteem made her susceptible to his manipulation.

He sweet-talked her into believing herself to be falling in love with him and she fell for it all. He had a tall tale about how he'd been unjustly arrested, set up by a detective who was out to get him and screwed over by a legal system slated against those less fortunate in life. Though now ashamed to admit it, Kate was pulled in by his story. Due to her emotional entanglement with him she chose to see only the best of him. She not only listened to his lies, she bought them; hook, line and sinker. After repeatedly being told how the detective had set him up and the legal system had unjustly convicted and incarcerated him, she became putty in his hands.

At this point in her story, Jeremy asked Leanza to get the man's name. A few moments later Kate said the name Thatcher Foreman and Jeremy's heart broke. Having seen with his own eyes what Thatcher was capable of Jeremy believed his baby daughter to be dead.

He became inconsolable and Leanza had to leave the interrogation room to be with him.

It took some time to get Jeremy to even hear her, let alone listen to her reasoning. When he had finally calmed down, Leanza reminded him they didn't have all the facts. Only then was she able to return to Kate and get the rest of the story.

To everyone's shock, amazement and great relief they eventually learned that Kate had not done with the baby what Thatcher instructed her to do.

As Kate's story unfolded, they learned she had initially applied for the position at the Austin, Texas, hospital without even knowing why Thatcher wanted her there. Infatuated with him she imagined he was transferring to a prison near its location and wished for her to be close enough to continue visiting him. Having taken control of her thinking her emotions robbed her of all rational reasoning.

By confessing that he spent time with some bad people before going to prison Thatcher won Kate's trust. This was his manipulative plan all along but Kate couldn't see that.

Once he knew she trusted him Thatcher told her Jeremy Alan was the man who had framed him for the horrendous acts he was accused and convicted of. Of course, he insisted he was totally innocent. He then told her Jeremy was the man who had actually done the things Thatcher was accused of. He said Jeremy was now about to become a father to an innocent little child.

Thatcher actually shed tears from concern for that baby. He convinced her the public life displayed by Jeremy and Marissa Alan was all a deceitful cover-up of Jeremy being a bad cop; a cop who framed people for crimes he himself was guilty of committing.

As embarrassed and ashamed as Kate now was to admit to it the truth was what it was. Thatcher succeeded in convincing her any baby born to the Alan's needed to be protected from them. He repeatedly said "that baby's parents are terrible folks! Someone has got to save that baby and you are the only one who can do it."

He told her there were many good people who wanted a baby. Kate knew that to be true. Thatcher told her all she had to do was sell the baby on the black market. It wasn't as bad as it sounded. He knew someone she could contact who would see to it that baby got a good home. Of course, she could keep the money. She could put it in the bank and live off of it. He was never getting out of prison so it wasn't like he needed it. She was doing the job. The money would be her reward. But her real reward would be knowing she'd protected that poor little baby.

Thatcher gave her the name and number promising these were people who would find the baby a good home. They weren't in it for the money, they just wanted to help children but everyone knows money is what makes the world go round. He assured her the baby would have a good life if only it were safe from that terrible Alan couple.

So that was the plan.

Everything went like clockwork the night she took the baby. The only snag was running into the night janitor in the stairway as she was leaving. At the time she thought sure that was going to come back on her but there was nothing she could do about it so she just carried on. She lived in fear of being found out for months but nothing ever came up about the janitor seeing her that night.

She was supposed to meet up with the baby buyers she had contacted right away. She wasn't sure what stopped her.

All she could tell Leanza was that after gazing into the baby's eyes she simply couldn't do it. It was like the baby hadn't been real during all those months of planning. Once she looked into its precious face everything changed. Once the baby was real to her so was the nagging feeling that she couldn't trust what Thatcher was telling her.

As soon as she admitted that she didn't meet up with the people she'd arranged to sell the baby to Leanza asked her what she did do.

Kate became very quiet. She'd looked very sad during the earlier interrogation. Now she looked miserable. Tears poured from her eyes and she sat silently wiping them away.

As the minutes passed Leanza became very concerned. On the other side of the two-way mirror Jeremy was about to lose his mind.

"Take your time," Leanza said. "I know this is very difficult."

"What are you doing?" Jeremy demanded in her ear.

"Whenever you're ready Kate, please just tell me what you did with the baby."

Finally, Kate raised her head and looked Leanza in the eyes. In the quietest, saddest voice the agent had ever heard Kate said, "I used my very best friend in the most terrible way."

"What does that mean?" Leanza asked.

"We became friends in elementary school and remained close for the rest of her life. She was a wonderful person. She remained my very best friend right up until the day she died. Her name was Amber Delaney.

A couple of years after losing her husband and little boy in a car accident Amber opened a children's home. I went there so often I was like a part of the family. Amber was an excellent mother and all of the children in her care were loved and happy. Because of our friendship I saw that. I knew how loved and well cared for those children were.

Once I had taken the baby, I knew I couldn't do what Thatcher wanted me to do with her. But I had kidnapped a baby! It wasn't like I could just take her back. The police were everywhere. Everyone was searching for her. If they found her - they would find me. I couldn't let that happen.

I was desperate. Not knowing what to do.

I only knew I couldn't let anything bad happen to that beautiful child. That's when I decided she had to go to Amber's children's home. She would be wanted and loved and cared for there.

But no one could ever know I was involved, especially not Amber.

I had to work the next day so I didn't have much time to deal with the baby. There was only one person I could trust. My brother and I had a cousin who grew up with us. We were close and we grew even closer after my brother went to jail. We already had a few secrets he had never told so I figured I could trust him with one more. As luck would have it, he and his wife had come to Austin on vacation. We'd gotten together a few times that past weekend. What other choice did I have? I called and told him I needed his help.

Just as I knew he would he came right over.

I lied, of course. I told him someone had turned to me for help. The baby's parents. They were involved in something dangerous and some very bad people wanted to kill them. They knew that if those people found out they had a baby their child would be killed, too. All they wanted was for their little girl to be safe and have a good home but no one could ever know where the child came from.

I gave him the number to The Delaney Children's Home. I told him to talk with the caretaker, Steven. He had to convince Steven the children's home was the only hope for this baby to survive. They must never reveal the circumstances under which they'd taken the child. I knew Ms. Amber couldn't turn a child in danger away and I was right. Arrangements were made and my cousin and his wife took the baby. They left for North Carolina that very night. He called me after the baby was delivered.

I had convinced him and his wife to believe our lives were all in danger, I made them swear that for that reason we would never speak of it again. Not to each other. Nor to anyone else. And we never have.

True to their end of the bargain the people at the children's home never told anyone a thing. I know this because Amber was my closest friend. She told me many things she never told another living soul but she never told me where that child came from. She just played it off like the state had given her another child to foster until a home became available.

Of course, I never told her what I'd done. I hated my deception and how I had used her but what was done was done and there was no going back.

The lies just kept coming. I told Thatcher I had done exactly what he told me to do. For the longest time I was afraid he'd find me out. I thought sure he would talk with the people whose number he gave me. To this day I don't know why he didn't.

My brother had tried to warn me not to get involved with him. It wasn't until afterward that I saw him for the evil man he really is. I told my brother how sorry I was for not listening to him. He asked for a transfer to the closest prison system to me so we could continue to visit without Thatcher's interference. It was granted and I never saw Thatcher Foreman again. If I ever do it'll be too soon."

"Whatever happened to the child you took? Do you know?" Leanza asked hopefully.

"I wish I could tell you," Kate said, her eyes brimming over with tears.

"If you only knew how much I wish I could tell you that. I don't know how Amber pulled it off but she raised that little girl until she was almost four years old. She was a beautiful, happy, delightful child. One day she was just gone. The other children said she'd been adopted and I never saw here again.

As with all the other children who were adopted from the Delaney Home for Children, I have no idea where she went. Amber already took confidentiality seriously. In this case, she believed that little girl's life was at stake. Based on that I can assure you she never told anyone where that child was placed.

I never thought I'd ever hear myself say this but I'm glad Amber's not here," Kate said with a sob. Her crying was almost inconsolable as she continued, "I'm thankful she will never know what I did. The guilt tore at me every time we were together. Amber was the kindest, most loving, selfless, caring person I've ever known and I used her for my own protection. I am so sorry! I cannot tell you how much I regret my part in all of this. I am so sorry for everything I've done. I wish I could make up for it but I can't. I know that." She took a deep breath and calmed herself.

"There's one thing I can promise you though, there's not a doubt in my mind that child went to a very loving family. Amber made sure of that with all of her children, but that little girl was very special so I'm sure she's had a wonderful life."

The good news here, Leanza thought, is that Jeremy's daughter is still alive. The main question now is; where is she?

CHAPTER 54

"It was the strangest thing I've ever experienced," Jovie said while rolling the dough to make a pie crust. As was their monthly habit, she and her mother were doing meal prep together. They were currently making chicken pot pies to put into the freezer.

"I can only imagine," her mom replied. "How are you feeling about it now?"

"I've got to be honest. I feel really drawn to that place."

"I'm not surprised. It makes perfect sense really. The memories you're having are happy memories. Your father, brother and I have already told you we could see how loved you were there. The first time we interacted with you was at a family visit we'd been invited to because of our quest to adopt. We didn't have much experience but had been to a few other children's homes before that one. I have to say, the home you were in didn't feel like the others at all. It definitely had more of a family feeling.

During that first visit we mostly just watched all of you little ones playing together as we talked with the adults. While we all ate, we interacted together with all of the children who lived there. After the meal your brother ran around playing with the rest of you. Your father and I occasionally came and played with you as well.

It was a very happy environment. We came back for family visits several times that summer hoping you would get to know us enough to feel comfortable coming home with us once we had everything ready and the legalities of the adoption were done.

Every time we left, we felt as though we'd just spent time with a very happy family. Never did it feel like those other children's homes we visited.

187

I can see how you would be feeling drawn to the place just based on what we experienced there."

"Thank you for being so supportive, mom. I can't imagine what it must be like for you and dad that I'm suddenly curious about my life outside of us as a family. I hope you know this isn't about anything missing from the life you've given me. You, dad and TJ are my family. There's no question about that and nothing is ever going to change it. You know this, right?"

"Yes, Jovie we know but thank you for saying it anyway. Your father and I have known a few adoptive families that have gone through tough times when the child wants to seek out their birth parents. We've always known there was a possibility that may someday be you. We decided a long time ago that if you ever felt that need, we would support you in your search. I know this isn't quite the same but we support you in it."

"That means a lot to me, so thank you. I'm not even sure where to go with this. The woman who ran the place, the one who I guess I would've considered my mother during those first three years of my life is gone. She died. That's basically the reason the children's home was closed.

My point is that this isn't going to result in us being reunited. I have been having some scattered memories of the others who lived there. Even if those memories were stronger, I would have no idea how to go about finding anyone. At this point, I'm thinking all I can really do is see the house and land. And I'm not even sure how to go about that."

"But you want to, right?" her mother asked.

Without hesitation Jovie answered, "Yes. I would really like to see the house and walk the property. It's been sitting empty and seriously neglected for a very long time. Getting inside the house and walking the grounds may open more memories for me."

"That could be a good thing," her mother said, quickly adding, "That's really all that can come of seeing the place, I suppose."

Jovie looked, and felt, a little uncomfortable. Dead space hung between them a little awkwardly. It stretched to almost a full minute before she spoke again. "I don't want to keep anything from you. You and dad have always been totally upfront with me. I owe you the exact same courtesy."

Her mother stopped mixing the pie filling and turned to give her daughter her full attention.

"If you have something to say, you can. There's nothing you can't tell me. Go ahead. Unless, you want your father to be here?"

"No, that's not necessary. I'm probably making too much of this. It's just that, well, okay, uh, okay let's start over here. You already know my future plans. We've talked about this before. I'm not looking to keep renting. That just feels like throwing money away. It's not entirely but it comes pretty close. You get nothing but a place to live from the payments you make and when you decide to move on you get nothing toward your next home. When you buy a place, you get money back when you're ready to move on. That makes it as if you lived there free of charge and I love that. I'm not telling you anything new here.

The only thing I haven't told you and dad yet is that I'm ready to buy my first home now. Still, this isn't a move you make without some level of fear. That being said, I've been a bit hesitant to get started. Although I've wanted to, I haven't called a realtor to get started looking.

I guess what I'm saying is; as crazy as this sounds, I'd like to find out who actually owns that place on the lake so I can look at it as a prospective buyer. I do want to see it because of the way I feel and the memories I'm having but maybe there's more to it than that.

The thing is, I love the setting. I know this seems crazy but I've been thinking about it a lot. If I actually like the house, well, the idea of bringing that old place back to life might actually appeal to me."

CHAPTER 55

As they sat talking after dinner on the day of the interview Leanza filled Vonda in on the day's events. Being the professional she was, she had always followed protocol by not using the suspect's name. With the interview resulting in a confession Leanza now thought nothing of saying, "Kate Reynolds has been placed under arrest."

Hearing the name of her long-time book-club friend Vonda was both shocked and saddened. How was this possible? Vonda had forgotten Kate had once been a traveling nurse. But then, even if she'd remembered, Kate wouldn't have come to mind when Leanza talked about the case. Vonda knew Kate as a fun, friendly, kind and caring person, for her to kidnap a baby was simply unimaginable.

Leanza assured Vonda that Kate was filled with regret. She listed the ways keeping such a huge secret for so long effects good people. Kate was no exception. The guilt, self-condemnation and remorse she felt were all common in someone who had made such a regrettable choice.

Having done this for a long time Leanza shared sometimes seeing things others missed. In this case, despite Kate putting up a good fight during the interrogation, Leanza felt strongly she'd been approaching her breaking point before she was even questioned. There had never been any doubt in Leanza's mind that Kate was going to confess. That was part of the reason she'd pushed her so hard and so fast.

Vonda immediately began praying for her friend. Before long she asked Leanza if it were possible for her to visit Kate at the jail. She was already facing the legal consequences of her actions but there was far worse to come. Vonda wanted to be there for her friend but was also filled with concern for Jeremy and Marissa, who were very dear to her, as well.

What a mess, she thought.

Still there was good news in all of this. The Alans now knew for certain that their daughter was most likely alive. She had been cared for at a children's home until she was adopted somewhere between the age of three and four years old. Who adopted her, where she ended up and where she was now was still a mystery that hopefully Leanza and Jeremy could solve.

At least now they had somewhere to start.

After speculating about what may happen next and empathizing with everyone involved Vonda and Leanza were both exhausted. Leanza from the demands of the case, Vonda emotionally. They said good-night and Leanza went to the guest room.

As she did every evening Lilly led the way to Vonda's bedroom and jumped up onto the bed. She then lay watching as Vonda went about her nightly routine.

Finishing up Vonda lifted Lilly into her arms and sat down on the edge of her bed. While cradling and petting Lilly softly Vonda talked with God. She very honestly told him how angry she felt at Kate for the years of suffering she had put the Alans through. The most recent book club meeting came to mind. Kate had showed them the monarchs. She made comments about honoring her friend by tending her milkweed garden all these years since her death. How was it possible that those two women were one and the same?

Human nature never ceased to amaze her. God's love never ceased to amaze her either. As shocked as she was by what Kate had done, God was not shocked. He'd known about it all those years and that whole time He was there ready to forgive. God loved Kate and Jesus died for her, already knowing what she was going to do in what was undoubtedly the worst moment of her life.

"Your love is amazing, God," Vonda said aloud. "Please help me love the way you do. I'm going to go see Kate tomorrow and I really want to be there for her. Please give me the words she needs to hear. Help me love her as you love me."

Vonda placed Lilly onto the bed and settled in beside her. Turning onto her side she pressed in close as Lilly purred contentedly. Soon they were both asleep.

After breakfast the next morning Vonda went to the Mount Tabor Police Department and was shown into a room used for visiting. As Kate was led into that same room, she saw Vonda and froze.

"I'm so ashamed," she said, seeming to wilt right where she stood.

Vonda's heart was immediately filled with compassion and she rushed to her friend. Placing her arms around Kate, Vonda gently embraced her. Sobs tore through Kate's body. Vonda could literally feel her shame as she began to speak soothing words into her friend's ear.

It took a little while for Kate's crying to quiet. When it did Vonda led her to the table. Vonda pulled her chair around to the same side of Kate's and sat down beside her.

Her sobs subsiding, Kate wiped her eyes on her sleeve and sadly said, 'You must hate me."

Looking her friend directly in the eyes Vonda said, "I don't hate you, Kate, and neither does God."

"I don't see how that could be true," Kate said through her tears.

"Well, it is. God loves us. It's our sin that separates us from Him and the guilt and shame of our sin eats away at us, until we're willing to admit what we've done and accept His forgiveness. It really is that simple. We're the ones who make it difficult.

From what Leanza has told me, you've been living with the regret of your choice for a very long time. It's been tearing you up inside, hasn't it?"

"Yes," Kate said as another sob rose up in her throat. "I don't know how I've managed to live with myself."

It took a moment before she could go on. "I tried to think of a way to fix what I'd done. There just wasn't one. Believe me, if I could go back, I would change so many things. But I can't. It will never happen but even if you could find that baby and her parents, they would never forgive me. How could they? I've cost them a lifetime together.

I know faith is a huge part of your life, Vonda. I have seen the peace it brings you and I've always been happy for you. It's not like I don't believe in God because I do. Even knowing it to be impossible I have tried to make up for what I did. But at the end of the day, it all boils down to one thing; God is good and I'm not.

I think I'm actually glad this has come out. I'm going to plead guilty and take whatever punishment the judge decides is fair. Maybe I'll feel better by actually paying for what I've done."

Vonda had been slowly shaking her head 'no' for some time. When Kate stopped speaking, she reached over and placed her hands over Kate's.

"Oh, dear Kate. The only thing you got right in all of what you just said is that God is good. Yes, He is. He is holy and good and we are not. That's the whole point. Romans 5:8 says this "But God demonstrates his own love for us in this: while we were still sinners Christ died for us."

Do you catch that, Kate? *While we were still sinners.* Before He enacted a plan to save us God knew the terrible things we were going to do. Jesus knew before He ever went to the cross what each of us was capable of. Knowing that – they collectively chose to show their love for us. That's how much they love you, Kate. And the same is true for me.

What you've said is true. There are lasting and life changing consequences to what you did. You're going to be held accountable and there is a price to pay. I know it feels like it to you, but what you've done is not unforgivable. In 1 John 1:9 the Bible says if we confess our sins, God is faithful and just and will forgive us our sin, and will purify us from all unrighteousness.

What that means is that once we accept God's forgiveness, He no longer sees us in our sin. When he looks at us, He sees his perfect, sinless, righteous son.

Jesus covers our sins, Kate.

Once you accept His forgiveness you will be set free, even in jail you will be free.

CHAPTER 56

Having been built on the furthermost point of the peninsula the front of the house faced Lake Spivey. On one end was a small combination back porch mudroom with lots of windows and an entry door. The driveway led directly to the back of the property facing that door.

Driving slowly up the barely visible drive, Jovie passed a wooded area off to her left before seeing an overgrown field that met up with the back yard. Spivey Lake could be seen to her right just past the high weeds and overgrown reeds and cattails lining the edge of the water. Due to years of little use the driveway was mostly grass but Jovie could still see the track for each vehicle tire. She followed them to where they ended and parked the car.

The Realtor wasn't there yet.

Stepping out of her car Jovie closed the door and stood slowly taking a look at her surroundings. As she had already known it to be, the land was overgrown and neglected. Contrary to what she'd expected, that became almost unnoticeable due to the natural beauty.

She just stood there taking it all in. The chirping and calls of birds in the trees, the lapping of the water meeting the shore, the leaves rustling in the gentle wind soon had her mesmerized. She'd just started to debate walking toward the house when she heard tires slowly coming up the drive behind her. Turning toward the sound she smiled at the driver who parked and disembarked.

Jovie walked forward and extended her hand.

"It's nice to put a face to the voice," the Realtor said. "I'm Lisa Evans. I'm so happy to meet you."

"It's nice to meet you," Jovie replied with a friendly smile.

"Have you been here long?"

"I pulled in about five minutes ago. I've just been standing here taking a slow look around."

"I'm glad. It's a good-sized property and as you can see there's great potential. I'm told this place was quite beautiful back in the day. Here's the information we've got on it," she said while handing a Real Estate flyer to Jovie.

After giving her a minute to look it over Lisa asked, "Would you like to check out the property or go inside the house first?"

"You know what, it's such a beautiful day outside I think I'd like to walk the property first," Jovie answered.

"Let's do it," Lisa said as the two women began a slow tour of the back area.

Across Lake Spivey at the end of the pier house Doctor Jaxson Delany was relaxing on one of the fishing benches. Leaning back his head resting in his hands which were linked at the base of his neck he had his long legs stretched out in front of him. Ankles crossed, feet resting on the railing; Jaxson loved watching the sunset in this exact position.

He was in the habit of doing this about twice a week. His eyes caught a slight movement across the lake and he leaned forward to get a better look. Almost immediately two women came around the side yard of his old homeplace.

Curiosity getting the best of him, Jaxson stood up and took two steps to the railing to look more intently. He had seen correctly. There were two women walking slowly around to the front of the house. He wondered what was going on as he continued watching. They walked out to the water's edge off to the left front of the house. Before long they moseyed past the front of the house over to the gazebo not far from the lakeshore. A few moments later they crossed the footbridge and moved toward the broken pieces of the wooden dock which jutting out of the water and stretched out across it ending at the weathered wooden platform. He watched as the one woman pointed and gestured, obviously talking about the damaged property.

What's happening? Jaxson asked himself, feeling just a small bit of alarm rising up in his chest. Is someone actually interested in the place? He had long wanted this to happen. So why did he find himself feeling alarmed? Had he gotten so accustomed to seeing it the way it was that he didn't want that to change?

Jaxson wasn't prone to making snap decisions but in that moment he did exactly that.

Hurrying down the dock he jumped into his vehicle, snapped his seat belt on and threw it in gear. Barely keeping himself from peeling out he hurriedly drove away. Half a mile later he turned onto Ten Mile Road, drove straight to Wildlife Club Road and turned left. Coming to its end he pulled in and parked behind the two cars already there. Recognizing one car as belonging to the Realtor he'd met once before he knew for sure the place was being shown.

Asking himself what he was doing he got out and walked toward the front of the property. He hoped the two women wouldn't mind the intrusion since he didn't seem able to stop himself.

Coming around to the front of the house he saw that they were just turning toward it not far from the footbridge they had earlier crossed.

"Hello ladies," Jaxson called out, trying to sound friendly enough to be welcomed as he slowed his pace and walked over to join them.

Recognizing him from their prior meeting Lisa said, "Hello Doctor, this is Ms. Jarvis."

She turned toward Jovie who smiled curiously and greeted him."

"Ms. Jarvis is interested in your mother's old place. I've been showing her the property but we haven't gone inside the house yet."

"Oh," Jovie said, "you used to live here?"

"I did," Jaxson said, smiling at the younger woman.

"I'm sorry," Lisa said. "I guess, I should've explained that and asked if you mind the doctor being here."

"Certainly not," Jovie said. "In fact, you're welcome to stay for the rest of the tour if you'd like. You're a doctor then?"

"Thank you, I think I will tag along. Yes, I'm a pediatrician. The result of growing up in a house full of children, I suppose."

"Oh, yes," Jovie commented. "I have heard this was a children's home. Your mother was the lady who ran it then?"

"That's right," Lisa interjected. "I suppose it must have been an interesting life to have all of those other children vying for your mother's attention."

Jaxson smiled. It was common for people to assume he was Ma's birth child since his last name was Delaney.

"Actually, I came to live at the Delaney Home for Children when I was six years old," he clarified.

Looking surprised, Lisa said, "I'm sorry. I just assumed..."

"No apology necessary. I understand. I took Ma's name as my own when I came of legal age. She was, in every way that matters, my mother. I don't know if you can understand that, but it's true. Taking her name was my way of honoring her."

"That's beautiful," Jovie said, softly. She found herself feeling a connection to the man. "Being adopted myself I completely understand what you mean. Family isn't about blood. It's about who is there for you."

"Exactly," Jaxson agreed, looking at her warmly.

"Well, here we are," Lisa said, stepping up to the front door. "Let me get this unlocked and we'll take a look inside this large family home."

It had been a good number of years since Jaxson had been in the house and memories were pushing in on him.

Stepping inside Jovie felt an even deeper sense of familiarity than what she had been feeling outside the house.

The living room was spacious with lots of windows. Jovie was a huge fan of natural light so the room appealed to her immediately.

Lisa led them through to the dining area which opened up to a large kitchen. A long wooden table with multiple chairs pushed up to it sat in the center of the room.

Talking and laughter suddenly filled Jovie's mind. For a split second she saw children seated in the chairs and dishes filled with food in the middle of the table. The lovely brunette woman she'd seen hanging laundry on her last visit was standing at the end of the table smiling. Another woman was at the stove in the background.

Jovie felt unbalanced for a few seconds and realized the doctor was looking at her strangely.

"Are you ready to keep moving?" Lisa asked, looking at Jovie quizzically.

"I am," Jovie answered.

Lisa turned to Jaxson and said, "I'm just thinking perhaps you should be the one to lead this tour, Doctor Jaxson. After all, you know this house much better than I do."

"You're doing fine," he said, flashing a smile at her. "I'll just continue to tag along."

Jaxson?" Jovie said in a whisper no one else heard. Was this the Jaxson from her memories? The boy who carried her on his hip while flying kites. Was this the older brother she kept asking her new family about after she was adopted? This was all getting confusing and Jovie was feeling a bit overwhelmed.

Looking into the smaller room off from the dining area Jovie visualized children spread out at different play stations. There was a small table where several were coloring, a rug and large pillows on which two children lay reading. In the corner were shelves and a toy box where a child stood deciding what to play with next. She shook her head to scatter the vision and turned aside.

"Before I take you upstairs let's cross through the kitchen and take a look at the mud room. This is the entrance into the house from the back yard," Lisa said.

Looking past her into the mud room Jovie immediately thought of butterflies. As she entered the space a strong sense of happiness flooded her entire being. In the right side of the room her mind saw tomato cages with netting over them. There was a boy of about eleven kneeling beside one. Jovie remembered standing in front of him while leaning back into him. Their heads were close together as they both looked intently into one of the cages. "Look Jovie, do you see it? It won't be long now and a beautiful butterfly will come from that," the boy said.

Turning to look away from the memory, Jovie's eyes met Dr. Jaxson's full-on. She felt as though she knew him. A quizzical look came into his eyes just before Jovie looked away.

"Let's head upstairs now," Lisa said, and the two obediently followed her.

At the top of the stairs was a small landing area, a bathroom as wide as the landing lay just beyond it. There were closed doors on either side of the landing.

Lisa placed her hand on the doorknob of the door to her left. "What was this room used for, doctor?" she asked as she opened the door. Jovie entered the room with Jaxson following close behind her.

Jovie's mind's eye immediately saw a long row of single beds covered in pink bedding of various patterns. At the far end were toy boxes and a large chalkboard on an easel. Toy baby beds with baby dolls covered in blankets lined the wall. Just that quick the vision was gone.

"This was the girl's bedroom," Jovie heard herself say walking further into the room. "Jovie's bed was right here," she continued as she turned to the doctor and added, "that's right, isn't it?"

With a look of surprise on his face, Jaxson said "That's exactly where Jovie's bed was. How did you know?"

Meeting his eyes with hers she said softly, "My name is Jovie."

CHAPTER 57

Jaxson's breath caught in his throat. He felt as if he couldn't breathe as her eyes held his.

"Jovie?" the name was barely audible he said it so softly. Taking a step toward her he said it again, louder and with more confidence.

"Jovie."

His eyes searched her face as he spoke just above a whisper, "Are you really my Jovie?"

Continuing to search her face for anything that would prove her declaration true his eyes pooled. He was totally unaware of the tear that slipped out and slid slowly down his cheek.

He had felt strangely drawn to her from the first moment they were introduced. She seemed familiar to him in some way he hadn't been able to put his finger on. He'd been watching her closely as they went through the house. Seeing that her interest was more than just in buying the place. She was reacting to the house at every turn. That made sense to him now. But was this really his baby sister? How could that be?

Lisa realized something significant was unfolding before her very eyes and was totally enthralled by what was happening. The room was charged with emotion as the two stood looking at each other. There were actual tears in the doctor's eyes.

Apparently, this was an unexpected reunion between two children who had once lived in this house together. I'm so glad I'm a part of this moment, she thought as she stood silently by and continued observing

"If you are the boy who carried me as we flew kites in this backyard and who taught me about butterflies, then yes, I am your Jovie," the lovely young woman said.

Wanting to grab her in the tightest hug she had ever experienced, Jaxson instead simply stared at her. He was in shock. Had his little sister really just walked right back into his life after all these years of wondering and praying?

The myriad of emotions playing across his face told Jovie she meant far more to this man than she could fathom. He seemed to be holding himself back from her. Without understanding exactly why she was doing it she took a step toward him and opened her arms.

His eyes moved to her outstretched arms and he took a small step forward.

As if a dam had suddenly burst, they then rushed to each other for the hug they both wanted. The hug Jaxson had been waiting for all his adult life.

As if suddenly awakening out of a stupor his hug became urgent and alive. When his arms tightened around her Jovie tightened hers as well.

"Is it really you?" she heard him whisper, his mouth next to her ear. She felt him suppress a sob. "Thank you, Father," he breathed shakily. "Thank you, God," he said more urgently. "Thank you for answering my many prayers. You've finally brought my baby sister home after all these years. How is this even possible?"

Unbidden tears welled up in Jovie's eyes, the emotion in his voice tearing at her heart. The connection she felt to this man was undeniable and beyond explanation.

Lisa's hands had risen to her face. Her fingers were now pressed to her lips and her eyes welled with tears. What a beautiful reunion.

CHAPTER 58

"Kate has been extradited back to Austin, Texas," Leanza told Vonda and Marshall as the three ate supper together. "She is to be held in jail there until her court appearance. At that time, she will be asked to enter a plea in the kidnapping charges the state is bringing against her. She plans to plead guilty. She is filled with remorse and says she will accept whatever the court decides.

I've looked into it and the crime of kidnapping is a third-degree felony in the state of Texas. Under certain conditions a person convicted of kidnapping may receive a grant of probation but even then, the statute calls for a minimum of one year of imprisonment. What Jeremy and Marissa decide to do will be factored in. If they want her to be shown mercy it will most likely affect the court's decision. It all depends on the judge. At this point it's anyone's guess what will happen."

"I've got to say this has been an incredible situation," Marshall said. "I know Vonda was completely blown away to learn of Kate's involvement."

"I was," Vonda said. "We've been in the same book club for a good number of years now. We've become a tight group of friends. Kate is fun and funny and such a kind person. It's hard to imagine her being capable of doing something like this. She told me, and it's obviously true, she's spent years trying to live in such a way as to make up for what she did so many years ago.

I was really angry with her at first, for the pain her actions have caused my friends. The Alans are wonderful people. Seeing her in jail and hearing how broken she was moved me more than I had expected it to. And, oh my goodness, what are the chances that I would know both the couple whose baby was taken and the person who took their baby. How does that even happen?

"It really is a bit of a stretch," Leanza said, pointing out that Kate was originally from North Carolina. She only took the temporary job in Austin Texas for access to Jeremy and Marissa's baby.

The three friends realized there were some pretty huge coincidences in all of what followed; Kate deciding to give the child to the Delaney Children's Home instead of selling her as Thatcher wanted, Kate's cousin being in Austin on vacation at that precise time, him believing the child's life was in danger and he and his wife's agreeing to drive the baby eighteen hours across the country to deliver her secretly and safely in the dead of night.

Kate being from North Carolina and Amber's friend since elementary school explained how she knew of the Children's Home, of course.

While enjoying the delicious meal Vonda had prepared, they continued to examine the strange circumstances involved in Leanza's investigation. What about the Alans choosing a small town in South Carolina just across the North Carolina border as their home? That was just the result of Marissa's love for the ocean and two trips they had taken to the Myrtle Beach area. After three years with no progress in finding their missing baby, grief had begun to rule their lives. They moved simply because they wanted a new start.

The final coincidence being that their move took them only two small towns away from the children's home their stolen baby had been taken to.

It was all pretty incredible, really.

They chatted more about the case as they cleaned the kitchen and dining areas. Vonda started the dishwasher and they each took a piece of Leanza Butterfinger poke cake to enjoy in the living room as they continued their visit.

"This is absolutely delicious," Vonda said, licking her fork to get every bit of whipped cream.

"It's very rich," Marshall said, wondering if he was going to regret having such a large piece but not sure he could resist eating every bite.

"Do you have any ideas on how to go about locating the Alans' daughter?" Marshall asked.

"Nothing concrete, yet," Leanza replied. "Since Kate didn't go through the channels Thatcher told her to there's no point in following up in that direction. I have looked into the children's home she was basically smuggled into but it closed down years ago. At this point I have no idea where the adoption records for that particular home may have been kept, if they even were. According to Kate's story there probably are no records anyway.

If the house mother found a way to have records compiled, they might be in the county courthouse but they may be sealed. There is a legal process involved in getting records opened. Jeremy will have to get into that. Open adoptions began to be a thing in the 1970's but it was a slow process. It seems safe to assume this wasn't an open adoption. I'm not sure how long North Carolina adoption records were kept prior to 2005 when it became policy that they be kept for one hundred years. Without knowing what kind of records there were in this case that seems the best place to start in trying to find her.

You should've seen Jeremy and Marissa when I told them we now know for certain their daughter was still alive at around three to four years old. I've never seen relief more clearly displayed on someone's face than on theirs.

They both admitted that as much as they've held onto that hope, they've often expected to get a call to the opposite effect.

Can you imagine what it's going to be like if those two are actually reconciled with their daughter?

CHAPTER 59

Lisa backed out of the room to give Doctor Jaxson and his sister some privacy. She walked across the landing and looked at the other bedroom. It was a mirror image to the first one. She assumed since the other room was the girl's bedroom that this one had been the boys. The blue walls bore that out.

Coming back into the landing she met Doctor Jaxson and Jovie. Their faces were a little red and tear stained but both were smiling.

"I wasn't sure I should come over here when I saw you two ladies wandering around on the property earlier, Lisa. But let me tell you I am so glad I did," Doctor Jaxson said, his face beaming.

"I am, too," Jovie said.

"I guess you figured out what was going on in there?" he asked.

"I think so," Lisa answered. "Perhaps you two can fill in the details. All I've done is piece together that both of you must've lived here as children. You were obviously close and lost contact once you were adopted," she was looking at Jovie as she finished talking.

"That's it in a nutshell. We need to fill each other in on the details, too, though," Jaxson replied.

"That's exactly right," Jovie said. "Are you in a hurry, Lisa? I don't want to keep you, but Jaxson and I do have a lot to talk about."

"I'm not. But we've just about finished the tour of the place," Lisa said, turning to head down the stairs as the other two followed. "If you two would rather talk without me I can leave you here but I'll have to lock the house up before I go."

At the bottom of the stairs Jaxson said "I'm fine with you staying." He looked to Jovie for her consent or disagreement.

Jovie nodded in agreement and all three of them went to the kitchen and sat down at the table.

In order to fill them both in with how she had come to be there Jovie described the feeling of familiarity that had come over her during the book club meeting weeks ago. She went on to share the snippets of memory last week when Kate brought them over to talk about the monarchs.

Jaxson was amazed to learn Jovie knew Kate. He asked if Kate realized who Jovie was. In response to her confused expression, he explained that since Kate was his mother's closest friend she was often at the house and had known Jovie as a very small child.

When Jovie asked Jaxson how it was that she had come to live at the Children's Home he seemed to go somewhere else in his mind. After a few seconds he said, "come with me. If it's still here there's something I think you'd like to have."

The two women glanced at each other curiously as they got up from the table and followed Jaxson back through the dining area and across the living room into a large room.

"This was Ma's bedroom," Jaxson said. He crossed the room to some built-in shelving. There were random sized plastic tubs on the various shelves. He stood looking at the tubs thoughtfully.

"I'm not exactly sure which box it's in so let me just look through a couple of them." He reached for a box, sat it on the floor in front of him, removed the lid and crouched down to look through it.

"When I was nine years old Ma told me I would soon be helping with a very important mission. I was to be the 'keeper of the treasure'. She helped me prepare for what I would be doing during the mission. I didn't know it at the time Jovie but the mission was your arrival and you were the treasure."

He put the lid on that tub and reached for another. The entire time he was talking he kept glancing at them as he searched through the tubs.

"The day of the mission finally arrived. I was excited all day. I had never been allowed to stay up until midnight and I had never been out on Spivey Lake so late into the night. Matthew and Steven, the men in our family" he explained, "and I took a canoe over to the beach shore. Those two went to get the treasure while I waited in the canoe. When they returned Matthew handed me the treasure, it was a tiny baby wrapped in a light green baby blanket. You, Jovie. I held you and kept you safe on the way home. Oh, here it is!" Jaxson looked up with a huge smile on his face. He lifted a fairly large zip-lock bag out of the tub, stood up and turned to hand the bag to Jovie.

As Jovie reached out to take it, he said, "Ma called me in here one day when I was about sixteen. She opened this tub and pointed to that bag. 'I want you to know this is here,' she said. 'It's what came to us with Jovie. I've put it into this bag to keep it fresh. If she ever comes back here, and someday she may, she will want to know how we came to have her. We will tell her the story of the night she arrived and give her this bag.'"

"Open it!" Lisa said excitedly looking at Jovie. "See how tiny you were when Doctor Jaxson first met you."

Jovie opened the bag and gently pulled the warm and fuzzy mint-green receiving blanket out. As she opened it something fell onto the floor. It was a pink baby onesie with long sleeves. Beside it lay a tiny pink, blue and white striped newborn hat. Lisa picked up the onesie and Jovie picked up the hat.

Holding the onesie up for the other two to see Lisa said, "oh, look, just look at how tiny you were!"

Jaxson took the blanket from her and opened it. He was telling her how the blanket was wrapped tightly around her with just her little face showing through a little opening.

Jovie was running her fingers over the tiny hat in her hand. This was a lot to take in and she was feeling quite overcome with wonder and emotion.

Jaxson continued telling the story of the night she arrived. He told how they all gathered in the living room and sat staring into the baby's face.

"After we told Ma how smoothly everything had gone. Ma asked us to tell her your name.'"

Jovie realized Jaxson suddenly seemed uncomfortable.

"What?" she asked. When he didn't answer, she asked more pointedly, "What is it?"

His eyes met hers and he said, "I'm sorry. I just realized this may be hard for you to hear. You didn't have a name. The people who gave you to us didn't tell us your name."

"What? What do you mean?" Jovie felt confused. "What were all of you told about why I was given to your mother's children's home? It seems very strange that a baby would arrive in the middle of the night. As if it were a secret, don't you think?"

"Yes," Jaxson said softly. "I've always thought it odd. Steven had gotten a phone call that a baby's parents were in danger. They didn't want anyone to know they'd just had a baby because the people who wanted to hurt them would probably kill their baby."

"Oh, my!" Lisa said. "That's like something out of a movie. Wow, I wonder who they were and why they were in such danger."

Jovie suddenly felt as if she were an alien being or something equally as strange. She didn't know what she had expected to learn about herself but it certainly had not been anything like this.

"I'm sorry if I'm upsetting you," Jaxson said, now regretting that he'd gotten so carried away in telling her everything. The poor woman looked a little overcome.

Jovie had been turning the tiny baby hat around and around in her fingers as she listened. Noticing it again now Jaxson thought it might be her nervousness.

"It's alright," she said in a somewhat shaky voice. "I don't know what I was expecting to hear but this is the truth of my beginning. It's okay, really. It is a bit surprising to learn I came to you with no name at all, though."

"I know. I was too young to understand at that time but still I could see that Ma and the men were shocked by that. Ma said it was okay though and we would name you ourselves."

"So that's what happened?" Jovie asked, looking at him in wonder.

"Yes. That's what happened. I gave you the name Jovie and Matthew and Steven and I chose Ma's middle name for yours. You became Jovie Lynn Delaney. So now I suppose you are Jovie Lynn Jarvis?"

"That's right," she said, nodding her head. Being reminded of who she was felt reassuring and she smiled.

"Well, I'd better fold this blanket back up so we can see if we can get it back into that bag for you," Jaxson said as he started trying to fold it.

Lisa offered to help him. She then laid the onesie onto the built-in shelf and took two corners of the blanket.

As she stood watching them Jovie realized she was absentmindedly rubbing her fingers against something inside the baby hat. She lifted it up and looked at it but saw nothing from the outside. Turning it inside out she saw a long and narrow bit of threading toward the very top of the little hat.

"What's this?" she asked quietly but loudly enough that the others heard her.

Taking the blanket from Jaxson Lisa reached for the onesie intending to put them back into the bag.

Jaxson stepped over to Jovie and said, "What?"

"I'm not sure," she said, lifting the hat for both of them to see more closely. "Oh, it appears to be embroidery. What does it say?"

"Looking closely at the lettering Jaxson read aloud, "Amy Lynn Alan."

CHAPTER 60

Jovie debated all morning about whether or not to attend today's book club meeting. She was still reeling from everything that had taken place yesterday and just didn't know if she was up to frivolous socializing.

On the other hand, she had a lot of respect for Deb and the other ladies in the group. They were her friends and with their life experiences they might be perfect for her to talk with about what was happening in her life.

She just felt very unsteady and unsure of where to turn next.

In all her life up to this point Jovie had never even considered seeking information about her birth parents but that was changing fast. Seeing the house, meeting Jaxson and hearing the circumstances of her arrival at the children's home had been a lot to take in. But she now felt as if that house and Jaxson were a part of her.

All of this had started at the book club meeting at Spivey Lake as feelings of familiarity took hold of her. Those feelings never subsided. Being on the grounds of the children's home at the next month's meeting brought flashes of memories to her mind. Going through the house yesterday and reconciling with Jaxson opened a floodgate of emotions and more memories.

What she was too young to remember Jaxson told her about. It was incredible to imagine arriving there at only a few days old, having no name and her life possibly being in danger. Was that true? If so, what had happened to her birth parents and why?

Hearing Jaxson talk about how he and the others in the family loved and protected her during the first four years of her life was really something. Finding her again was obviously having a profound effect on Jaxson.

Without even knowing him Jovie trusted him. They shared a strong connection and as crazy as it seemed she was already thinking of him as her big brother.

Still, none of the rest compared with learning that her birth name was Amy Lynn Alan. She and Jaxson were both amazed over her middle name being Lynn both at birth and when named at the children's home. What are the chances of something like that happening?

With all of this circulating through her thoughts she'd gotten very little sleep the night before. In spite of that, and everything else, she decided to go to the book club meeting. She was uncertain whether or not she would share what was going on once she was there. Time would tell.

Vonda had arranged a variety of coffee mugs on her kitchen counter next to two full coffee pots, one regular and one decaffeinated. The selected book featured a coffee-drinking main character solving a mysterious death in her favorite coffee shop. This begged a coffee theme for today's meeting. There was a good variety of sweeteners, creamers and syrups to flavor the coffee and whipped cream to top it off. Along with the scones and muffins Vonda had made, it was a nice, and tasty, display.

As soon as everyone arrived, they were invited to get refreshments and gather in the living room to begin their book discussion.

As Jovie sat listening, she was glad she'd decided to come. It was good for her to have this distraction and she grew more and more relaxed as the meeting progressed. Looking around the room she realized Kate was missing. There would have been two missing if she hadn't come. Despite the meetings being preset for the second Thursday each month it wasn't unusual for someone to miss occasionally.

After discussing the book, the ladies began to talk about other things going on in their lives. It wasn't long before Jovie decided to share what she was going through. Assuming that not all of these ladies knew she had been adopted she shared that information first. She then went into how she'd felt the day the meeting was held at Spivey Lake, reminding them that she'd had a strong sense of déjà vu'. Most of them remembered that.

As Jovie continued to share, their expressions told her they were fascinated with her tale. It felt good for her to be talking it out. She was thankful she had decided to come today.

After sharing everything that had happened the day before Jovie talked about how it was making her feel. She shared many of the thoughts she'd struggled with throughout the night.

Unlike everyone else, Vonda knew Kate had been arrested for kidnapping a baby and extradited to Texas. The case had not been made public in North Carolina yet. If it had hit the media in Texas, she wouldn't have heard about it. As she sat listening to Jovie's fascinating story Vonda began to suspect an even more unbelievable story was about to unfold in the young woman's life.

Could Jovie be the baby Kate had taken from the hospital? Her mind told her that wasn't possible. It was crazy enough that Vonda knew both the couple whose baby had been taken and the woman who had taken that baby. It was totally improbable she also knew the young woman that baby had grown up to be. It seemed absolutely impossible!

Vonda fought to keep her mind from going into overdrive, getting ahead of the story and making assumptions that weren't true. The last thing she wanted was to complicate Jovie's life by assuming these two situations tied in with each other if they didn't.

Jovie was now telling them about the man who joined her and the Realtor when she looked at the old children's home. He showed her the baby items his mother saved from the night Jovie came to the children's home. She said she was holding a newborn baby hat in her hands when she felt something on the inside of it.

"When I turned that little hat inside-out I saw there was something embroidered inside the top of it. It was a name. Ladies, I now know my birth name. It's Amy Lynn Alan."

Vonda felt as though her heart had skipped a few beats. Oh, my heavens, she thought. This *is* Jeremy and Marissa's daughter!

"The thing is," Jovie continued. "I don't even know what to do with this information. I guess that's why I'm telling you about it. I just found this out yesterday. I haven't even told my parents. I was so overwhelmed when I got home last evening. I just felt like I needed to process the information myself before getting my parents and my brother involved. To be honest, I wasn't sure about coming here today but I'm glad I did.

I can't thank you all enough for letting me talk about this. I know you're all trustworthy. You are my friends. I know you won't go talking about this to other people, this is my story to share and you understand that. Thank you for being here for me."

Each lady was shaking her head in agreement, some leaned forward, those closest touched her hands in assurance. Each person's body language expressed their care and support.

"I know you probably don't, but do any of you have any idea where I should go with this name? I'm thinking maybe the police station has a system that could search for a missing child by that name during the year of my birth. Maybe that would reveal the parent's names? Is that where I should go, do you think?"

Vonda spoke up before anyone else could, "I think I might be able to help you, Jovie. You may remember me mentioning my friend who is visiting from Virginia right now. She's actually an advocate for missing people. I'm sure she will know what you need to do. Would you like me to talk with her? Better yet, would you like to come over and meet her and talk with her yourself?"

"Oh, that would be wonderful," Jovie said. "I can't thank you enough Vonda. I haven't had any idea what to do with this information."

The ladies were all nodding in agreement. As they said it to her, Jovie certainly couldn't dispute her life being as interesting, if not more interesting, than the book they had just finished discussing.

Jovie thanked them again for being there for her and assured them she would fill them in on whatever she learned going forward.

Deb and Jovie stayed a while after everyone else left. As usual, Jovie planned to stay and visit her parents when Deb dropped her off at their place to get her car. Today her plan was to tell them everything that had unfolded the day before. Vonda and Deb encouraged her to stick with that plan. Deb even offered to stay with her for moral support. Vonda promised to call Jovie and tell her what Leanza thought her next steps should be.

As soon as the two women left Vonda let out the breath she felt as though she had been holding. While cleaning the dishes and putting the left-over refreshments away, she made plans on how to fill Leanza in when she returned to the house in a few hours.

Lilly had walked to the front door with Vonda as she'd seen her guests out and was just moseying back into the kitchen. Vonda took one look at her and said, 'This is unbelievable! Lilly, do you realize what's about to happen?"

Picking Lilly up, Vonda hugged her and said, "Jeremy and Marissa are about to learn that the lovely young woman I know and have grown to love is their missing daughter. I am so happy for all of them!"

Lilly purred contentedly in Vonda's arms as Vonda began to pray for Jovie and her parents, all four of them; Owen and Myla Jarvis and Jeremy and Marissa Alan.

CHAPTER 61

When Leanza came home a few hours later, she found Vonda waiting to talk with her.

As Vonda finished sharing Jovie's story Leanza understood her eagerness. Like Vonda, Leanza was amazed to realize Vonda knew all the people involved in this crazy situation. The two women put their heads together to come up with a plan.

First, Vonda called Jovie and offered to be at the Mount Tabor Police Station to introduce her to Leanza the next day. Jovie accepted the offer. Jovie mentioned the data of missing persons information possibly being used in the search for her birth parents. Vonda responded once Leanza knew who her birth parents were she would invite them to meet Jovie; she speculated that could happen as early as tomorrow so Jovie may want to come prepared, just in case.

Once Jovie agreed the two moved on to the second part of their plan. Leanza made a call to Jeremy and Marissa telling them she had very strong reasons to believe their daughter had been found. In response to their questions, she said it appeared she had been adopted by a very nice family and given a good life. Leanza explained she was still in the process of confirming everything. Once everything had been verified, they may actually get to meet their now adult daughter the next day at the police station. Amid their relief and excitement Leanza set the time for them to arrive as one hour after the time Vonda had set with Jovie.

The phone calls done they began supper preparations as usual. Marshall arrived and they filled him in. The three went about enjoying the evening together as was their daily habit. A few hours later Marshall said his goodbyes and headed home.

Going into their own bedrooms, the ladies each were excited for what the next day would hold. Both women were thinking of the many prayers about to be answered as they drifted off to sleep a short time later.

Where Deb would normally have just dropped Jovie off at her parents after the book club meeting, she went inside with her. Jovie told them what happened when she went to see the property on Spivey Lake the day before.

The only thing she didn't share was that she had now learned her birth name. When Jovie walked outside with Deb to thank her for staying Deb asked Jovie why she didn't share that. Jovie didn't have a clear answer. She guessed it was because her birth last name was Alan. There was a family at church with that last name. The chances of that couple being her birth parents was so slim that Jovie didn't want her parents to even go there. It just seemed better to wait and see what happened. Deb agreed that made sense. The two women hugged and Deb left. Jovie visited with her parents a while longer before going home.

After hanging up from Vonda's call that evening Jovie called her parents.

"Hello," Myla Jarvis said into the phone.

"Hey, mom, is dad close by?" Jovie asked immediately.

Once both of her parents were on the call Jovie told them about her appointment at the Mount Tabor Police Department the next day. She explained she might not learn anything but if they wanted to be there, she would like them to, just in case. Of course, they agreed to meet her there.

The next day Jovie, Owen and Myla Jarvis arrived at the police station and introductions were made. Jovie introduced Vonda to her parents. Then Vonda introduced each of the Jarvis family to Leanza. Leanza then led them all to her temporary office.

Thinking it best to start at the beginning Leanza explained that she had recently been approached by friends of hers. The couple wanted to enlist her help in a final effort to find the baby who had disappeared from the hospital nursery two days after birth almost twenty-five years ago. The man was a police detective in Austin Texas when the child went missing.

Vonda shared that she and Leanza met the year before when Leanza rented a condo in Vonda's neighborhood. She was in the area to help the FBI solve a missing persons case in Myrtle Beach.

216

Leanza picked the story back up at that point, telling them her current investigation had led to a traveling nurse living in this area. Naturally, she took the opportunity to visit Vonda. When confronted the woman confessed to kidnapping the baby and was arrested.

Vonda gently broke the news to Jovie that their book club friend, Kate, was that woman. Jovie was shocked to learn Kate was now facing kidnapping charges in Texas.

At this point, Leanza began to point out the similarities in the case she had come here to work on and Jovie's backstory. Jovie, Owen and Myla had already began making the connection. A baby was kidnapped at only two days old near the same time Jovie, only a few days after her birth showed up at the Delaney Home for Children.

"So, what you're saying is that I'm the baby who was taken from that hospital in Austin, Texas?" Jovie asked.

"That's what I'm saying," Leanza answered.

Myla reached out to take her daughter's hand. With concern in his eyes Owen studied both of these women he so deeply loved.

Jovie sat silently looking down at the intertwined hands resting on her leg. A few seconds passed before Jovie raised her head, looked at Leanza and said, "Let me get this straight. What you're telling me is that I was kidnapped from my birth parents at a hospital in Texas at only two days old. I was immediately brought to the town of Mount Tabor in North Carolina where I was secretly given to a children's home.

That doesn't make sense. Why? Why would anyone do that?"

CHAPTER 62

"That's the exact question we asked Kate when she confessed," Vonda said. "You're absolutely right, Jovie, what happened to you makes no sense," she turned toward Leanza in expectation.

"You were taken in an act of revenge. Your birth father was, at that time, an excellent police detective who spent years working diligently to discover who was behind a long line of abductions and brutal attacks. Over time the unknown suspects' crimes advanced to vicious killings.

It was your father that discovered who he was, tracked him, arrested him and gathered evidence for a conviction. The man is named Thatcher Foreman and he's currently serving a life sentence. Wanting nothing more than for the man who put him behind bars to suffer, Thatcher found a way to make that happen. He made the detective's firstborn child disappear."

"Incredible," Owen Jarvis said, shaking his head sadly. "This is unbelievable."

"Yes, it is," Leanza said. "But it's true. Thatcher had a far worse fate in mind for you, Jovie. but Kate couldn't do it. Her best friend, Amber Delaney ran a home for children. Knowing you would be loved and cared for Kate found a way to get you there without Amber knowing she was behind it. The good news now is that we have found your birth parents. If you want to meet them today, we can make that happen."

"I can't imagine what they've been through all these years not knowing what happened to their child," Myla said. Turning to look at her daughter, she added, "You do want to meet them, don't you?"

Jovie looked from one to the other of these two wonderful people who were her parents. They had given her a secure and happy childhood, teaching her right from wrong, encouraging her to have faith in God. They supported her dreams and helped her achieve her goals. Even now, when she was a grown woman, they were still here, offering their love and support. No one would ever take their place in her life. Looking at them now Jovie's heart was full of love. She could not be more thankful for the life she had as Jovie Lynn Jarvis but, yes, her mother was right. She did want to meet these people.

Myla leaned in to look her daughter in the eyes. "We are not upset that you're about to meet your birth parents, Jovie. They've been through a terrible loss at no fault of their own. It is well past time they have you in their lives."

"That's right," Owen said, taking a few steps over to where Jovie and her mother were sitting. "We are here for you and the three of us are going to be there for them now."

"You two are the most wonderful people. I love you so much," Jovie said as the three of them hugged.

When they broke apart, Jovie turned to Leanza and said, "Okay. Yes, I would very much like to meet my birth parents. What's more, I want everyone in this room to meet them along with me, can that be done?"

"Absolutely," Leanza answered. "This office isn't very big and it's already pretty full. I need you all to come with me. I'll put you in the visiting room until we can make that happen."

Everyone followed Leanza down a long hallway and into a room with a table and chairs in the center of the room and chairs along two walls.

"There are plenty of chairs here so just have a seat. I'm going to see if the Alans have arrived yet. I won't be gone long," Leanza said.

After Leanza left the room Myla turned to Jovie and asked, "Did she say the Alans? I wonder where they're coming from. If they still live in Texas, they've come a very long way. Do you think they could be related to the Alans we go to church with, Jeremy and Marissa?"

Jovie said, "yes, that's what she said but I'm sure there are many people with that last name. The chances they would be related are probably pretty slim. I don't see why we can't ask them though."

Vonda simply could not believe what she was hearing. She had no idea the Alans went to the same church as the Jarvis family. This situation just kept getting more and more interesting.

Meanwhile, the Alans were due to arrive in ten minutes. Leanza had just gotten to the front entrance when the door opened and the couple stepped inside. Hurrying forward she greeted them and led them to the office the others had just vacated. She motioned for them to sit down and took the seat across from them.

"Is she here?" Marissa asked softly.

"Yes, she's here," Leanza said as Jeremy reached over and took his wife's hand.

"Are you certain this person is our daughter?" Jeremy asked. Leanza got the distinct impression he was trying to protect his wife from further disappointment and pain. She could certainly understand that.

"I am," Leanza answered seeing the fear in their faces change to hope

"I know this is an incredible day for you two," she said. "Still, it can be a bit overwhelming. You've been through so much for so many years. As I mentioned on the phone, I believe you'll be happy with the way your daughter was raised. Her adoptive family is very loving. They're good people with faith similar to your own. You're going to get to meet them. Her adoptive parents are here with her not because she's afraid or doesn't want to meet you though. They are here to support her and they all are happy to be meeting you. I've explained what happened and why she was taken. All of them are aware of what you've been through and they're hearts go out to you. Are you ready to do this?"

The two of them looked at each other and nodded their heads.

"Alright, let's do it," Leanza said as they stood up to follow her. They were almost to the visitor's room when Marissa asked, "What's her name? I want to know what to call her when we meet."

"Her name is Jovie," Leanza answered.

"Jovie," Marissa repeated. "That's very unique."

"Yes, it is," Jeremy agreed.

Arriving at the visiting room Leanza opened the door and, after a quick knock, stepped into the room with the Alans close behind her.

As soon as she saw Jovie, Leanza turned toward her to make the introductions. Instead, she saw recognition register on the young woman's face. Confused she followed Jovie's gaze to Jeremy and Marissa.

"JJ?" Jeremy asked, with a look of bewilderment. Marissa turned to Jeremy meeting his quizzical look with her own as Jovie stared at them in disbelief.

"Jeremy?" Owen said standing up from where he'd been seated along the wall.

Leanza was totally confused. Was it possible these people already knew each other?

CHAPTER 63

It was as if none of them had even heard Owen speaking.

Jeremy, Marissa and Jovie stood looking from one to the other almost as if they were all in shock. They were definitely in disbelief.

It was Marissa who finally spoke.

"JJ? What's happening?" Slowly turning toward Leanza, she queried, "You said our daughter's name was Jovie."

"It is," Myla said, now standing next to her husband slightly back from the other three. Marissa and Jeremy looked at her.

"Her name is Jovie Jarvis – JJ. Our son Tyler Jarvis was nicknamed TJ very early on. It didn't take him long to start calling Jovie JJ. It just stuck."

Coming out of a fog Jovie said, "I went by JJ all through school and at church, basically my entire childhood and as you know, I'm 'Coach JJ'. In my adult life, when I started college and now in my job as a Social Worker - I am Jovie.

"So, she really is our missing daughter?" Jeremy asked, addressing Leanza again.

"Yes, she is. I'm sorry for the confusion. I had no idea all of you already knew each other."

Being too taken aback to believe it Marissa said, "I'm sorry. I just don't understand how this can be."

She turned to Myla and Owen, "she's adopted? You adopted her?"

"Yes, just before she was four."

"I'm sorry," Marissa said, looking directly at Jovie. "It's not that I don't want you to be our daughter, JJ. I'm just having trouble taking it in since we were expecting a complete stranger. Of course, we will be thrilled if you are really our lost little girl. I'm just having trouble believing it."

Jovie smiled at Marissa and said, "I understand. This is crazy. I don't know how else to say it. It's crazy."

She gave a shaky little laugh.

Jeremy found himself staring at the dimple in JJ's left cheek. How many times had he looked at it and found himself reminded of Marissa.

Before he could put his thoughts into words JJ said in a voice that was just short of a shout, "Oh, wait!! I know. I know exactly what we need."

She rushed over to the table where she had been sitting while waiting for her birth parents to arrive. She unzipped the large purse she'd carried in with her and pulled out a good-sized zip-lock bag. After tossing a fuzzy green baby blanket onto the table she grabbed the other items and hurried back to Marissa and Jeremy. Do you recognize these baby clothes? My brother Jaxson gave me these. I was wearing them the night I came to live with him at the children's home."

Marissa looked in passing at the onesie before reaching for the newborn baby hat. Taking it from Jovie's hand she immediately turned it inside-out.

"Look," she said, holding the hat up in front of her husband's face. "It's my embroidery of her name."

Tears streamed from her eyes as she turned toward Jovie, reached out and laid her hand on Jovie's cheek, "Amy Lynn," she said. Turning toward her husband she now said, "Jeremy, she's Amy Lynn."

Crying now, she opened her arms and Jovie went into them. "You're my baby girl, JJ, you really are!" Marissa said as Jeremy stepped forward wrapping them both in his embrace. Tears were streaming down their faces. Everyone watching had tears in their eyes.

Owen put his arm around Myla and pulled her against him as they stood watching their daughter's reunion with her birth parents; this couple they knew, respected and cared deeply for.

A silent observer to all that was taking place, Vonda whispered ever so softly, "Thank you, Lord."

Jeremy, Marissa and Jovie went from hugging to looking into each other's faces and back to hugging. They were crying and then laughing. This went on for several minutes. Backing out of a group hug one more time Jeremy turned to Myla and Owen and said, 'get in here you two! This is a family moment."

Wiping their tears away the couple rushed to join their daughter and their friends in a tight hug.

A few moments later the group broke up and Jeremy reached out to shake Owen's hand, "I am so thankful God placed her in your home, Owen. Marissa and I have talked often through the years about what a wonderful couple you and Myla are. We've often admired your family. I can't think of anyone I could have trusted with my own daughter more than you two."

Marissa reached out and hugged Myla, "That's exactly right. What a blessing that our daughter became yours."

CHAPTER 64

The women cheered as Marshall made it to first base after hitting a ground ball. It was the sixth inning and the Old Timers had the upper hand over the Middle Agers and were hoping to take the game. It felt good to be doing something normal after the week they'd all had.

Three days ago, instead of meeting their birth daughter, Jeremy and Marissa discovered they'd known her and her adoptive family for most of her life. Jovie was actually JJ who was actually Amy Lynn Alan. What a crazy situation! The women were still discussing the ins and outs of it all.

"When I told her Jovie was the baby she kidnapped, Kate admitted she'd begun to suspect as much," Leanza said. "She admitted she was thrown when Deb brought Jovie to book club that first time. Jovie is such a unique name that Kate's first thought was to wonder if they could possibly be one and the same. But nothing about Jovie supported that until the meeting at Spivey Lake when she said everything felt familiar. Seeing her reaction to the lake brought everything back to Kate's mind. Her deeply buried guilt feelings began to resurface in the form of unsettling dreams. When she took some of you ladies to the Delaney Home for Children property and Jovie asked what the place used to be Kate was almost certain Jovie was the baby she'd kidnapped.

Over the following weeks the mere possibility of Jovie being the baby made her think about turning herself in. Her guilt was playing against her fear of the consequences almost constantly. She really believes, and I'm inclined to agree, that if she had been further along in that process, if she'd just had a bit more time before I brought her in for questioning, she would've confessed immediately."

"That's incredible," Vonda said when Leanza finished speaking. "Can you imagine realizing the baby you kidnapped is someone you now know and they have no idea what happened or that you were involved?"

"Let's go Mason!" Stacey's shout caused Vonda to realize her future brother-in-law had just stepped up to home plate. The three women shouted and whistled their support when he got a solid hit and made it to third base bringing two other men home.

"They're really playing a good game tonight," Leanza said, clapping along with Vonda, Stacey and the other spectators. "I love this! We never get to the ball field at home. Chrystian and I are going to have to change that when I get back."

"I'm sure there are city leagues you two can get involved with," Vonda said.

"I still haven't gotten over the fact that you knew everyone involved in this entire kidnapping/adoption scenario," Stacey said to Vonda.

"I know," Vonda agreed. "I would seriously like to know what the chances of that happening really are."

"I know you would, but I don't think we ever will. Suffice it to say it's extremely rare," Leanza assured.

Despite the fight the Middle Agers put up the Old Timers took the game and wow, were they excited!

Stacey joked it was too bad the concession stand wasn't open on Thursday evenings. "We could've treated them to free ice cream bars like we do the boys when their team wins," she said, laughing as Mason came over to join her.

After everyone else had cleared out Vonda and Leanza helped Marshall gather up the equipment and get it locked up. He gave them both a hug and insisted he was bringing supper to the house for them the next evening. The two women had been cooking some very nice meals together since Leanza's arrival and Marshall wanted to treat them for a change. After saying goodnight, he headed home.

On the walk home they picked up where they'd left off in conversation earlier.

"I'm just so thankful so much good is coming from this entire situation," Vonda said. "Talk about answered prayers! They're all over the place."

"They really are," Leanza agreed with a light laugh. "I mean Jovie's entire childhood is answered prayers. Not only were Jeremy and Marissa's entire family praying all these years but so were Dr. Jaxson and the other men in Ms. Amber's household. That's a lot of praying over one little girl."

"God could not have answered all those prayers any better. For Jovie to be chosen and adopted by Owen and Myla Jarvis was awesome in and of itself. In their household she gained a big brother who was just as involved and loving as Jaxson had been. She and her brother TJ are as close as siblings get. TJ says the look he saw on Jaxson's face when he hugged Jovie goodbye inspired him to love and protect his new sister as Jaxson had done before him. TJ's only two years younger than Jaxson. He was ten when they took Jovie home, old enough to understand the connection he saw between those to, remember it and live by it.

"It's amazing what children are capable of comprehending," Vonda said.

"What's amazing is how God provided everything the people who loved her were praying for," Leanza said.

"And now he's actually brought her back into a relationship with her big brother, Dr. Jaxson and her birth parents, who not only live in the same area but go to church with her adopting family. Don't forget that Jovie actually coached her twin sisters in gymnastics and has been to her birth family's house for celebration pizza parties! I mean, really? Does it get any better than this?"

"I've seen a lot of things as a missing person's advocate," Leanza said. "So, to answer that question; no, I honestly don't think it gets any better than this!"

CHAPTER 65

Jeremy and Marissa's oldest son, Ryan, loved his career with the Fire Department and it was going very well. His parents were happy for him and certainly proud of him and his achievements.

If Ryan wasn't working a twenty-four-hour shift he was usually at church on Sundays. To Marissa's delight he had never gotten out of the habit of coming back home for lunch with the family after Sunday morning church service.

Understandably so, with the girls still being in college they didn't make it home most weekends. Wanting to be sure everyone was there for Easter, Marissa put the word out that she was cooking a large feast this coming Sunday. They would go to church as a family and enjoy lunch together afterward.

Marissa was an excellent cook and enjoyed nothing more than family gatherings. She decorated the table and completed most of the meal preparations on Saturday.

When Ellie asked why there were so many places set, Marissa shared that the Jarvis family would be joining them for lunch after church. They hadn't seen JJ in quite a while so Ellie, Marie and Aiden were happy to hear it. Marissa smiled at her husband who winked at her from across the room. It was fun sharing such an important secret.

The next morning Marissa set the crock pots with the mashed potatoes and corn onto the kitchen counter and turned them on high. She put the ham in to bake right before the family headed to church. The only thing left to do upon their return was to bake the rolls.

The whole day felt like a celebration. The music was wonderful and it seemed especially fitting that the sermon was about new life. Everyone enjoyed the service.

Owen Jarvis pulled into the driveway behind Jeremy and everyone got out of their vehicles. The two families went into the house together. While their children talked with the Jarvis family Jeremy helped Marissa get the ham out of the oven. She popped the rolls in to bake and they went about slicing the ham and putting it onto a large platter. Once everything was lined up on the counter Marissa asked everyone to gather at the dining room table and take their seats. She explained that they were eating smorgasbord style today. After the prayer they would each take their plates to the counter and help themselves.

Jeremy asked their oldest son, Ryan if he would pray before the meal. As the family always did, everyone joined hands around the table and they each bowed their heads.

"Thank you, God, for this day," Ryan's strong voice filled the room. "Thank you, for what Good Friday and Easter Sunday represent since they are the basis of our faith. Thank you that Jesus not only laid down His life for us but through your power He rose again. He is your promise and our example. Through our faith we have new life here on earth and will spend eternity with you when this life is over. That's what we celebrate today, Lord, and we are grateful.

And now, as I so often do, I think of my older sister, Amy Lynn, mom and dad's first child. Thank you, Father, that though we don't see her and we don't know where she is, you do. Please be with her, protect her and bless her with love and happiness until that day when we are all together.

Thank you for our friends, the Jarvis family who have joined us today. Thank you for mom and all this delicious food she's cooked for us to enjoy.

We love you, Lord, and we thank you for every blessing. Amen"

"What a wonderful prayer," JJ said looking across the table to meet Ryan's eyes as she reached up to wipe her tears.

A hush had settled over the room during the prayer and it wasn't lifting. The Alan children noticed that their parents and the entire Jarvis family all had tears in their eyes. And yet they were smiling.

"What's going on?" Marie asked, looking from one to the other.

"Yeah, what gives?" Ellie asked just a second before Aiden commented, "You all look like you're in on something we're not."

"That's exactly right, son," Jeremy said. "We have some wonderful news to tell you."

"You do?" Ellie asked with a soft laugh. "Oh! I love surprises, y'all know I do! What's going on?"

Looking around the table and seeing all their smiling faces Marie said, "Hey, this is something big, isn't it? You all look so happy."

"Come on!" Aiden chimed in.

Looking directly at Ryan, Aiden asked, "Do you know?"

Ryan smiled but was shaking his head slightly from side to side while answering, "I don't know. We seem to be the only ones in the dark here so somebody spill it."

"I will," JJ said looking at her birth parents questioningly.

"Yes, go ahead," Jeremy and Marissa said in unison.

"I loved that prayer you prayed for your sister just now, Ryan," she said with a huge smile on her face. "My family and I have only just learned about your sister, Amy Lynn. It's kind of funny because even though we've all known each other and gone to church together for so long you're about to learn something you don't know about me, too. I was adopted into this family when I was almost four years old. It seems like kind of a fun coincidence to me."

As they nodded their heads in agreement, she continued, "Only it's not a coincidence, very few things are. But this definitely isn't. This was actually God's plan."

Glancing quickly at her parents, all of them, JJ grinned and said, "Okay, I'm just going to come right out and say it. Thank you, Ryan, for praying for me today. In fact, I want to thank everyone in your family for all the prayers you've been praying for me my entire life."

Knowing what she was talking about the adults looked closely at the Alan children's faces as they waited for understanding to register.

Looking at each other they looked slightly confused.

JJ went on, "You all know me as JJ – which is short for Jovie Jarvis. But the name I was given by my birth parents is Amy Lynn Alan."

Understanding came into their eyes immediately as Jovie quickly added, "That's right, you're getting it now! I am Amy Lynn Alan, your sister.

CHAPTER 66

Jaxson caught a glimpse of the scene on his back deck as he turned from the refrigerator to sit the sweet tea onto the table. He simply could not keep from smiling.

His little sister Jovie was here!

At this very moment she and Steven were getting reacquainted. Matthew, Ruby and the kids were due to arrive any time. The family that adopted her, as well as her birth parents and their other children, were all here.

Almost overnight his sister had gone from having one brother; him - from many years ago, to four brothers in total and twin sisters. Not to mention going from one set of parents to two and adding a whole slew of other family and friends.

This is the biggest crowd I've ever had for a cook-out, Jaxson thought as he headed out the back door with the sweet tea, ice bucket and cups.

Within the past hour Jaxson had met Leanza, the missing person advocate responsible for finding his sister, as well as Jovie's friends, Vonda and Marshall. More new faces and names kept coming for him to remember but he wasn't complaining. Jaxson had always dreamed of having a large family and with Jovie's return that dream was coming true.

"I sure do wish you were here to see this, Ma," Jaxson heard himself say softly. As he walked up to join the group Steven pulled Jovie into the crook of his arm and she smiled up at him. He and Matthew were telling her about her life in the Delaney Home for Children and how much she'd been missed after her adoption.

"I simply cannot tell you how good it is to see you again," Steven said. "If I'm honest, I wasn't sure we ever would. Talk about answered prayers!

But this guy right here never lost faith, and man did he miss you that first couple of years."

"That's for sure," Matthew added. Both men were looking at Jaxson. "We all did, the place just wasn't the same without you. You were such a bright and happy little girl and look at you now!" Turning to the others he said "Can you believe this? We really can look at her now."

Meeting Jovie's eyes again he said in wonder, "I still can't believe you're really here."

"I can hardly believe it myself," Jaxson said. "I keep thinking this is a dream I'm going to wake up from any second."

"No, it's real!" Jovie said, smiling at her big brother. "I'm back and you're stuck with me so you might as well get used to it."

"You'll never hear me complaining!" he replied.

"Hey everyone!" a shout rang out as almost every head turned in the direction of the sliders between the kitchen and the deck. "I heard there was a party going on so I just came on through the house to find you!" Lisa laughed as she stepped out onto the deck and headed into the group.

"That's exactly why I left the front door unlocked. The more the merrier!" Jaxson answered. "You got here just in time. We're about to get the steaks off the grill and chow down."

"Perfect!" The Realtor answered, spotting Jovie and heading in her direction.

The two women spoke privately for a few moments while everyone else began filling their plates with the various side dishes and lining up at the grill to get their steak.

Jaxson joined Steven at the grill. Being the last to fill their plates Lisa and Jovie walked to a deck table. Lisa sat down but Jovie stood looking over this crowd of friends and family all talking, laughing and eating together. She wasn't sure her heart had ever felt this full before. It was a wonderful feeling.

"No time like the present," she said to herself and raised her voice to call out for everyone's attention.

The chatter and laughter began to die down as heads turned in her direction.

"I'd like to say something, if y'all don't mind."

"We don't mind!" Aiden called out in reply.

"Have at it!" Ryan said with a huge smile on his face.

"Go right ahead!" TJ shouted.

"Well, there you have it! Looks like you've got the floor, sis!" Jaxson added.

Looking from one to the other Jovie laughed and said, "Okay, well, you all heard it, my brothers have spoken! The floor is mine but don't let me keep you from eating while your food is good and hot! There's nothing like a good steak right off the grill."

She went on to thank everyone for coming. Her shout-out of thanks to Jaxson for having such an awesome cook-out was met with whoops, hollers and applause.

"It's been quite an exciting couple of weeks, hasn't it?" Jovie asked and couldn't keep from smiling as heads began to nod in agreement. "I must say, it all feels pretty great to me!" She paused through more whoops and hollers before continuing, "Who would've thought a month ago we would all become this huge wonderful family? I mean, some of you I've known and loved most of my life. The rest of you knew, loved and missed me all during that time. Thank you for remembering and praying for me for so long. It's nothing short of amazing." Jovie was looking at the people she was referring to as she spoke. With great emotion in her voice, she continued, "How blessed I am to have each and every one of you. The ones who have been a constant part of my life; and those of you who were part of my forgotten home."

Looking directly at Jaxson she saw a flicker of sadness and pain cross his face at those words. It left quickly as she continued, "I've recently been regaining my lost memories and every one of them makes me smile. The Delaney Home for Children was a wonderful home to live in. I can only imagine how hard it was for those of you who remember losing Ms. Amber; then to see the home we all shared sitting empty and in such disrepair. That being said, let me be the first to tell you that's all about to change! I've just gotten great news and I want to share it with my family, all of you; my whole family at the same time! Are you ready?"

The sudden shift and promise of good news had people looking at one another questioningly as smiles crept onto their faces.

"Well, are you?" Jovie shouted. She laughed out loud when they began shouting in reply.

"Yes!"

"Let's have it!"

"What is it?"

"Okay, I hope you're ready because here it is! Our good friend, Lisa, who as you all know is the Realtor who's been handling the Delaney Home for Children has just given me the awesome news. My forgotten home is about to become my actual home. The offer I made has been accepted! Not only that, with my social services background and my love for children I'm planning to reopen the Delaney Home for Children."

Jovie was thrilled to see the surprised and happy expressions on the faces of her guests. Some even had tears in their eyes, Jaxson included.

This cookout had just turned into a celebration party!

By the end of the evening Marshall volunteered one of his Davidson Construction's crews to do the renovation work on the house. Steven, Matthew, Jaxson and Ryan were all on board for tackling the repairs to the property. In fact, they couldn't wait to get started.

Those repairs would include replacing the Gazebo since it was most likely beyond repair. It also meant repairs and a new paint job for the footbridge; as well as rebuilding the dock and the wooden platform at the end of it.

It seemed everyone had an idea of how they could help. Jovie's mothers were excited about the landscaping, already planning which flowers would work best around the house. Vonda volunteered to make curtains for the windows. Jovie's fathers promised to provide the food for the work days that were soon to come as long as their wives were willing to cook it.

You want to talk about a family project coming together?

Jovie's new home was looking to be a big one.

CHAPTER 67

The weeks immediately following Jaxson's cookout and Jovie's new home announcement were busy on all fronts.

It didn't take Leanza long to tie up the loose ends on the case. She then spent a few wonderful days having fun with Vonda and their friends before flying home to Virginia.

After locating Thatcher, Jeremy paid him a visit at the prison where he was serving his life sentence. With great satisfaction he looked the man in the eyes and told him his intricate plans to make Jeremy suffer for the rest of his life had ultimately failed.

Not surprisingly, Thatcher hadn't changed at all. He was enraged to learn that while he continued to suffer through his incarceration, Jeremy was enjoying a relationship with his daughter.

Thatcher was shocked to learn the baby he meant great harm to, and her adoptive family, had been a part of Jeremy's life the entire time. He was outraged to learn they'd not only been reunited but were fast becoming one big happy family.

Everything Thatcher had done was now undone and it angered him to the core. Despite the years that had passed he was still blaming Jeremy for his situation. It was clear he would never accept it as the consequences of his own actions.

Jeremy told Thatcher he had been, and would continue, praying for him to turn away from bitterness and hatred to embrace God and His love. If Thatcher was touched by that at all, he didn't show it.

Jeremy later told Marissa that walking out of that prison felt like leaving it all behind; all the hatred and evil Thatcher had spewed onto him but mostly all the pain he'd poured into their lives. It was all finally just part of the past. Leaving that prison was one of the best feelings he had ever experienced. He finally felt totally free!

Marissa said God was simply keeping His promises. He was using even that terrible situation for good in their daughter's life and in their own.

The two of them were still floating on the happiness of learning JJ was their missing daughter. The joy of having her back in their lives overrode everything else. All they wanted was to enjoy their family and friends and the love they all shared from that point forward.

Since Kate had entered a guilty plea her court appearance was set quickly. The judge would be sentencing her based on her plea and the evidence the state would present against her. In her steadfast determination to accept whatever the judge decided she had refused to petition the court for mercy.

Upon Leanza's advice she did submit a statement in regard to her great regret and remorse for her actions. Kate was deeply surprised, shocked and humbled on the day of her court hearing. Vonda, Stacey, Monica, Lynda, Dianne and Deb - her entire book club group was there. She was amazed to see so many of her Carolina friends enter the courtroom.

When Leanza entered, Kate was astounded to see that Jeremy, Marissa and Jovie had come as well. As if that weren't enough, when those Kate had wronged were given an opportunity to speak, Jeremy spoke on behalf of himself, Marissa and Jovie. After acknowledging what Kate's actions had cost them as a family, he talked about her immediate regret and lifelong remorse. He then shared with the judge what he now knew about the life Kate had lived between the time of the kidnapping and her arrest.

Kate was moved to tears as she sat listening to Jeremy petition the court to allow her to serve her sentence in Raleigh, North Carolina. He said doing so would allow those who loved and cared for Kate to visit her. He then shared that each of them wanted to encourage Kate to continue the good life she had been living, once she'd fulfilled the court appointed consequences of her actions.

He reminded the judge that Kate had entered a guilty plea and was fully prepared to face the consequences of her actions. She had repeatedly expressed her willingness to accept whatever the judge ruled as fair punishment.

Jeremy then pointed out the fact that he, Marissa and Jovie were the ones this crime had affected. He emphasized that the three of them wanted grace and mercy for Kate. Since those who were most deeply wounded wanted that it was his hope the judge would oblige.

When Jeremy sat down, he felt satisfied that he'd done everything he could. The outcome was now in the hands of the court and God.

When the final sentencing came through the judge granted Kate's transfer to the North Carolina Prison. Everyone rejoiced! Kate was completely overwhelmed at the love of her friends and those she had victimized. She cried openly in the courtroom causing everyone in attendance to be deeply moved.

Kate was allowed a few moments with her friends before being taken away. There were hugs all around as she thanked each one for being there and they assured her of their love and support. She was told it would only be a matter of days before she was transferred to the North Carolina prison.

Despite the circumstances involved, it ended up being a wonderful day.

CHAPTER 68

The changes made to Jovie's house were unbelievable; especially considering the short amount of time that had passed since she gained possession of the property.

At Jovie's request Jaxson was meeting her at the house. Having spent most of his life at the Delaney Home for Children she wanted him to be part of the home renewal project.

The way she saw it, he knew what worked from the perspective of a child and what needed to be done from the perspective of an adult. Who better to offer input?

Marshall's crew assessed the damage that had been caused by the house sitting empty for so long and pinpointed the unrepairable sections. Jovie went over the specifics of the renovations she envisioned, asking Jaxson for his input throughout. Based on this information Marshall did a sketch of the redesign. After Jaxson and Jovie left, he went over the sketch with his crew. Demolition immediately commenced in which all damaged and unwanted parts of the house were torn out. All the demolished materials were removed.

Materials donated from the Davidson Construction Company were delivered as quickly as the next morning and the renovation began.

Over the following weeks the crew went to work on the inside of the house.

It was exciting to see the beauty of the property restored as the outside crew took to the landscaping. Myla and Marissa, her two moms, did a beautiful job choosing and planting flowers around the grounds together.

The huge undertaking of rebuilding the dock went smoothly, as well as the repair and repainting of the foot bridge leading out to it.

It was going to be a picturesque setting when it was completed.

Just as he had done many years ago, Steven constructed a large picnic table to be placed in the center of the new and larger gazebo. Seeing the Gazebo back in its rightful place to the left front of the house completely washed away Jaxson's mental images of Ma's last hours. Finally, his memories of happier times in the gazebo were able to take their place.

After a good cleaning, a new coat of dark stain and clear coating were applied to the oversized dining room table making it, once again, perfect for the huge kitchen. Steven couldn't suppress a smile as he ran his hands across its smooth top. Memories of Ms. Amber giving him her exact specifications all those years ago warmed his heart. He found himself anxious to see children sitting around the table again. Nothing could honor Ms. Amber's memory more.

Each work day was filled with fun, food and fellowship as new memories were made and the old place came back to life.

Steven, Matthew and Jovie had been working together on a secret project this entire time. Now that it was finished, they were having trouble keeping it from the others. No one could believe they'd managed to keep Jaxson out of the mix.

As usual, Jovie's moms had made a wonderful assortment of food for this final work day. Most everyone was enjoying the fruits of their labor and they were all getting close to being finished with this project. Realizing everyone involved had come out for the day. Jovie, Steven and Matthew decided it was time for the big reveal.

Since he'd stayed busy finishing the repair to the dock Jaxson had not been kept up on the clearing of the grounds around the milkweed garden. In fact, he and the other men were on the dock right then making sure everything was holding up well. This being the perfect time Matthew and Steven brought the surprise out and positioned it. As Jovie headed out front word of what was about to happen spread. Not wanting to miss this, everyone began to make their way around to the rear of the property.

Walking across the footbridge Jovie called out to those the dock.

"So, what's the verdict? Is this dock going to stand the test of time? Not to mention the footfalls of lots of children in the years to come?"

"You bet it is!" Jaxson answered, lifting his arm in a silent invitation to his sister. Jovie walked to his side and he lowered his arm across her shoulder and gave her a tight squeeze.

"It looks and feels great!" Jovie declared. Jumping up and down slightly she added, "It's very secure! Great job guys!"

"Well, listen," Jovie said, motioning for them to join her as she walked toward the house, "we're in need of a few able-bodied men around back. Can I get you fellas to lend a hand?"

"Of course," they were all saying in unison as they followed her lead.

Rounding the edge of the house Jovie was pleased to see that everyone had lined up in front of the surprise and were facing their direction.

"Huh, looks like they're waiting for us. I wonder what's going on," she said with a chuckle in her voice as Jaxson and his buddies began to realize something was up.

"Matthew? Steven? Would you two come on over here and tell us what's up please?"

Stepping forward the two met up with Jovie and Jaxson. Realizing this was a surprise for Jaxson the others fell back a few steps but continued to follow.

Matthew spoke loudly so everyone could hear him. "We wanted to do something special in memory of your mother, Jaxson. Her milkweed garden seemed to be the best spot for it. We sure hope you like what we've done."

Just as they arrived at the milkweed garden the crowd parted to reveal a beautiful high-backed bench with a large Monarch butterfly engraved, painted and sealed into the weather resistant material of the bench. Above the Monarch was the inscription: In loving memory of Ms. Amber Delaney ~ forever in our hearts and memories ~.

It was obvious from the look on Jaxson's face that they could not have chosen a better memorial gift.

CHAPTER 69

While getting ready for the final walk-through meeting with Marshall at her renovated home Jovie thought about her friends. During recent book club meetings, a variety of beautiful locations had been suggested for the wedding. She was frustrated that Vonda had yet to react as if any were a good choice for their special day.

Vonda went with Marshall to his meeting with Jovie. Arriving early, they parked at the back of the house and walked around to the front. Talking it over, the two of them decided to wait for Jovie in the new gazebo. As they sat side by side at the picnic table taking in the view of Spivey Lake they began to talk about their wedding.

Shortly after their engagement and unbeknownst to everyone else they chose a date. They made an agreement not to tell anyone what date they were thinking of until they decided where to have the wedding. Months had now passed with no location agreed upon.

As they sat there alone together Vonda said, "This may seem silly to anyone who doesn't know our story Marshall, but it keeps coming to mind that we should get married where you proposed."

Marshall's head turned toward her in surprise as a smile slowly spread across his face. "Really? You would be alright with that?"

"I would," Vonda answered, meeting his smile with her own. "The ball field is, after all, where all of this began. If I hadn't clumsily lost control of my lunch the day we met, spilling cola all down your arm, this wedding wouldn't be taking place at all."

Marshall laughed out loud.

"Excellent point," he said. "Did I ever tell you why I chose to propose to you on the pitcher's mound?"

"You did not. I'd love to hear it."

"When I got the idea to start the Old Timer's League it was just a way to get the fellows in my age group to be more active. Myself included. I've always enjoyed a good game of baseball and the Parks and Recreation department of Logan agreed to let us use the field at no cost. It seemed a good way to get the guys to be interactive, have a bit of fun and stay physically active.

Obviously, it was a good idea. I mean, look how well it's worked out. While I was trying to do something good for others it didn't take me long to see it was good for me, too, especially after you ran into me," he said, nudging her gently with his elbow.

"I was already enjoying the games but I really enjoyed them once you came along; something about having you calling my name out as you cheered me on from the bleachers. I found myself looking at you before each pitch. Seeing you chatting with those around you, smiling and watching me pitch; well, it just brought me joy. I proposed to you on the pitcher's mound because I wanted to make you feel special in the same spot you had made me feel special so many times.

"Oh, Marshall, I didn't know. Thank you for telling me that." Vonda put her hand through his arm and rested it on his hands that were folded together on the table. Marshall smiled at her.

"Is it settled then?" he asked. "Are we really getting married on the pitcher's mound of the ball field?"

She turned to look him in the face and they both started laughing.

"Let's do it," she said. "Why not? Now we just need to find a meaningful place to have the reception afterward. Concession stand food just doesn't seem the way to go."

"I have an idea," a voice from behind said startling them both.

They turned to find Jovie walking around to the front of them.

"Why don't you have your wedding reception here? I'm sorry but I've been eavesdropping on you two for the past several minutes. I didn't mean to. You didn't hear me coming up behind you and I wasn't around when you two met and got engaged so I got caught up in listening. I didn't know about the ball field. I think it's a wonderful idea for you to have your wedding there. And I don't know about you two, but I think this property would be perfect for your wedding reception, especially since you want something meaningful. What could be more meaningful that a newly renovated home for children? I really hope you'll agree to let me hostess the reception for you."

Not only did they agree to Jovie's offer but when Steven, Matthew and Jaxson made another suggestion they happily agreed to it, as well. Since their wedding reception was going to be very small it seemed like a wonderful idea.

And so it was that advertisements went out by way of newspapers, television and radio announcements and on all social media outlets. Any and all children who spent time during their childhood living in The Delaney Home for Children were not only invited but encouraged to return for a reunion at the home's reopening.

Vonda and Marshall's wedding reception was to be a joint event with the Delaney Home for Children Reopening/Reunion.

With the support of her family and friends Jovie went about making it all happen. She was soon settled into her new home and everything that needed done for her to begin receiving children was completed. Jaxson volunteered his Pediatric services and it was now just a matter of time.

Ever since their engagement Vonda had been condensing her belongings to just what she would take with her. She and Marshall began moving the remaining items into the home they would share in Stokesbury. Vonda was very happy when a young couple with a new baby purchased her house in record time after she listed it for sale. The real estate closing was set for just a few days before the wedding.

Vonda accepted Jovie's invitation for her and Lilly to stay with her for those few days between the house closing and the wedding.

The day before the closing, Marshall and Mason drove a small moving truck with the last of Vonda's belongings to Stokesbury. After sharing a soft kiss Marshall left Vonda alone to walk through her house on Anderson Avenue in Logan, South Carolina for the last time.

Lilly followed close as she wandered from room to room. She found herself once again embracing the joy of choosing this house with Stanley not that many years ago. The spirit of their life together was revived in memories of finding their way around, visiting churches and planning a happy future together. She felt herself flounder as she relived the sudden loss of Stanley. She let grief flow through her again at the memory of the lonely times that followed.

Opening the sliders, she stepped out onto the back deck and stood looking over her back yard. A smile played at her lips as she remembered helping Stanley put the new shed together shortly after moving in. She turned toward what had once been open fields. At the thought of watching the new homes begin to be built an unsettled feeling washed over her. Thanking Him again, Vonda didn't let herself dwell on the terrifying time God had brought her through back then. The empty field was gone now and new houses stood everywhere she looked. New families would soon be living in each one of them. They would make wonderful memories here just as she had done through the years.

Stepping back into the house Vonda closed and locked the sliders. She couldn't help smiling as she remembered the Christmas morning Marshall surprised her with her very own wind spinner. It was already in the yard at their house in Stokesbury. Feeling Lilly's soft fur brush against her ankle Vonda leaned down to pick her up.

"Have you said your goodbye's yet, Lilly?" She asked her sweet feline companion. "We sure did have some good years here together, didn't we girl?"

Vonda carried Lilly to the front door and opened it. Turning to take one last look into the now empty house she said softly, "Thanks for all the good times. You've been such a great home! Don't you worry now, your rooms will be filled with the love of a new family and the laughter of children very soon."

And with that, Vonda stepped across the threshold and walked away.

CHAPTER 70

As Pastor Mike stood smiling on the pitcher's mound a guitarist to his left played a medley of selected songs. The guests included Vonda and Marshall's families, Marshall's business partners, Old Timers team members and all the family that went with them along with friends of both the bride and groom.

The planned number of folded chairs arranged behind home plate had increased as the envisioned small wedding continued to grow. This was a result of being as well loved as today's couple.

A lovely white wedding-arch trellis covered in vines stood ready. The greenery was interlaced with lavender lantana flowers, seashells and a variety of beautiful silk butterflies. A few living butterflies occasionally flew close enough to check it out as well.

Large swaths of dark material covered both dugouts to hide the wedding party until the fast approaching appointed time.

Marshall's nephew Caleb came out of the dugout on the left side of the baseball diamond and sheepishly grinned toward the guests. Smiling and waving the entire way as he walked to the dugout on the right side he quickly ducked inside. Appearing again he walked to the pitcher's mound and whispered to Pastor Mike who grinned broadly and patted the boy's shoulder. Caleb then scurried back to the left-side dugout.

"Okay folks," Pastor Mike said as he turned to the guests and raised his voice. Pretending to make a pitch from the mound he playfully announced, "it's time to *play ball!*"

Caleb appeared again, grinned and hurried to the front row where he joined his brother Declan.

Marshall walked out of the left-side dugout toward Pastor Mike who motioned for him to stand inside the arched trellis.

Mitch, who had been following Marshall, passed him on his way to the right-side dugout where Leanza stepped out and joined him. She looked beautiful in a dress with a subdued lavender floral pattern. The two of them walked to Pastor Mike and took their places on either side of him.

Mason, who had followed behind Mitch, went to the right-side dugout to be joined by his lovely wife. Stacey looked as beautiful as he had ever seen her in the soft floral lavender dress the ladies had chosen especially for this occasion. The two of them took their places on either side of Pastor Mike as well.

The moment Marshall and everyone else was waiting for finally arrived.

Vonda stepped from the lady's dugout.

She looked stunningly beautiful in a lovely ivory colored empire-waist dress featuring soft lavender butterflies sparingly spaced throughout. Most of her gorgeous hair was held up in a butterfly hair clip. A thin layer of long hair flowed across her shoulders with curled tendrils gently circling her face. She was the picture of loveliness and absolutely took Marshall's breath away. As he stood gazing at his radiant bride he knew, for the first time in his life, what it meant to feel completely blessed.

Vonda joined him beneath the trellis and reached her hand out to his. Marshall could not stop smiling as he took her hand and looked deeply into her eyes.

Pastor Mike welcomed everyone to the first wedding he'd ever performed on a ball field. Marshall, Vonda and their guests laughed with him as he shared the story of how they had met just as it had been told to him. The rest of the ceremony was somewhat traditional even as it was lighthearted and fun with Pastor Mike making a series of ball park references.

After kissing his bride Marshall picked up on that theme by announcing that he had just won the game. Amid the laughter and applause that followed everyone was invited to join the happy couple at Jovie's home for the reception.

The caterers Jovie hired did a wonderful job and the spread of food was both plentiful and delicious. According to the published announcements

The Delaney Home for Children Reunion was set to begin one hour after the start of the wedding reception.

As the hour approached Jaxson, Steven, and Matthew anxiously kept a watch toward the back of the house for signs of approaching cars. They had no way of knowing if any now-grown children had seen or heard the advertisements for today's reunion and would come but they were hopeful.

CHAPTER 71

All of Kate's book club friends had proven faithful to their promises of visiting her in prison. She was now just over halfway through serving her sentence.

Stacey and Vonda being directly involved in the wedding left Monica, Deb, Lynda and Dianne working together on a video of the day's events. Since Kate couldn't be there for the nuptials her friends were taking the day to her on film at their next visit.

They had already shared the renovations to Jovie's new home by video. Kate cried when she saw the memorial bench for Ms. Amber by the milkweed garden.

During that visit Jovie shared how happy she was that her new property backed up to Kate's. She also said she hoped Kate was willing to continue tending the milkweed garden as she had done all through the years in memory of her best friend. She invited Kate to help her teach the children in her care about growing Monarch butterflies in the years to come as well.

Kate was overwhelmed and thankful to be welcomed into Jovie's life and the new Delaney Home for Children family. It also gave her so much to look forward to when her sentence was finally served and she was able to return home. The thought of reliving the wonderful times she'd shared with Amber in that house with her family filled her heart with warmth.

Monica was filming some of the wedding guests in the back yard when a car turned into the driveway, drove up to the parking area and parked. She stopped filming and watched as a tall young man got out and looked toward the house.

It dawned on her that he might have come in response to the public invitations for those who had spent time at the Delaney Home for Children during childhood. Not wanting him to feel out of place she started forward with the intent of welcoming him. Out of the corner of her eye she saw Jaxson, Matthew and Steven walking toward him so she fell back. The man seemed to be searching their faces intently and it appeared they were doing the same with him.

Hearing another car approaching Monica turned to watch it pull in and park as well. Two women got out of the car, looked at each other and started toward the house.

Dianne came up beside Monica saying, "It looks likes things might be about to get interesting."

"I was just thinking the same thing," Monica replied. Both ladies continued observing the new comers as Deb and Lynda joined them.

The men were now standing in a group talking with one another. Matthew had been studying the younger man's face intently when suddenly he moved forward and grabbed the fellow in a tight hug. Jaxson and Steven were moving in quickly and all of them were smiling and talking at once.

Monica heard Matthew say, "Robby? Is it really you?"

"I can't believe all three of you are here!" the young man said over their heads.

The two women approaching the men looked at each other and began to smile.

Deb heard one of them say, "Jaxson? Sarah, look! It's Jaxson!" and then both ladies rushed forward. Reaching the men, the one who wasn't Sarah said, "Jaxson! It's me, Lisha."

"Lisha!" Jaxson cried out in a happy response, immediately releasing the men and turning to hug her.

"And it's me, Sarah," the other woman said laughing out loud as Jaxson moved to hug her and Lisha turned to hug the other men. "Who else is here? Oh, I was so afraid to hope! Now I'm just very glad I came." Tears flowed from Sarah's eyes. She and Lisha looked from face to face as recognition continued coming to them.

"Hey girls, there's another car coming. I can hear it in the distance," Deb said, startling her three friends who were intent on the scene unfolding before them.

"I can't look away," Monica answered. "This is too good! I don't even know who these people are but I feel so happy for them."

"Me too," Dianne answered swiping a tear from her own cheek.

The man who got out of the car that had just pulled in walked over to the milkweed garden. He stood taking it all in for a full moment before running his hand along the back of the tall bench. He seemed almost to be caressing Ms. Amber's name and the inscription that followed it.

Tired of being an observer Monica was walking toward him.

"Hello," she said in a friendly manner. "Welcome! May I introduce myself and my friends? I'm Monica, this is Dianne, Deb and Lynda. And you are?"

"It's very nice to meet you ladies. I'm sorry though, none of those names sound familiar to me. I guess I wasn't living here when any of you were."

"Oh, no. We never lived here." Monica said.

"We're, well, you know what? It doesn't really matter who we are right now. Let's get you to some people that probably will matter to you," Deb stepped forward and placed her hand under the young man's elbow. She began steering him toward the group huddled together half-way between them and the house.

"I have someone here the rest of you may want to talk to," she called out loudly. As all heads turned to look in their direction she asked, "What did you say your name was again?"

"I didn't," the young man chuckled. "And I don't think I will just yet, if you don't mind."

Meeting up with the group that had been approaching them Deb said, "y'all figure it out. That seems to be the name of the game, so good luck!"

The woman named Lisha took one glance at the young man and said excitedly, "Carter! Oh Carter, I'm so glad you came!"

Turning toward the rest of the group she practically shouted, "It's Carter everyone. He's here!" Then the entire group descended on Carter with laughter, hugs and tears.

By this time Jovie had joined the others. Before long a young man named Asher arrived. Everyone was having a wonderful time listening to the memories of the adult children who were reuniting. Asher told about the time he named the first butterfly to break through its cocoon. When he said he'd named it Char the others remembered and began to share the names they had given their butterflies.

There were so many wonderful and meaningful memories shared. It gave those outside the group a small glimpse into the life Ms. Amber had given the children. A life filled with love and good times together.

Occasionally, Jovie saw a shadow cross Carter's face. She didn't understand why until a little bit later.

Over the next two hours eight more people who had been part of Ms. Amber's household stopped by. Thirteen came, in all. Each one talked about being saddened throughout the years when they'd returned to find the place closed up and left in such disrepair. Some had only learned of the tragic loss of Ms. Amber upon their return.

Those who lived at the Delaney Home for Children during Jovie's three-year stay were very excited to see her again. Everyone was thrilled to learn she was honoring Ms. Amber's legacy by re-opening the house.

To say it was an exciting afternoon would've been a gross understatement.

The happy couple, the wedding party and all of their friends celebrated the future while an entirely different group of people reminisced over the past. Emotions were high, tears flowed, laughter rang out and love was everywhere.

While standing back to take it all in Jovie was overcome with the goodness of God.

CHAPTER 72

Having spent several hours sharing happy memories and catching one another up on their current lives the reunited group of adult children walked together over to the milkweed garden. As they talked about Ms. Amber and looked at the memorial bench their tears flowed freely. Jovie shared that the bench had been made as a surprise for Jaxson from Matthew and Steven in honor of his mother.

It was only natural, at that point, for the conversation to shift to the tragic storm that took Ms. Amber's life. As the story unfolded Jovie began to understand why that shadow continued to cross Carter's face. This was the child Ms. Amber went out into the storm to rescue.

As the other's listened intently Lisha shared how terrified she was when Ms. Amber put her in charge. Ms. Amber repeatedly sought her assurance that she would do what was being asked of her. She was commissioned to keep the other children safe until Ms. Amber returned safely with Carter.

Lisha turned to Carter and said, "I was so relieved when I heard you scream my name and rushed to find you huddled in the living room floor. I had never been so happy to see anyone in my entire life. I am so thankful you survived that storm!" She moved over to him and hugged him tightly.

"I cannot tell you how glad I am to see you, Carter. I loved you so much when we were children. I have loved you all through these years we've spent apart. I've never stopped thinking of you. We must never lose touch with each other again!"

Carter was moved by Lisha's words and embrace. He had no idea he meant so much to her. Still, he was, as he had so often been through the years, overcome with guilt that his actions had cost their house-mother her life.

Jaxson saw the look of guilt cross Carter's face. Although he was sure there were those who may not think it the thing to do, he had to address it.

"Her death was not your fault, Carter." He said simply.

Carter's eyes met Jaxson's. Wordlessly they said, 'Yes, it was.'

"No," the ones having lived through that tragic day with him joined in saying.

"Jaxson's right Carter! Nothing that happened that day was your fault! Ma would not see it that way either." Lisha spoke the words as she went over and sat beside him on the memorial bench. She was so thankful to be face to face with Carter as she hoped against hope that he would believe her.

Looking him directly in the eyes Lisha continued, "She loved you - just as she loved all of us. We were only children back then and any one of us could've done what you did that day. Besides which, God had already appointed the number of days in Ma's life. It was her time! What happened was nothing more than that. As she had been doing all of our lives, she continued to the last moment of hers. And that was simply to love each of us completely."

As Lisha had been speaking a large monarch butterfly had fluttered over to the group. It was now gently fluttering in and out among them.

"Yes, it's true," Sarah stepped forward and said "She gave her life to protect you Carter, but she would've done that for any one of us. And, even now, from her place in heaven, she undoubtedly counts it as an honor."

The monarch gently passed Carter's head and alighted ever so softly atop his right hand where it lay over his left. Its movements had caught the eyes of everyone in the group. They watched it gently opening and closing its wings as if it sitting there with Carter were the most natural thing in the world for it to do.

"It's Ma," Sarah said softly. "She's here. She wants you to know she's here with us."

"Yes," Jaxson agreed. "More specifically, Carter, she wants you to know she's with you. She's agreeing that nothing that happened was your fault."

Steven finished with what all of them were thinking, "She wants you to know you're not to blame for her death. She loves you!"

As if on cue the Monarch arose and fluttered over to Carter's chest where it attached itself to his shirt directly over his heart.

Carter's eyes went from the Monarch to those standing around and about him. "You're right," he said confidently. "I mean, look at this. How can I deny what's right in front of me?"

Amid the soft laughter the monarch arose from Carter's chest, circled over their heads, and flew away.

Just then a car turned into the driveway attracting everyone's attention.

Jovie began walking toward it almost as if she were expecting someone.

A rather handsome man got out of the car. He turned and looked at her with the most piercing blue eyes she'd ever seen. "Are you Jovie Jarvis? The owner and proprietor of The Delaney Home for Children?"

"I am," Jovie answered, meeting his smile with her own. "Is there something I can help you with?"

"Yes, ma'am there certainly is," he said, stepping toward the back of the car and opening the door. He leaned into the back seat and withdrew with a baby carrier.

Still smiling he turned to Jovie, lifted the carrier and said, "You can give this little lady a home. She was abandoned at our fire station today."

Jovie's smile was radiant as she looked into the child's face and reached out to take the carrier. Turning around she saw that everyone was slowly moving toward her.

Stepping up to her side Jaxson said, "Somehow this seems very fitting to me."

"It's more fitting than you may realize," Steven said as he joined them.

After leaning down to look into the little girl's face, he lifted his eyes to meet Jovie's. "The first child Ms. Amber ever took into this house was a little girl who had been abandoned at the local fire station. The child was delivered here by a fireman."

Jaxson reached out and took the handle of the baby carrier from Jovie's hand. Turning toward the crowd he began to scan their faces; from the reunited adult children of Ms. Amber's home for children, to newlyweds Vonda and Marshall and all of their friends and family, to Kate's book club friends, then to Jovie's birth parents, adoptive parents and her combination of siblings and finally to the man who had made this delivery.

Lastly, his eyes rested on Jovie and he grinned.

Sitting the carrier onto the ground Jaxson lifted the baby out of it. In a dramatic gesture he held the child up for everyone to see. His grin spread to a wide smile.

Loud enough for all to hear Jaxson said, "Welcome to The Delaney Home for Children little one. It's time to meet your family!"

VS Gardner

The author enjoys reader feedback. She invites you to contact her through Messenger at her Facebook Author page, VS Gardner or via email to vsgbooks2020@gmail.com. Referrals to other readers and/or ratings/reviews on Amazon, Goodreads, (etc.) are greatly appreciated.

As in her first two novels the setting of this book echoes VS Gardner's home in beautiful South Carolina where she lives with her best friend/husband. She loves spending time with her family and is thankful for life's many blessings.

In 2020 VS Gardner was excited to achieve her lifelong dream with the publication of her first book A KILLING ON HARDEE STREET, whose mystery centers around the main character, Vonda Graham. Although each book is a stand-alone, containing its own mystery, Vonda's story continues in A BRICK TO REMEMBER and concludes in THE FORGOTTEN HOME.

Be sure to follow the Author on Amazon and/or her Facebook Author page; VS Gardner for notification of future publications.

You are greatly appreciated!
May God continually bless you and yours!

Made in the USA
Middletown, DE
02 April 2023

27457197R00158